HARD GOING

The murder comes – much to Slider's family's disgust – during his week off, saving him from the horrors of a trip to the shopping centre with his two older children. The late Mr Lionel Bygood, who looks, to all intents and purposes, like an old-fashioned sort of gentleman, has been bashed in the head with a bronze statue, in what Doc Cameron describes as 'our old friend the Frenzied Attack'. It soon emerges that Mr Bygood was a philanthropist, well-known locally for giving help and advice to all who needed it, from all walks of life. But with all signs pointing to the victim knowing his killer, Slider and his team find themselves embroiled in an investigation that provides scant evidence or possible motive, but all too many suspects...

Recent Titles by Cynthia Harrod-Eagles from Severn House

THE COLONEL'S DAUGHTER
A CORNISH AFFAIR
COUNTRY PLOT
DANGEROUS LOVE
DIVIDED LOVE
EVEN CHANCE
HARTE'S DESIRE
THE HORSEMASTERS
JULIA
KATE'S PROGRESS
LAST RUN
THE LONGEST DANCE
NOBODY'S FOOL
ON WINGS OF LOVE
PLAY FOR LOVE
A RAINBOW SUMMER
REAL LIFE (*Short Stories*)

The Bill Slider Mysteries

GAME OVER
FELL PURPOSE
BODY LINE
KILL MY DARLING
BLOOD NEVER DIES
HARD GOING

HARD GOING

A Bill Slider Mystery

Cynthia Harrod-Eagles

Severn House Large Print
London & New York

This first large print edition published 2014
in Great Britain and the USA by
SEVERN HOUSE PUBLISHERS LTD of
19 Cedar Road, Sutton, Surrey, England, SM2 5DA.
First world regular print edition published 2013 by
Severn House Publishers Ltd., London and New York.

British Library Cataloguing in Publication Data

Harrod-Eagles, Cynthia author.
Hard going. -- (A Bill Slider mystery)
1. Slider, Bill (Fictitious character)--Fiction.
2. Police--England--London--Fiction. 3. Murder--
Investigation--Fiction. 4. Detective and mystery stories.
5. Large type books.
I. Title II. Series
823.9'2-dc23

ISBN-13: 9780727897183

ONE

Quietus Interruptus

Slider's wheels were in dock. Atherton came to fetch him, elegantly suited as always, but wearing a – in Slider's opinion – lamentable pair of suede shoes.

'There's nothing wrong with suede shoes in the right context,' Atherton protested, following the direction of his eyes. They had had this conversation before. Of course, when you'd worked together for a long time, you'd had most conversations before.

'I must have been frightened in the womb by Kenneth Clarke,' Slider said. Atherton followed him back into the kitchen. Five pairs of eyes turned on them: Slider's father, wife Joanna, children from his first marriage, Kate and Matthew, and baby George. No doubt if the foetus in Joanna's womb had developed eyes yet, they too would be rolling in their direction in mute accusation.

Slider had been going to take Matthew and Kate to the Westfield shopping centre – which, oddly, they regarded as a treat.

'At least it came at the *end* of his week off,' Atherton offered.

'He hasn't finished breakfast,' Joanna said with wifely reproach. There was half a slice of toast and marmalade on his plate displaying a profile of his dentition that would have made a forensic scientist burst into song.

'I drove as slowly as I could,' Atherton said meekly.

'What is it?' Matthew pleaded. 'Is it a big case?'

Big case. Slider tutted inwardly. They all watched too much telly.

'It's a murder,' Atherton admitted.

'Cool!' said Matthew.

'Gross!' said Kate.

'Can I come, Dad?' Matthew pleaded.

Slider's father answered for him. 'Course you can't. And it's not "cool". Some poor soul is dead.'

Matthew blushed – he was terribly sensitive about being told off, even in the mildest terms – but Kate merely rolled her eyes. It was her response to everything. She must have eye-muscles like a boxer's biceps, Slider thought.

'I'm sorry, kids,' he said. 'It can't be helped. Your mother will be fetching you tonight.' He looked at his father. 'Are you all right looking after them?'

'Looking after us?' Kate said derisively. 'What are we, little kids?'

'Are you working today?' Atherton asked Joanna.

'Rehearsal for tonight,' she said. She was a violinist with the Royal London Philharmonia. 'Festival Hall. All-Prokofiev programme. First violin concerto, symphony number one and the Scythian Suite.'

Atherton was a classical music buff from way back – unlike Slider, who'd had to learn as he went along: when he first met Joanna he could barely tell the 1812 from Beethoven's Fifth.

'I don't know the Scythian Suite,' Atherton said. 'What's it like?'

Joanna thought a moment. 'Like The Rite of Spring's lesser known younger brother.'

'Good?'

'Twenty minutes of agony. Too many dots!' she moaned.

'I meant, to listen to?'

'Some of it's not bad,' Joanna said, 'but mostly it's tinsel.'

'Tinsel?'

'Gretel's lesser known gay brother,' Slider suggested.

'At least it finishes with a fortissimo,' said Joanna, 'so the audience will know when to clap. Quiet endings confuse them.'

'We're so shallow,' Atherton scoffed.

Slider intervened. 'We must get going.' He bent to kiss her and she kissed him back with enthusiasm.

'Eeuw!' Kate complained routinely. 'Get a room!'

Slider ignored her. 'Don't get too tired,' he said.

'Now he tells me,' Joanna retorted.

'And don't skip lunch.'

Atherton lashed round a dithering Ford Focus,

missing it by a coat of paint, and asked, 'Is she all right? Joanna, I mean.'

'She gets tired,' Slider said, 'but she won't admit it.'

'That's a big programme,' Atherton commented. 'All Prokofiev. No nice go of Haydn to rest your brain.'

He skimmed between a big red bus and a lurking traffic island. The incoming Labour council had installed hundreds of them to use up a budget surplus left by the outgoing lot. Locals called the new administration the Road Island Reds.

'You look tired too,' said Slider. 'You look like hell, in fact. Everything all right?' He knew Atherton's girlfriend Emily, a freelance journalist, was away again, and wondered if he were missing her.

'Me? I'm fine,' Atherton said, which was the equivalent of a 'Keep Off' notice.

'Do we know anything about the shout?' Slider asked instead.

'Only that it's in Shepherd's Bush Road,' he said.

'Well, that's nice,' said Slider. 'We can go home for lunch.'

Shepherd's Bush Road was the main north–south road

from Shepherd's Bush to Hammersmith. With two of its four lanes dedicated to buses, it was barely adequate for the traffic in the first place; filling the space in front of the house with a variety of police wagons and do-not-cross tape had terminally fouled up the flow. Slider slapped on the spinner and Atherton used the bus lane, but even so they had to wiggle through side roads at the end to get near enough.

The house they were looking for was halfway down, in a block just before Brook Green: a tall, handsome Victorian façade, yellow London brick and white stone facings, shops on the ground floor, and flats above. As well as hiding the roof behind a curious ornate parapet, the original builder had ambitiously named the block Empire Terrace, with raised lettering on a white stone panel topped by a sort of decorative pineapple. That'd cause some fun if it ever fell, Slider thought.

The shops in Shepherd's Bush Road became posher the further you got from the Bush end, and in this block, as well as the inevitable estate agent, there was a tapas bar, a high-end Italian restaurant, a fishmonger's also selling expensive kitchen equipment (inevitably called The Kitchen Plaice), a dress shop with a double-barrelled name, and a knick-knackery sort of gift emporium called Ludlow Hearts and Crafts.

'Well, you can't get more upscale than Ludlow, now can you?' Atherton commented. 'Down our end there'd've been an Asian supermarket, a kebabery, a newsagent's, a betting shop and a caff specializing in chips.'

'We're not in Kansas any more,' said Slider.

A uniformed PC, big, blond Eric Renker, was guarding a smartly painted red door between the Italian and the dress shop, and a number of other woodentops were hanging around, some ready to man the barriers if the crowd of happily concerned citizens pursuing their right to gawp got bigger, and two resignedly directing the traffic round the blockage. Among the vehicles Slider recognized the forensic wagon up alongside the nick's own Sprinter, and the sleek Jaguar belonging to Freddie Cameron, the forensic surgeon.

Two of Slider's own DCs were there. Phil Gascoyne, newly transferred from Uniform, tall and fit from years of chasing drunks round Shepherd's Bush Green, was chatting to Rita Connolly, a peaky-faced Dubliner who looked almost too slight to be a policeman, though she was tough enough in reality. She had recently had her pale hair cut really close, giving her head the frail look of a Christmas tree bauble. Since Gascoyne regularly shaved his own fair locks to a stubble, an accidental head-clash between the two of them would probably cause a ringing in more ears than theirs.

'Doc Cameron's just gone up,' Connolly volunteered as Slider and Atherton arrived. 'And forensic's still in there.'

'What do we know about the deceased?' Slider asked.

'We've got a name, sir – Lionel Bygod,' said Gascoyne, and spelled it.

'A "y" instead of an "i"?' said Atherton. 'That's unusual.'

'Unusual is good,' said Slider. Made it easier to be sure who you were talking about when the subject wasn't called Smith, Brown or Robinson. 'Who found him?'

'His cleaner, housekeeper, whatever you'd call her,' said Connolly. 'Fine class of a woman with a chip on her shoulder. Half eight this morning. Back of his head's bashed in. His lordship Bob Bailey doesn't want us in there yet,' she added with scorn. She didn't like the crime scene manager for personal reasons, but they were often resented because they were civilians and not subject to police command. 'So here we are, hangin' around like the smell o' gas, waiting on his pleasure. Will I go and get the teas?' she concluded resignedly.

Her tone said *because I'm the woman*, but Slider liked to surprise. 'No, Gascoyne can go. But later. I'm going in.'

A steep flight of stairs led to the first floor where Bob Bailey intercepted them and told them that what he gratuitously dubbed 'The Murder Room' was the big reception room at the front. 'But you can't go in. My boys and girls haven't finished yet.'

These days the forensics experts were trying to discourage detectives from visiting crime scenes at all, and to have them rely instead on photographs and possibly virtual reality walk-through reconstructions. However, as Slider sometimes had to point out, this wasn't *CSI Miami*, and the forensic department didn't conduct the entire investigation.

He gave Bailey a sturdy look that said he didn't get clothed up in the Andy Pandy suit and attractive shower cap just to pull the girls.

Bailey wavered. 'You can take a look from the

door,' he compromised.

The room was large and well-proportioned, with a high ceiling and handsome mouldings. It was decorated and furnished in appropriate Victorian style, with a brownish patterned wall-paper, a Turkish carpet covering the floor, and heavily framed oil paintings on the wall. A leather Chesterfield and two club chairs were grouped around the mahogany chimney-piece, and in the alcoves to either side were book-shelves crammed with books. There were nice little tables and lamps here and there, a bust of Caesar on a marble column in one corner, and an aspidistra on a stand with barley-sugar legs in another. It felt rich, comfortable, and very masculine, like a gentleman's club.

In the window was a massive mahogany desk, on which Slider could see an electric typewriter, a telephone, a wooden stationery-holder, and what looked like a brass shell-case containing a variety of writing implements. To one side of it stood a two-drawer filing cabinet, on top of which was a small document safe, its door ajar and the key in the lock. And in the large, leather chair the victim was sitting, slumped forward over the desk as though he had fallen asleep. Judging from the length of arms, legs and back, the late Lionel Bygod had been a tall man.

Bending over him was Freddie Cameron, another ghost in white coveralls among the busy wraiths fingerprinting and photographing.

'Bill!' he said in cheerful greeting. 'He can come over, can't he?' he added to Bailey.

After some negotiation, Bailey graciously

allowed Slider to cross a designated path to the desk. Atherton he made to wait at the door.

Cameron had had to shed the jacket of his grey two-piece to put on the plastic suit, but nothing could dim the radiance of his neckwear, which shone through it, flamboyantly pink, purple and yellow.

'Ah,' said Slider, 'one of the ties that blind.'

'It's from the Matisse collection,' Freddie said.

'Glad it's not the Jackson Pollock collection. I've just had breakfast.'

At closer inspection the late Lionel Bygod was very thin, and Slider wondered whether it might be a recent development because his suit was not a new one, but seemed loose on him. It was a nice-looking three-piece in light pepper-and-salt tweed, and he was wearing a lovat-green knitted tie with it and – Slider stooped to look – well-polished brown brogues. Slider remembered Atherton saying once that a gentleman could wear brown shoes in London as long as Parliament wasn't sitting. He had probably been joking – it was sometimes hard to tell with Atherton – but still, Mr Bygod was dressed like a gentleman as far as Slider was concerned.

He had had a decent head of hair, grey, thick and wavy. The massive blow to the back of his skull had mashed hair, bone and blood all together in a sticky mess. Blood had trickled down the side of his face and under his head, soaking into the leather-bound blotter and pooling a little on the polished desk top.

'Several blows of considerable force,' Cameron said. 'Our old friend the Frenzied Attack.

Depressed fracture of the skull, and no doubt cerebral contusion and laceration. It's not the fracture that kills, you know, it's the brain damage. Most of all the shearing stresses.' He straightened. 'When the head is rotated by a blow – and virtually every blow has some rotational element – the layers of brain tissue slide over each other.' He demonstrated with his palms. 'The old grey matter can't take it.'

'Would death have been instantaneous?' Slider asked.

'With blows of this force, unconsciousness would have been immediate. Death would have followed quite rapidly – a couple of minutes at most. You can see there has been bleeding, but not much. When was he found?'

'This morning, when the housekeeper came in.'

'I'd say he's been dead at least twelve hours,' Freddie said. 'Twelve to eighteen hours, so you're looking at yesterday afternoon or evening. Anything else before I get going?'

Slider stared, and thought. The top half of the body was obscuring what, if anything, was lying on the blotter. 'I'd like to know what he was doing at the desk when it happened. People don't usually just sit. Was he reading, working, what?'

'I'll call you when I move him,' said Freddie.

Bailey intervened eagerly. 'We've got the murder weapon.' He produced an evidence bag. It was a bronze statuette of a woman with tight curly hair, wearing a flounced, straight-skirted, nip-waisted dress that left her impossibly round bosoms bare. The face and head of the subject were obscured unpleasantly with bits of Mr Bygod.

Freddie hefted it gently. It was about fifteen inches high and heavy. 'That'd do it,' he said. 'It's a genuine bronze, not spelter.'

'It was lying on the carpet just there.' Bailey pointed to a spot a couple of feet behind the chair. At a nod from Slider he took it across to show Atherton. 'Greek goddess or something.'

'Not Greek. That's a Cretan costume,' Atherton said. 'It's Ariadne.'

'How on earth do you know that?' Slider asked. He was always surprised by the things his bagman came up with.

'It's written on the base,' Atherton pointed out.

'Creet or Greekan,' Bailey said, 'grip it round the legs and you've got a good weapon.' He demonstrated with what looked like a drive to deep extra cover.

Slider was looking round the room. 'Over there. There's a space on the mantelpiece.'

The mantelpiece was otherwise crammed with *objets d'art* of china, jade, and ivory, some rather dim-looking Etruscan bronzes, an onyx bull, and two little figurines that were, or were meant to look like, Sèvres. In the centre was a space, about the right size. It was easy to imagine Ariadne as the centrepiece of the eclectic display.

'Any fingermarks?' Slider asked without hope. Any two-bit criminal knew enough to wear gloves these days.

Bailey shook his head. 'Chummy wiped the bottom half of the thing, where he'd held it, with some sort of cloth. Handkerchief or something.'

Slider met Freddie's eyes with hope. 'If it was a handkerchief and not clean, we might get some DNA transference from it. What about the rest of the room?'

'Cleaner does a good job,' said Bailey. 'There aren't many marks anywhere. But we'll lift what we can.'

The house was a thing of strange contrasts. To begin with, though it was usual in London for the floors above commercial properties to be divided into several flats or even a multiplicity of bedsits, this was all one home, over three floors. Given the cost of housing in Hammersmith these days, its size ought to have made it quite valuable; on the other hand, not everyone wanted to live over a restaurant. It was hard to guess what it might fetch on the market, but it wouldn't have been cheap.

At the back of the first floor was an L-shaped kitchen-dining room; on the second floor the master bedroom was in front and a large bathroom, obviously made by sacrificing a second bedroom, at the back. On the third floor – the attic behind the parapet – were two maids' bedrooms with a sliver of a modern shower room tucked between them. One was empty; the other seemed to be used as a storage room, containing suitcases and cardboard removers' boxes full of personal possessions.

The main bedroom was decorated and furnished, like the living room, with grand, heavy old furniture in the Victorian style, very much a man's taste; yet the kitchen and bathroom had been done out fairly recently in modern style and at some expense, with a lot of tile, marble, chrome, and a profusion of gadgets.

The kitchen in particular roused Atherton's envy. 'Every damn thing that *ouvres* and *fermes*,' he remarked. He loved to cook, but living in a tiny two-up-two-down he hadn't the space for a kitchen like this, even if he could have afforded it.

Slider had often noted that, as a rule, the posher the kitchen, the less it was used, but this kitchen, though it was spotlessly clean, was obviously cooked in.

'I wonder if Mr Bygod was another of these epicurean bachelors who like to cook,' Slider mused.

'Don't look at me when you say "another",' Atherton objected.

'If the chef's hat fits,' Slider said. 'There's no sign of a woman's touch in the bedroom or reception room.'

A further anomaly was that flight of stairs at the bottom. The front door was heavy, and was controlled by an entryphone system, the upper end of which was beside the door inside the living room. It was recently painted and sported well-polished brass furniture – quite a grand door in its way – but behind it was a tiny lobby, lit only with a bare light bulb hanging from a long flex. And while the upper hall and stairs were carpeted, these lower stairs were covered with linoleum that looked old and worn, and the walls were painted with a dingy pale green emulsion that was much scuffed and marked with traffic.

'You'd think, given the flat must have cost quite a bit,' said Slider, 'that he'd want to make a better impression.'

'Perhaps he didn't entertain,' Atherton said. Then, 'That was a nice suit he was wearing. Bespoke.'

'How could you tell from that distance?'

'I can tell. Might be interesting to talk to his tailor.'

One of Bailey's ghosts found them to tell them that Doc Cameron had moved the body and wanted them back, so they returned to the living room. The corpse was off the desk and on the floor, on its back, in a body bag, waiting to be zipped up. Slider took a look at the face – the first time he'd been able to see it. Thin, with high cheekbones, a prominent nose and full, carved lips: distinguished, he'd have said. A strong face, and while not exactly handsome, it was agreeable to look at – probably women would have found him attractive, he thought.

He stared down for a long moment, aware that this was the last the world would see of Lionel Bygod, whoever and whatever he had been. From here he would go to the morgue, where he would be unemotionally cut up and analysed, no longer a person but a case, a piece of evidence in an investigation; and from there into a coffin, his final disintegration taking place unseen within the oak, pine or mahogany, depending on the next-of-kin's propensities or finances. That zip would zip closed his time on the stage, like the final curtain on the last night of a play. All that he was and had been was over and done with. And Slider had yet to discover if anyone cared. It was a melancholy moment.

'Ah, there you are.' Freddie disturbed his reverie. 'Well, there were no other visible injuries, so I think you can take it it was the head trauma that killed him. *Ceteris paribus* and subject always to post-mortem.'

'Ever my cautious Freddie,' said Slider. But they'd had cases between them before, more than one, where all was not as it seemed. He walked to the desk. 'And what was he doing, sitting there?'

'That's rather curious. It appears he was writing a cheque.'

There it was on the desk, the cheque book, the edges of the pages stained with blood. The victim's body had shielded it; but paper acts like a wick and had drawn it up from the wet blotter. A rather nice fountain pen, dark green marble effect with gold bands, was also lying there, uncapped. He had got as far as writing the date, Slider saw.

'The pen was actually in his hand,' Freddie said. 'The right hand. It was hidden under his torso when he fell forward.'

'So he was actually writing it when he was killed,' Slider mused.

'Yesterday's date. If only the blow had miraculously stopped his watch as well, we'd have the exact moment of death pinpointed,' Freddie said drily.

* * *

Outside, Slider discovered his boss, Detective Superintendent Fred 'The Syrup' Porson, walking up and down, his autumn raiment – a beige raincoat of wondrous design, covered in flaps, straps and buckles – swirling around him like a matador's cape. He had abandoned the eponymous wig when his dear wife died, but his bony pate served only to emphasize the lushness of his eyebrows, as lavishly overgrown as Sleeping Beauty's hedge, and whipped up into peaks like hoary meringue.

He was talking to Swilley, another of Slider's DCs, who had to pace with him and looked as though she didn't like being made to look foolish in that way. He swung round as Slider emerged with Atherton behind him, and barked, 'Only just made it!'

Slider was stung. 'I came as soon as I heard, sir – or as soon as my lift arrived.'

Porson waved that away. 'Over there. Checkpoint Charlie.' He gestured towards the next side turning. 'Border between us and Hammersmith. Only just the right side of it, or they'd have got it instead of us. Thankful for small murphies.'

Slider forbore to comment. Only the upper echelons could actually *want* a murder case.

'I've already had friend Grunthorpe on the ear'ole to me this morning,' Porson rumbled on. 'In the person of DS Carthew of course. They think it ought to go to Hammersmith's murder squad.'

Grunthorpe was Porson's equivalent at Hammersmith, and Trevor 'Boots' Carthew, his right hand man, was famous for his dedication to his master's interests. Grunthorpe was known to be always on the lookout for prestigious cases to boost his reputation – or easy ones to boost his clear-up rate.

Slider frowned. 'But the deceased wasn't anyone important, was he?'

Porson shrugged. 'Not as far as I know, but that's irrevelant. I think they're jealous about the Corley case. Touch of the green-eyed wass-name.' In his impatience with life, Porson's way was to take random swipes at language, like a bored waitress wiping tables in an airport eatery. 'We did ourselves a bit of bon with that, and they want some of what we've got. Give 'em half a chance and they'll be all over this like a cheap rash. So I want the investigation done by the book and double-quick time. Don't want any excuse for Mr Wetherspoon to cast nasturtiums on our efficiency. What's it look like so far?'

Slider shrugged in his turn. 'No obvious signs of burglary. And it doesn't look professional.'

'Domestic? Blast,' said Porson.

Slider concurred. Human passions took a lot more fathoming out, and amateurs didn't tend to have their prints or DNA handily on record. They might be more liable to leave traces behind, but you had nothing to compare them with until you'd identified them by other means. And other means tended to take time.

Porson looked round at the immediate area. 'And this is a bad place.'

Slider knew what he meant. At intervals along the pavement edge trees had been planted, the tall, handsome London planes beloved of Victorians, which had now reached magnificent full size. It was a soft, early autumn day and the buttery sunshine was filtering through the leaves, turning them to glowing shades of lemon and lime. Beautiful – but they would restrict any view of the door from across the road, either by a casual gazer-from-the-window or a CCTV camera, should there happen to be one. Nearby there was a bus camera on a tall pole, but of course that was focused straight down the road. Some of the posh shops might have cameras pointed at their doors which could possibly show people walking past, but without a precise time of death, that might not narrow the field in any meaningful way.

Porson came out of his reverie. 'Still, we've got it and they've not, and a nod in the hand's as good as a wink. And I want to keep it that way, so I need you to stay on your toes.' There was a furious clicking sound, like a troupe of asthmatic cicadas, heralding the arrival of the press, and Porson glanced over his shoulder, then gathered his coat around him in a curiously dainty gesture. 'The Bavarians're at the gate. I'm off. Keep me in the picture.'

He scuttled off, the better, Slider reflected, actually to stay *out* of the picture.

Slider called Swilley to him, and briefed her about the disposal of his personnel.

TWO

Don't Cry for Me, Ardent Cleaner

Having dispersed the available troops on canvass, DC Kathleen 'Norma' Swilley took the Italian restaurant for herself. She was a tall, athletic woman, good looking in a blonde, small-nosed, wide-mouthed, Californian way. From the beginning she had had to fight her way through the various misogynies of the Job – even now, marriage and motherhood hadn't discouraged the chancers, or those who insisted that because she rejected their advances, she must be a lesbian. But she had found refuge in Slider's firm. Slider only cared that she was a good policeman, and was the one work colleague who had never hit on her, so he had her undying loyalty.

The restaurant was unimaginatively called Piazza but was obviously a posh one. She found the door unlocked, but it was not yet open: the lights were off, it felt cold, and the only sound came from the gloom of the far interior, where a man was clinking about with bottles, setting up.

'Hello?' she called out.

He came hurrying towards her at once, dressed in the pan-global uniform of white shirt and black trousers, a tall man, with thinning fair hair, and the sort of knobbly peasant face that looked as if it had been roughly marked out of clay with thumbs, then decorated with a small, bristly moustache like desert grass.

'*Bella signorina*!' he cried as he approached. 'So much regret! *Siamo chiusi*! We are closéd. But you will come back later, please, so beautiful *signorina*!'

He beamed at her, a smile that seemed so genuine it made all the difference from being called *bella signorina* in any other Italian restaurant. She almost found herself smiling back.

'It's all right, you can drop all that stuff,' she said, showing her warrant card. 'Police.'

But he continued to smile, and his eyes seemed kind. 'But it is true, you are beautiful,' he insisted. She made a discouraging face, and he went on, 'To tell you truth, I am not Italian anyway.'

'No kidding,' said Swilley.

'I am from Kurdistan,' he admitted modestly.

'Is that right, Mr—?' Swilley enquired, for the notebook.

'Here I am called Cesar,' he said. Now he had dropped the *eh, Luigi!* stuff, his accent was faint and unclassifiable, residing more in his cadences than anything specific.

'Real name? For the record,' she said.

'Sinar Serhati. I will spell it for you.' When she had it down, he asked, 'Is there some trouble? I see so many police outside.'

'I'm afraid there is. It concerns the man who lives upstairs.'

His eyes widened. 'Mr Bygod? Has something happened to him? Please God he is all right?'

'I'm sorry to say he was found dead this morning.'

Serhati's face registered immediate concern and dismay. 'Oh, please, no! This is terrible! He was such a nice man – and very kind to me.'

This was good, Swilley thought – he evidently knew Bygod more than casually. 'I'd like to ask you a few questions about him, if I may,' she said.

'Of course,' said Serhati, still with the sorrowful cast. 'Please sit down, and would you like some coffee? I'll ask Naza to bring some.'

Swilley assented, and watched him go to the back and call out to someone out of sight. He returned and sat opposite her at a small table, gave her a searching look, and said, 'Was it his heart?'

'Why do you say that?'

He shrugged. 'Only that at his age it is usually heart.'

But she could see from his expression he didn't think it was. Of course, the police would hardly come asking questions about an infarct. It was a problem in the Job, that simply turning up alerted people to the fact that something was wrong, and put them on their guard.

'I'm afraid it looks as though someone killed him.'

Interesting. He didn't look as shocked at that as he might have. He sighed. 'These are bad times,' he said quietly. 'So much trouble in the world.'

'What was the nature of your relationship with Mr Bygod?' she asked.

'He was a customer,' he said at once, 'but he was also very good to me. He helped me buy this place.'

'He gave you money?'

Serhati looked hurt. 'No! I would not ask him for money. He helped me get loan from the bank. Told me where to go, how to apply. Helped me write a business plan. All sorts of advice. You see, I was a waiter here. Ever since we came to England – Naza, my wife, and me – I have been waiter, and Naza worked in kitchens, but our dream was to have our own restaurant. We saved and saved but never enough. Then I came here, and after a year I was made manager. The owner, Mr Batelli, he owns four restaurants, he can't run them all himself. He liked me, and I did well for him, and then one day he said, "How would you like to buy?"'

'An *Italian* restaurant?' Swilley asked.

'No-one eats Kurdish food – not even the Kurds,' he joked. 'But the business is the same. Naza and I are Kurdish, my chef is Spanish, his assistant is Greek, I have one Polish waiter, one from Kosovo, and one from Portugal. Mr Bygod used to call it United Nations. But restaurants are like that everywhere. Catering is the great melting pot, Mr Bygod used to say.'

A little, round woman came scuttling from the back with the coffee and a plate of thin cinnamon biscuits. She cast one nervous look at Swilley, Serhati said something to her in a very foreign language, and she scuttled away again.

'My wife, Naza. She doesn't speak so good English.'

Which sounded to Swilley like a warning off. But there seemed no reason yet to interview her and she let it pass. She sipped her coffee, which was excellent. 'Was Mr Bygod a good customer?'

'The best sort. He loved food, he appreciated it. We like people who enjoy what we serve them. And always good wine. He knew a lot about wine. He helped me make up the wine list after I bought the place.'

'So was he well off, do you think? Had plenty of money?'

Serhati shrugged. 'There was no show about him. He wore nice clothes, but not flashy. His house was comfortable the same way. I would call him an old-fashioned English gentleman. He spoke like that – like a lord, like Oxford-and-Cambridge. Maybe he had money – I don't know. I don't think it mattered.'

She understood what he meant, or thought she did – that someone like Bygod would be the same whatever his circumstances. But money always mattered. Nice clothes cost money at some point in their history. So did an Oxford education. She wondered if Serhati knew that Oxford and Cambridge were separate places.

'Why do you think he helped you?' she asked.

'Because he was a good man,' Serhati said with faint surprise, as if she shouldn't have needed to ask.

'He liked you,' she suggested.

He shrugged. 'I suppose he did. But it was not

only me. One of my waiters, too, a boy from Syria – he had trouble with the immigration. He's gone now,' he added hastily, 'but Mr Bygod helped him with the papers.'

What Swilley was getting from this was an unusual degree of involvement with a local restaurant by a customer, particularly a Londoner. She decided to probe a little further. 'So you've been in his house,' she said casually, not making it a question.

He paused the fraction of an instant as if weighing his response – a suspicious pause, it could have been, except that he came from an oppressed people, where such caution was probably a survival tactic; where simply coming to official attention was all you needed to find yourself in trouble. He seemed to settle into his skin a little as he concluded the truth had to be told. She recognized the look as an act of courage – or perhaps of hard-won trust. 'He asked me up there several times when he was helping me with the bank papers, and once when I had a problem with the Public Health inspector. It was not a social thing.'

Yes, what about the social thing, Swilley wondered. 'Did he eat here often?' she asked.

'Often for lunch, at least once a week, sometimes more. Not so often for dinner. But I think he ate out a lot. Like I said, he liked food.'

'Did he come here alone? Or did he bring friends?'

'Most often alone. Sometimes with friends. Men around his own age – English men. I think they talked business. But they seemed to know each other well – they laugh and joke a little too.'

'So, always men,' Swilley suggested. 'Never women.'

He did not seem to find that a pointed question. 'Maybe he took women somewhere else,' he hazarded. 'But last week he brought a lady. I was pleased. She was not young, but beautiful, and—' He waved a hand, searching for the word. 'Glamorous. Like film star, maybe, but not so much. Beautiful for a woman of her age, the way sometimes French women are, do you know?'

'When was that, exactly?'

He thought. 'Thursday? Yes, I think Thursday. Lunchtime.'

'Do you know her name?'

He shook his head regretfully. 'He didn't introduce.'

'What did they talk about?'

'I don't hear, but I think maybe business – serious mostly. But I saw him hold her hand once across the table, and she smiled at him. I think they were fond of each other.'

'Was that the last time you saw him?'

'No, he came in to lunch on Saturday. Alone. That was just like usual.'

Swilley lost interest. Serhati seemed like a dead end. She wound up the interview with questions about the previous afternoon. He was not much help. The restaurant closed between three and seven and he and his wife and all his staff had gone home as they usually did between sessions. He hadn't noticed anyone going to Mr Bygod's door during the hours he was here, but then he wouldn't notice when he was working. People passed by all the time, and he couldn't see Bygod's door unless he stood right by the window, which he never did.

'If you think of anything that might help us, please get in touch,' Swilley said, giving him a card, and he hurried to open the door for her. As she passed him, going out, he touched her arm, briefly and shyly.

'How did they do it? I mean, was it – bad?' She froze him off with a look, and he said instead, humbly, 'I'm sorry. I only pray he didn't suffer.'

And, surprisingly for her, she took pity on him and said, 'I think it was quick.'

The cleaner's name was Angela Kroll, and she called herself Mr Bygod's housekeeper. She had had blood on her clothes, so they had been taken away and she had been given coveralls and slippers to wear until her husband could collect her and bring a new set. 'But they've put her in the soft room and given her coffee,' Atherton reported when they got back to the station.

In Atherton's view the soft room, which is what he called the interview suite where they took witnesses rather than suspects – people they *didn't* want to intimidate – wasn't any great shakes, but it was better than the bare rooms behind the front shop. It had carpet and upholstery and smelled of air freshener rather than feet and vomit.

'Kroll is the German word for someone with curly hair,' Atherton went on chattily as they trod up the stairs. 'So what we have here is a curly-haired angel. You can't get any purer than that.'

'Try not to let it prejudice you against her.'

Atherton smiled sinuously. 'How well you know me.' He looked keen, like a pointer in the presence of the guns. Slider could almost read his mind. Wouldn't it be nice if the suspiciously named angel had done it? They'd find a motive, prove that the pattern of blood on her clothes could only have come from wielding the weapon, and – bingo! All done and dusted in time for tea.

And of course, sometimes it happened that way. And often you got a confession to boot. People who had done someone to death in a moment of wildness, even where they had tried to cover up afterwards, were curiously eager to talk about it. And who was more willing to hear than your friendly plain-clothes police officer?

Angela Kroll had nothing particularly angelic about her appearance, though glamour was not enhanced by the coveralls and a face scrubbed of make-up. She seemed to be in her late forties, a stringy, whippy sort of woman with large knuckly hands, a pale, indoors face, poor teeth, and no-coloured hair, straight and dragged back tight to her skull into a ponytail. It was hard to tell if she was upset about her employer's death. Her eyes were jittery and her expression was guarded, but even the most innocent of civilians could get a little nutty in the presence of the police. Who didn't have secrets in their lives? It was one of the ways you could spot the professional criminal under questioning: they were too much at ease.

Slider started her off with the easy stuff to get her loosened up – name, address, marital status. She lived in Acton Vale with her husband, had three grown children, one still at home. Her husband was a builder. Kroll – no, it was a Polish name. She had a flat, North London accent and tended towards the terse and monosyllabic, but whether that was habitual, or nerves, Slider couldn't tell.

'How long have you worked for Mr Bygod?' he asked.

'Ten years,' she said with a shrug that meant 'more or less'.

'And you're his – housekeeper, you said?'

'I clean, do his laundry, cook sometimes.'

'You go in every day?'

'Not weekends. Eight thirty till two, Monday to Friday.'

'Is he married?'

'Ex wife. Before my time.' She seemed to read something into the question and bristled slightly. 'I'm his housekeeper, that's all. I know nothing about his private life.'

'You seem to keep the house beautifully clean,' Slider said soothingly.

She shrugged again. 'There's not really enough work, but I stretch it out. He likes me to be there.'

'To answer the door for him,' Slider suggested.

'When he's out. If he's in, he does it. With the entryphone. If it's the postman or something, he sometimes asks me to go down.'

'He didn't like the stairs?'

'He never went down to answer the door. He buzzed people up. Or not. Depending.'

'On what?'

'On whether he wanted to see them,' she said witheringly.

'Did he go out much?'

'Sometimes. I don't know what he did in the evening. I wasn't there.'

'But he had visitors while you were there.'

'I didn't say that,' she objected.

'You said he buzzed people up.' He spread his hands. 'I'm not trying to catch you out, Mrs Kroll. I'm just trying to establish a pattern of who might have come to the house.'

'Yes, he had visitors. If you could call them that,' she said with palpable disapproval.

'Why do you say that?'

'People came to him all the time for advice and help. Parasites.' She sniffed. 'Sucking the blood out of him.'

'Did he give them money?'

'No!' she said scornfully. 'Or not that I knew, anyway. But there's such a thing as wearing a person to death. Everyone in trouble, everyone wanting something. Always at him. Never a bit of peace.'

'You were fond of him,' Slider suggested.

'I worked for him,' she said. 'Fond doesn't come into it. What do you want from me?' She gave him a burning look.

'You said they were wearing him to death?'

She met his eyes for a fraction of a second then looked away, as if she regretted having given so much. 'Figure of speech.'

'Did you know any of them?'

'I never saw them, except in passing.'

'What did they look like?'

'Every sort. Old, young, rich, poor. Looked like right low-life, some of 'em. Wouldn't be surprised if some of 'em hadn't been inside – done time. I kept out of the way. I didn't want to get sucked in.' She sniffed again. 'He didn't seem to mind.' She looked about, grabbed a tissue from the box on the table, and blew her nose thoroughly.

Slider caught Atherton's eye over her shoulder. All these people tramping in and out, and some of them low-life, if Mrs Kroll was to be believed, was going to make a real cat's-tangle to unravel.

'You say he was divorced. Did he have any female friends?'

'I told you, I don't know anything about his private life.' She hesitated.

'Yes?' Slider encouraged. 'You thought of something.'

'Sometimes a woman phoned for him, didn't sound like one of the parasites. Posh voice, sort of low and sexy.'

'Name?'

'She'd just say, "Tell him Nina rang."'

'So you answered the phone for him?'

'When he was out,' she said indignantly. 'I told him to get an answer-machine, but he didn't like stuff like that. Old-fashioned, he was.'

'There was no computer in the house,' Slider mentioned.

'He didn't want one, said all he needed was his

typewriter. I said what about the Internet, but he said there were books for information, and people should talk face to face or on the phone. He said talking to machines would destroy society.'

Slider remembered something Atherton had once quoted him, originally said by Albert Einstein: 'I fear the day when the technology overlaps with our humanity. The world will have a generation of idiots.' You only had to see a group of youngsters out for the night, all texting away instead of talking to each other, to suspect old Al had a point.

'If you ask me he was dotty,' Mrs Kroll went on. She started to heat up. 'Got no TV either. Who doesn't have a telly? Got this old radio he carried round to listen to the test match and the news. God knows what he did in the evenings.'

Slider wondered too. Reading, or gadding about? 'Was he a well man, would you say?'

'Seemed all right. He never complained.'

'He could get about all right? Or was he frail?'

'Frail?' she said derisively. 'He wasn't that old.'

He saw Atherton make a gesture, and asked, 'Was he hard of hearing?'

'Not that I know of. Look, he may have been getting on, and he may have been weird about computers and such, but there was nothing wrong with him as far as I know.' She stirred restively. 'Is my old man here yet? I want to go home. I can't sit about here all day talking to you. I've got stuff to do, you know.'

'They'll ring up to us when your husband

arrives,' Slider said soothingly. 'Just tell me what your usual routine was. You arrived at eight every morning?' He said the wrong time deliberately so she would have to correct him. It would get her going.

'Half past,' she said promptly. 'I'd clear up the kitchen from his breakfast, and the night before if he'd cooked for himself. He went out to eat a lot, but he liked cooking as well.'

'So you'd know from the dirty dishes if he'd had people in.'

'I suppose so,' she said sulkily.

'Go on. You cleaned the house?'

'Hoovered, dusted, polished. Made the bed. Bathroom. Put his laundry in the machine and ironed the dry stuff. Cooked him lunch sometimes if he wasn't going out. Left at two sharp. That was it. Like I said, there wasn't that much work – you don't really need to clean a house every day – but he wanted me to be there.'

'Even when he wasn't there? When he went out?'

'That was when I got the chance to clean his study properly. When he was in, he always sat in there. I cleaned round him, but it's not the same, and if I was Hoovering and the phone rang I'd have to stop. Which it did, a lot.'

'And if visitors came?'

'I'd leave the room. Keep out of the way.'

'That must have been annoying for you,' Slider said kindly, 'when you wanted to get on.'

She shrugged. 'Every job's got its drawbacks.'

'He was a wealthy man, I suppose?' he slipped in casually.

But she looked wary. 'I never asked.'

'Did he keep any valuables around the house?'

'What you asking that for?' she said sharply. The burn was back. 'Mr Bygod trusted me, he left me alone in the house many's the time. I was with him ten years.'

Slider laid calm over the troubled water. 'I'm just thinking that if word had got round that there were valuables in the house – and you said some of the visitors were "low-lifes", maybe ex-cons...'

'Oh,' she said warily, unsure whether to believe him. 'Well, he didn't have anything like that as far as I know. Just his knick-knacks, his books, his crappy old pictures and such. Who'd steal *them*?'

'Did he have a safe?'

'Only that little one in the study.'

'I noticed the key was in it.'

'He never locked it. He said it was just to keep documents safe if there was a fire. There was no money in it or anything.'

'How do you know?'

She looked affronted again. 'He told me. Anyway, he had it open most of the time when I've been in there, and I could see. Just papers, that's all.'

The phone rang. Atherton answered it, and nodded to Slider over her shoulder.

'Your husband's arrived,' Slider said.

She scowled. 'And *he'll* be in a temper, getting called from work.' Something occurred to her. 'And I suppose I've got to tell him I've lost my job as well.'

'I'm afraid so,' Slider said.

'Bloody hell,' she muttered below her breath. 'As if I didn't have enough to put up with.' Aloud, she said, 'Can I go now, then?'

'Just a few more questions. This morning, when you went in – you have a key, I suppose?'

'That's right,' she said.

'You went upstairs, and into—?'

'The kitchen first. I go in there, take my coat off, put the kettle on, before I go and see him.'

'Did you call out to him?'

'Top of the stairs. "It's only me," I said, though who else it'd be I don't know.'

'Were you surprised he didn't answer you?'

'Not really. I thought he was reading or something.'

'What did you see in the kitchen?'

'Nothing. It was all tidy.'

'No dirty dishes.'

'He went out for lunch, Tuesday. Went off about half eleven, wasn't back before I left.'

'No supper dishes? So he didn't eat in, in the evening?'

'I suppose not.'

'And no breakfast things.'

'Well, there wouldn't be, would there? He was dead.'

'Didn't it surprise you? There were usually breakfast things for you to wash up.'

The weary look again. 'I didn't think about it. One less thing for me to do, that's all. I just went along to his study to see if he wanted anything and—' She stopped, her face tight and hard, which might have been the attempt to control emotion. But what emotion?

'Was the study door open or closed?'

'Open. It always was, unless he was having a meeting in there and wanted to be private.'

'So you saw him from the door.'

She nodded.

'Why did you go over to him?'

She bridled. 'To see if he was dead, what d'you think? He might've still been alive, then I'd've called the ambulance. I shook his shoulder and called him, tried to lift his head up, but it was no good.'

'Don't you know you aren't supposed to move anything at a crime scene?'

'I said, he might've been alive!' she said angrily. 'God Almighty!' She stood up. 'Can I go now? Or are you accusing me of something?'

'Not at all,' Slider said, standing up too. Her face was red, and she was bristling. He nodded to Atherton, who went to open the door. As she reached it, he said, 'By the way, do you wear rubber gloves while you're cleaning?'

She only turned at the neck, and the single eye he could see glittered. 'What you asking that for?'

'Answer the question, please.'

'For doing the bathroom, and washing up,' she said, as if trying to work out what he wanted.

'Not otherwise?'

'Why you asking?'

'We'll need to eliminate your fingerprints from among any we find in the house,' he said smoothly. 'That's all.'

'Oh,' she said, with a faintly baffled look.

Outside, Lawrence, one of the uniformed policewomen, was just arriving to escort her out. Slider called Atherton back quickly. 'Have a look at the husband,' he murmured. 'And get a background search started on him. And the rest of the family.'

Atherton nodded and went away.

Mrs Kroll had something to hide, Slider was sure of it, but it was a wearisome fact that civilians habitually tried to hide things that were nothing to do with the case they were being questioned about. If her husband or son were dodgy in some way, that could account for her wariness.

Or she might know more about Bygod's death than she was going to let on without official encouragement.

But she had not shed a tear for him, despite the ten years.

THREE

Huddled Masses

'We've got a para in the *Standard,*' Norma said, sitting on a desk swinging her lovely legs. One of the uniforms at the back of the room followed the movement with his eyes like a pendulum. 'Local hero murdered. The man who helped everyone, blah blah. "Mr Bygod was well-known locally for giving help and advice to all who needed it."'

'Right little boy scout, wasn't he?' McLaren said, unpeeling the end of a Mars Bar. 'That's what you get for helping people.'

'People are morons,' said Connolly impatiently. 'Try to help them and they spit in your face.'

'*He* was a moron,' McLaren countered. 'Letting them in like that, just anyone off the street. People are rotten.'

'The wretched refuse of your teeming shore,' Atherton said, strolling in with a take-out cardboard cup of coffee. 'Good to know compassion is alive and well in the modern-day police service. Send these, the homeless, tempest-tost to me.'

'Where'd you get that?' Connolly asked, eyeing the cup.

'Went out for it,' Atherton said.

'And y' didn't ask anyone else? God, what're you like?'

'You've got a kettle. Maurice, don't put that Mars Bar in your mouth like that. You look as if you're having oral sex with it.'

McLaren pulled it out quickly – which was not any sort of improvement – and said peevishly, 'What you want me to do? Can't eat it without putting it in me mouth, can I?'

'Bite a bit off, for God's sake!'

'Thank you, Jim,' Swilley said. 'At last. It comes to something when you have to give a colleague eating lessons.'

'Well, I haven't got your brain,' McLaren said sulkily.

'Whoever's got yours ought to give it back.'

'Ah, you're always givin' out to the poor oul culchie,' Connolly stepped in. 'Would you not give him a break once?' McLaren stared at her with his mouth open. No-one had ever stood up for him before. She looked at him kindly. 'Shut your mouth, Maurice, for feck's sake. I can see the last three meals you've eaten.'

Mackay looked up from the racing pages of the *Sun*. 'Anyone got anything for Lingfield tomorrow?'

McLaren saw the chance to take the attention off his eating habits. 'Two thirty. Horse called Make Or Break. Dead cert.'

'Like the last dead cert you gave me?' Atherton asked. He liked a flutter on the ponies now and then. 'Remember Bredon Hill?'

'Bredon Hill's a good horse,' McLaren said stubbornly.

'I'm sure he's very handsome. What I complain about is his serene, almost Buddhist approach to racing.'

'You wanted an outsider,' McLaren pointed out. 'No point betting at five to four on, that's what you said.'

'It's your own fault for asking him,' Swilley said. 'I've no patience with anyone who gambles. It's a mug's game.'

'You wouldn't understand,' said Atherton. 'A man has to have his pleasures.'

'Yeah, right,' McLaren agreed glutinously, through the chocolate, caramel and fondant melting round his tonsils.

Slider came in. 'All right, settle down everybody.' He spotted Atherton's cup. 'Anybody get me one?'

Swilley gave Atherton a pointed look that failed by several furlongs to make him blush, and said, 'I'll go, boss.'

'No, never mind now. I'll have one later. All right, Lionel Bygod, age sixty-six, lived alone, apparently divorced, done to death by blows to the back of his head, several, while sitting at his desk. Some time yesterday afternoon or evening. Found by his housekeeper this morning. There seems not to be any other disturbance, no sign of break-in. He was wearing a very nice watch, and his wallet was still in his pocket with seventy pounds cash in it.'

'So apparently not a burglary or robbery from the person,' said Hollis, his other sergeant, who generally acted as office manager. His thin hair and scrawny moustache always had an unconvincing look, like the feathers of a chick just out of the egg, but he seemed more than usually dishevelled today, and his rather bulging eyes were reddened, as if he hadn't been having much sleep lately.

'So how'd they get in?' asked Fathom, newish, callow, a big sweaty lad given to hair gel and powerful aftershave. 'Those doors with the entryphone, you can't slip the lock on 'em.'

'Either they were let in, or they had a key,' Swilley said impatiently. 'Keep up!'

'According to forensic,' Slider said, 'we can be certain from the blood pattern and lack of other traces that he wasn't moved from somewhere else. That means he was killed where he sat.'

'So someone crept up behind him,' McLaren said.

'That's a lot of creeping up,' said Norma. 'All the way up those stairs, on lino.'

'And there's a floorboard on the landing that creaks,' Atherton said.

'He'd hear them coming. Unless he was deaf.'

'There's no suggestion he was deaf,' Slider said. 'You ignore small sounds from behind you made by someone you know is there, whereas if you think you're in an empty house you're likely to turn round to investigate. So I think it's much more likely the murderer was someone Bygod had let in himself.'

There was a little murmur around the room about that. Most of them knew about Bygod's habit of giving advice and help to people who came in off the street; the others were soon enlightened by their neighbours.

'There's another thing to take into account. The murder weapon – the bronze statuette – was taken from the mantelpiece in the room. The murderer wiped his fingermarks off it afterwards and left it there. Which means—?'

'An amateur,' said Gascoyne. 'A professional would have taken the weapon away with him.'

'A professional would have brought his own weapon with him in the first place,' Norma pointed out, 'not relied on finding something when he got there.'

'Unless it was spur of the moment,' Atherton said. 'He came to see the victim for some other reason and just did it when the overpowering emotion arose. *Crime passionelle.* Don't you think that sounds like a fruity blancmange?'

'Or,' said Slider, 'he'd been there before, and made a mental note that the statuette would do the job. However, the fact that he didn't put on gloves does suggest a degree of lack of planning.'

'Maybe there wasn't time,' Norma said reasonably. 'Maybe moments when Bygod was sitting down with his back turned didn't come all that often.'

'I'll take that one,' said Connolly. 'Sure, if your visitor starts puttin' on the marigolds while you're chattin' about the weather, you might cop on that he's up to something.'

'Speaking of marigolds,' Atherton said, looking at Slider, 'you do realize the prime suspect has got to be the housekeeper, the angelic Mrs

Kroll? She has a key, she has every right to be there, she can wander in and out of his room pretty much at will and pick her time. Any noises she makes behind him he'll be programmed to ignore. We don't know exactly what time he was killed, and we've only got her word that he went out that morning and wasn't back before she left. She had the perfect excuse to have his blood on her clothes – and if she's left any fingermarks anywhere, so what?'

'All true,' said Slider. 'Except that she also had the perfect excuse to be wearing gloves and not to have to wipe fingermarks off the statue.'

'She didn't wear them for housework,' Atherton said, but his face showed he immediately saw the problem.

'Again, we only have her word for that,' said Slider.

'Well, she's still the prime suspect,' Atherton said.

'I don't disagree. We should look into her background and movements. See if we can find any evidence of when she actually did leave yesterday. Did you get a look at her husband?'

'Very tasty. Big, butch, and angry,' said Atherton.

'Other lines of enquiry, guv?' Hollis asked, making a note of the Krolls.

'I'm not sure the local canvass is going to yield anything – people pass up and down the street all the time, in and out of the shops – but you never know. CCTVs – McLaren, see if any of the shops have got one that shows people passing. I know we haven't got an exact time of death, but for now start collating from two o'clock yesterday afternoon. Fathom, see what London Transport's got. Their buses have cameras that may have caught something.'

'Right, guv.'

'And forensic may have something to tell us. We should get some fingermarks, at least.'

'If he did have a lot of ex-cons visiting him, that might prove interesting,' Atherton said.

'Otherwise – find out more about Bygod, obviously,' Slider went on. 'Basic background search. Was he retired? What did he do before that? Who were his friends? If he did go out to lunch yesterday, who with? There's a diary and an address book coming over when forensic have finished with it. Connolly, that's yours. Also the chequebook – Norma, see if there's anything interesting in that. And look into his financial position. Was he, in fact, wealthy, and if so, where did the money come from and where did he keep it?'

'When are we going to get a look at the contents of that document safe?' Atherton asked.

'When forensic have finished with it.'

'Guv, I've been thinking,' said McLaren.

'The first time's always the worst,' Slider comforted him.

'He was writing a cheque, right? I mean, there's no doubt – he'd written the date when he got whacked.'

'The pen seems to have been in his hand, and the cap was off,' Slider said.

'That's probably how the murderer got him to sit down with his back turned,' Mackay said.

'Good point,' Slider said. 'I'm not sure it helps, unless we can work out who he might have written a cheque to. Of course, it might have been one of the visiting lowlifes. Mrs Kroll said he didn't give people money, but again that's just her view.'

'But guv,' McLaren objected, 'my point is, if chummy did persuade him to write him a cheque, why didn't he wait for him to finish, so's he could have the money as well?'

'Janey Mac!' Connolly rolled her eyes – evidently it was a thing all girls could do, Slider observed with interest. 'It'd be a bit of a dead giveaway, wouldn't it, ya gobshite, if he goes hoofin' down the bank with the last cheque your man wrote?'

McLaren stood up for himself. 'There'd be nothing to say what time of the day he wrote it. Even if it was the last. If it was me, I'd have waited and took it.'

Slider took a minute to phone home, and got Joanna.

'I wanted to catch you before you left. All serene?' he asked.

'I've been resting, with my feet up, if that's what you mean,' she said defensively.

'Dad all right with the kids?'

'He's only just back with them. He took them out, even George. You'll never guess where.'

'Where?'

'The Tate.'

'He took *my* children to an art gallery? We are talking about OMG Kate and Footy Mad

Matthew, aren't we?'

'Turns out he was going there anyway today, to meet his lady-friend, and didn't see any reason to put off his date for a brace and a half of grandchildren. They had lunch, looked at paintings, came home on the top of the bus. A good time was had by all. He should have been a general. The army could do with his marshalling skills.'

'I hope he hasn't worn himself out,' Slider said guiltily.

'He seemed all right. He's gone back to his flat for a rest. The kids are packed and Irene'll be here any minute. I'm going to get George fed and in bed before your dad comes back over. He won't have anything to do but watch telly until you get home.'

'Sounds like the army's missing you, too. I won't be late home. I'm just finishing up some paperwork here.'

'How is it?' she asked. 'Sad or bad?' It was a shorthand they had.

'More sad than bad. It seems the chap was a bit of a philanthropist, and may have been whacked by one of his philanthropees, probably for some petty reason.'

'All reasons are petty, weighed against a human life,' she said.

'Good luck with your concert. Don't get too tired.'

'Tell it to Prokofiev,' she replied. 'I have no say in the matter.'

Just before he left, Porson sent for him. The old

man looked tired, after a day with his seniors and the press officers.

'Not much in the media yet, thank God,' he said as Slider came in. Unusually, he'd got his bottle of White Horse out of the filing cabinet. Porson was not a big drinker, but it was going-home time in the real world, and his nerves were obviously strained. 'Drink?'

'No thank you, sir,' Slider said.

Porson poured himself a modest noggin. 'I thought they'd have been all over it. Kind man bitten by the hand that feeds him, that sort of thing. Makes a good story. Lucky they had their minds in the usual place. MP caught cottaging in Hyde Park, so they've all run away to play over there. The local papers'll be on ours, but we can live with that. What about this cleaner woman?' His sharp eyes came up to Slider's face. 'She's got to be a possible.'

Slider explained the various matters relating to keys, fingermarks and choice of weapon.

Porson looked gloomy. 'She'd be a bastard to prove unless you get a good strong motive. She could leave herself behind all over the place and it wouldn't mean a thing. Mind you, if it was me in her shoes, I'd've worn the gloves, cleaned the statue and put it back on the mantelpiece.'

'Unless she wanted to make it look as if it *wasn't* her,' Slider said. 'We'd have found traces on the statue eventually, and that would have put her squarely in the frame.'

'Point. Except that they never think like that – lucky for us. Well, carry on. Hammersmith's lost interest a bit what with one thing and another, and given it wasn't anyone famous, but it only takes a slow news day and we're back in the spotlight. The bugger of it is,' he concluded gloomily, 'showing someone was there isn't going to get us anywhere.'

Slider had already made the acquaintance of that particular bugger.

He made Joanna go to bed as soon as she got home from the concert, and took her up a mug of Ovaltine.

'Oh, Daddy!' she simpered, fluttering her eyelids, but he could see how tired she was. They were too much, these long days and the strain of trying to be perfect in a fiercely competitive world; but he had expressed his doubts already, and could not press them without disrespecting her right to self-determination. He got on the bed beside her with his own mug, and she opened the batting – to keep him, he guessed, from saying the things he had just decided he mustn't.

'So how did it go? What's it looking like?'

'It's looking like a long haul.' He told her some of the details.

'The housekeeper, obviously,' she said at the end of it. 'All you need is a motive.'

'All!'

'Well, you know what I mean.'

'In any case, motives are usually the feeblest of things. It could be something as small as him telling her off about not cleaning something properly. How would you ever find that out? And any forensic evidence about her is automatically out of play because she had every right to be there.' He sighed. 'I don't see this one coming in quickly.'

She sipped, and then as he drew breath to speak she got in first. 'What about your dad's escapade today? Isn't that intriguing?'

'I'm more amazed than intrigued. Kate voluntarily went to an art gallery? Which Tate was it – Original or New Improved?'

'The Modern,' Joanna said, 'so I expect she'd heard of it somewhere on the "cool" spectrum. I'm more intrigued that he wanted to inflict them on his girlfriend.'

'Which one was it?'

'Oh Bill,' she said reproachfully, 'it's been Lydia Hurst for ages. Lydia from the Scrabble club?'

'Oh,' he said, recalibrating. 'Do you think it's serious?'

'Introducing your grandchildren?' Joanna said. 'I think it's a senior's version of taking her home to meet the parents.'

'He's not brought her to see us yet,' Slider complained.

'Doesn't want to frighten her off, maybe. This was a toe in the water. If she survived the children intact...' She shrugged.

'Well, it'll be nice for him to get married again, I suppose,' he said, wondering what was the appropriate reaction – wondering, indeed, what he felt about such a notion. His mother had died so long ago, and his father had lived an almost monastic life in the farm cottage where Slider had been born, until his recent move to a granny-flat attached to their new house. In all those years he had never seemed to want female companionship, and the only woman Slider had heard him speak about was his mother. Then, suddenly, transported to Chiswick, he had blossomed out into a new social life, and the zimmer-dollies had been all over him.

'I don't know if they'd get married or just live together,' Joanna said, slightly shocking Slider, who was old-fashioned about such things – well, anyway, about one's own father living in sin: the rest of the world could do as it pleased. 'But either way, we have to consider how it might affect us.'

'How could it affect us?' he asked, puzzled. 'You don't think his flat is big enough for two?'

'Who says they'd even live there? She may want him to live in her house. Or they might want a new place entirely. And wherever they end up, don't you think it's certain to mean he's not available, at least on the old basis, for babysitting?'

Now Slider saw it.

She went on, 'We've been spoiled, having him here and on tap at any time of the day or night. He cancels his plans at the last moment for us, stays on when we're late back, and never a word of complaint.'

'But he loves doing it. He loves having time with George.'

'Whether he does or he doesn't, we've become dangerously reliant on him. And what about when the new baby comes? He's not getting any younger, and two is a lot more than twice the work of one, especially when one of them is about to hit the terrible twos. I just don't think we can afford to blithely assume everything's going to go on the same way.'

He saw all the problems lined up ahead, along with the delicate emotional minefields through which a way would have to be picked. His dad, of course, would protest that he loved taking care of his grandchildren, and being of the polite generation he would say it whether it was true or not – which was the problem with extreme politeness. It was hard to know where you stood. On the other hand, the suggestion that he was not up to the task might hurt his feelings; while on yet another hand the assumption that he was automatically free to babysit as if he had no private life of his own could mine yet another rich seam of hurt and resentment.

But what Slider saw most immediately was that Joanna was already tired and fraught and the last thing she needed was to start worrying about childcare this far ahead of the game.

'We'll sort something out,' he said. 'Don't start worrying about it at this stage.'

She looked at him sidelong. 'Have you any idea what childcare costs these days? Even if there *were* childcare to cover our particular set of fractured circumstances. Neither of us works a nice tidy nine-to-five.'

'We'll work it out,' he said firmly. 'People do, all the time, all over the world. Even if it's a juggling fest. It's worth it, isn't it?'

There was a brief pause during which his blood ran cold. He was afraid she was going to say, *we should never have had this baby*. In the end what she said was not much better. 'Worth it, even if it means I have to stop playing? Because that's the bottom line, isn't it? My career isn't as important as yours.'

'I've never said that.'

'But that's what it'll come down to. I'll have to give up playing and take a job that will fit round the childcare.' She made a grimace. 'Giving violin lessons in the sitting room.'

He managed not to say that lives went through different phases or that lots of people enjoyed teaching and found it rewarding. 'We're a long way from that point yet,' he said instead, 'and we may never reach it. If Dad and Lydia do get together, they might *both* really like babysitting, have you considered that? Two for the price of one.'

She shook her head at him. 'Oh Bill! What is all this chirpy Dalai Lama optimism? "Everything'll be all right, everything'll be fine!"'

'It will be. Trust me,' he said. 'Never trouble trouble, till trouble troubles you.'

She began reluctantly to smile. 'Jiminy Cricket, that's what we should call you.'

'No, that was conscience – a different sort of getting into trouble.'

She put her mug aside and turned to him. 'Well, why don't we try that sort instead, just for a change? I'm already pregnant, you can't make things worse. Enjoy the free ride while you can.'

He put his own mug down and kissed her tenderly. 'Nothing about this is trouble,' he said, hand on her bump. The world he inhabited by day was a variously unpleasant and hostile place, and Joanna was his tranquil garden of refreshment. But she might not want to hear that just now, so he used his lips without words instead.

Morning brought Bob Bailey, calling in himself with the fingerprints. This was not kindness or especially good service, more that he was running a campaign of trying to get into Connolly's pants. He was recently separated and keen to get back in the saddle. He wasn't a bad-looking bloke – though not as good-looking, according to the women in Slider's firm, as he thought he was – and evidently reckoned he had a chance with Connolly, despite her undisguised hostility.

Slider's door was open and he heard the exchange from the CID room. Bailey's opening gambit was straightforward. 'Where's the lovely Rita? *Lovely Rita, meter maid*,' he warbled. 'When are you going to give me that date?'

Connolly managed to be quite robust without raising her voice. 'Go out with you? What are you, headless? I wouldn't date you if it was gold plated.'

'Ah, come on. I'm not talking about a cheap date. I'm ready to spend money on you. Anywhere you like. You can name your place.'

'And you can feck right off with yourself,' Connolly returned firmly. She crossed Slider's vision as she went out of the room.

Bailey appeared in Slider's doorway.

'There are baboons with more subtle mating rituals,' Slider said, glaring at him. 'How many times does she have to say no?'

Bailey was unabashed. 'She'll come round. Persistence pays.'

'Not if you call her a meter maid. She'll deck you, and I for one will cheer.'

'I like a girl with spirit,' he said with a mixture of lust and sentiment.

'Well, I won't have you harassing my staff.'

'Asking a girl out isn't harassing.'

'It is in the workplace,' Slider warned, and saw it sink in. Bailey was a civilian and not under his command, but employment law applied to him just the same.

Bailey became brisk and professional. 'Right, I've got the lifts for you. The place is very clean – that housekeeper does her job all right – so there aren't as many marks as you might expect. A lot of marks and smudges up the staircase wall and the handrail. Marks on the desk that may be the victim's. Recent marks in the kitchen look like a woman's, so probably the housekeeper's. And a lot of marks on the door of the Murder Room.'

'Can we not call it that,' Slider intervened in a pained voice.

Bailey shrugged. 'Whatever. Study, if you like. Like I said, madam housekeeper cleans and wipes, but nobody polishes up a door, do they? Now the doorknob's been wiped clean, both sides, but on the edge of the door there's quite a few marks, and about shoulder height there's a fresh thumb and all four fingers which are over the top of anything else, making them the latest. Like this.' He demonstrated the position on

Slider's office door.

Slider got it. 'He gripped the door to steady it while he wiped the doorknobs?'

'In my humble opinion,' said Bailey with an unhumble smirk.

'So,' said Slider, 'if they were left by the murderer, he didn't wear gloves, but having done the deed, tried to cover himself by wiping the weapon where he'd held it, and the door knobs. He managed to think that far, but not far enough.'

'It's a fair assumption,' said Bailey.

It wasn't as much as that. Anyone could have gripped the door by the frame in the act of closing it, and the fact that there were no marks over the top of these didn't give any evidence about when they had been made. But it was something. And if they came up with a match in records...

'It's a lead,' Slider allowed. 'Possibly.'

Bailey shrugged at such parsimony. 'I thought you'd be happy.'

'I'm ecstatic,' said Slider.

Bailey trickled out, hoping for Connolly to come back. 'Contents of the safe and the desk are on their way. And I've brought the diary and address book, and his wallet.'

The phone rang. It was Cameron to say that he had nothing yet to add to yesterday's conclusions. Death had been caused by the blows to the head: three of them, forceful and probably delivered rapidly given the small spread of the injuries – which by the way matched the superficies of the bronze statuette, so there seemed no doubt it was the murder weapon.

While Cameron was talking to him, Slider saw, through his open door, Connolly come back in, and beckoned to her. She came in and waited until he finished the call, then said, 'Did you want something, boss?'

'Yes – is Bailey annoying you?'

'No, boss. He's just an eejit.'

'I can give him a formal warning.'

'God, no – no need. I can take care of it.'

'I won't have you harassed.'

She grinned. 'I know some fellers who wouldn't be long putting manners on him for me, if need be. I've only to ask.'

'Now I'm wondering whether he needs protection from you,' Slider said.

'Female of the species, sir,' she said, and went perkily out, leaving Slider feeling better about her.

Nicholls, the relief sergeant on duty downstairs, rang through. 'Bill, there's a bloke come in, says he's a friend of your deceased. Says he was supposed to have seen him last night. Any use to you?'

'Could be,' Slider said. 'Might be a chance to get a handle on the man, maybe even some leads. We don't even know the next of kin yet.'

'Shall I put him in an interview room?'

'What's he like?'

'Like a 1950s BBC newsreader.'

'Better not, then. Might fry his circuits. Can you have someone bring him up here?'

'Will do.'

FOUR

Private Citizen

The man who was escorted upstairs by a uniformed officer was one Reginald Plumptre. He spelled it for them carefully. 'But it's pronounced "plumter". Most people try to make me a plum tree,' he added with a shy whimsy.

He was tall and thin, what Slider's father would have described as 'a long drink of water'. He appeared to be in his sixties, or perhaps older – it was harder to tell these days, when old people were so much more active. He was bald on top but had good thick linings all around at ear level, making it look as if he'd stuck his head in a bowling alley ball-polishing machine. He was wearing a conventional grey suit and a red tie, both of which seemed to have seen long service, but his cufflinks and watch looked quietly expensive and he spoke with an RP accent. Slider put him down as one of the army of office workers who had retired on good pensions before the bottom fell out.

'I'm Detective Inspector Slider, and this is Detective Sergeant Atherton. How can I help you, Mr Plumptre? Won't you sit down?'

Plumptre hesitated, looking at Slider but not at

him, his eyes absent with some suppressed agitation. 'I have to ask you first,' he said, 'is it true? I saw something in the paper – I can't believe – it seems too ... Is Lionel really dead? Someone killed him?'

'I'm afraid it's true,' Slider said. 'Please sit down.'

Plumptre's legs took the initiative, and he collapsed into the chair. He put hand to his head as if steadying it. 'I can't believe it,' he muttered shakily.

'Would you like a glass of water, or a cup of tea, or something?' Slider asked.

Plumptre visibly pulled himself together, sitting up straighter, licking his lips, clasping his hands together across his front. One of the old school: he was here to do his duty and would jolly well do it. 'No – thank you – no. I'm quite all right. It's a shock, that's all. You never expect something like that to happen to someone you know.'

'You knew Mr Bygod well?' Slider asked, to get him started.

'He was my friend,' Plumptre said. 'A good friend and a very fine man. I can't believe anyone would be so wicked as to harm him. I was supposed to be seeing him two nights ago, but even when there was no answer at the house, it never occurred to me...'

'You went round to his flat in Shepherd's Bush Road on Tuesday night? What time was that?'

'It was just after ten to seven. I rang the bell and waited for him to answer, but he didn't. That's when I looked at my watch, to see if I was on time. I waited until seven exactly, in case he had been in the bathroom, perhaps, and rang again. When there was still no answer, I stepped back to the edge of the pavement and looked up, and saw there was no light in any of the windows. So I thought he must have forgotten, or gone out and been delayed, or had something urgent come up, so I went home. I telephoned later from home but there was no answer. I expected him to ring me the next day and apologize – he was punctilious about such things. But when I walked down to the corner shop yesterday afternoon to get some milk, I saw the item in the newspaper. I was so shocked, I had to go straight home and have a cup of tea and lie down. And then, in the middle of the night, I woke up wondering whether I ought to tell anyone that I'd been there. Not that there's anything I can tell you, really, but I thought it might be useful to know that there was no answer to the doorbell at seven o'clock. A *terminus ante quem*, so to speak.' He gave a faint, apologetic smile. 'I am rather fond of golden age detective stories.'

He stopped. Talking seemed to have steadied him, and he looked less shaky.

'You did quite right to come in,' Slider said. 'What were you going to see Mr Bygod about?'

'Oh, just a social meeting. He was going to cook supper – he enjoyed cooking – and then we planned to play a little piquet. We're both keen card players. We used to play bridge together regularly until my wife died two years ago, and at about the same time his partner, who was quite an elderly person, went to live in Northampton with his son and daughter-in-law, so our little meetings lapsed.'

'His partner?' Slider queried.

Plumptre gave him a questioning look. 'Bridge partner,' he elucidated. 'It's harder than you might think to find an agreeable person to play with, someone at the right level of skill who takes the game seriously enough but not too seriously. So we rather gave up bridge. Since then, when we meet, just the two of us, for cards, we play piquet, or sometimes bezique.'

'How long have you known Mr Bygod?'

'Oh, it must be ten or eleven years now.' He looked to see if Slider wanted more, and seeing his receptive look, went on conversationally: 'We first met at a Residents' Association meeting. He'd just moved into the area. We got talking, and took a liking to each other. He said he wanted to busy himself with useful things now he'd retired, so I persuaded him to volunteer for the Home Visit Club – it's a charity I'm involved with. You visit housebound people and read to them, or talk, or do little errands, whatever they want. He helped with the office work, too. And it went on from there. He got himself involved in local campaigns, and charity things. Various committees. We're both collectors for the Royal British Legion. I suppose there isn't much charitable or volunteer work around the area that he *isn't* involved in. He's that kind of man – a genuine pillar of the community.'

In his enthusiasm he had slipped back into the present tense, and his face was relaxed and happy. He'd forgotten why he was talking about

Bygod, here and now.

'You haven't mentioned a wife. Was he married?'

'No – well, never since I've known him. I don't know much about his life before that. He didn't talk about himself, really. But he never mentioned a wife.'

'What about family?'

Plumptre shook his head. 'I never knew he had any. He never mentioned anyone.'

'So you can't help us with who his next of kin might be?'

'Oh dear, I'm afraid not.' He put a hand to his cheek. 'It hadn't occurred to me – of course you would want to ... but I really don't know. I could ask some of our other friends if they know. Perhaps he might have mentioned someone at some time.'

Slider digested this. Men were, in any case, deeply incurious about each other's private lives, and probably the older you got the more entrenched the habit became. It might not even be remarkable that Plumptre didn't know whether Bygod had ever had children.

He moved on. 'So was he already retired when you first met him?'

'Yes – we had both retired early, which was another bond between us, I suppose. I worked in the salaries department at Beecham's on the Great West Road. I was there before the SmithKline takeover, but when Glaxo took over the lot, I was eased out, so I took an early pension.'

'And what did Mr Bygod do before he retired?'

‘I believe he was a solicitor. I don’t know why he retired early – as I said, he didn’t really talk about himself. Perhaps he’d just had enough. He seemed very happy with his life the way it was.’

‘You knew about his habit of giving advice to people who came in off the street?’

‘It wasn’t quite like that,’ Plumptre said. ‘They were people he’d met elsewhere, or who were introduced by other people he knew. Word got round, of course, but he didn’t let complete strangers in.’

‘What sort of advice?’

‘Legal and practical – how to deal with the local council, what your rights were in disputes, faulty goods, that sort of thing. Who to go to and where to find information – rather like the Citizen’s Advice Bureau. Not lonely hearts stuff,’ he added, permitting himself a small smile. ‘He wasn’t an agony aunt.’

‘Talking of lonely hearts,’ Slider said, ‘did he have any women friends?’

‘Oh, there are women in our group all right – of course there are. But if you mean in the romantic sense – I don’t think so. I never saw him with anyone.’

‘Your group?’ Slider queried.

‘Of friends,’ Plumptre said with a clear look. ‘We’re on committees together and meet for drinks and meals and go out sometimes. It’s a very nice circle. Of course, we’ve all known each other for years. Everyone was so kind and supportive when my wife died.’

Slider was feeling his way towards an idea he couldn’t yet see. ‘Have you met any of Mr

Bygod's friends from outside that circle? Maybe people he knew before you met him?'

Plumptre considered, and a little frown pulled down his brows. 'Well – no. Now you come to mention it. He does like to entertain, and he gives wonderful parties, but whenever we go to his house, it's all the same people – my friends, and friends of theirs. Someone from before?' He pondered again, apparently fruitlessly, for he concluded, 'I think he said that he lived in Islington.'

Islington. Famous place, squire, Slider thought. London was not one place but a series of villages, and Islington was a long way, at least in spirit, from Hammersmith.

'Of course,' Plumptre said, with an air of being satisfied by the conclusion, 'he might have seen his old friends separately. No reason we should know everything he did.'

'Of course,' Slider agreed. And it was true – he wouldn't be the only person to have separate circles of friends which didn't intersect. He might even have gone back to Islington to see his Islington friends. But it was, at the lowest reckoning, odd that there should have been no mingling of the groups, if groups there were, at social gatherings he initiated. When you asked people to your house for a party, would you segregate so rigidly?

He wasn't sure where the thought was leading, so he left it to mash at the back of the stove, and asked, 'The people that he gave advice to: were there any – how should I put it – suspicious characters among them? People you felt he should be wary of? Criminals out on bail, or ex-convicts on parole?'

'I couldn't really say,' said Plumptre. 'I wouldn't be surprised, given that he knew about the law, but I don't know for a fact that there were. Although, wait...' He thought of something. 'I don't know if it's relevant, but the only time I knew him to turn down voluntary work was when one of our friends, Molly Shepherd, asked him to get involved in prison counselling with her.' He looked at Slider. 'I don't know if you can draw any conclusions from that. After all, I imagine most people would hesitate about going into that environment. But he turned her down flat. Molly was a bit miffed, but we all thought afterwards that he had so much on his plate, he probably didn't have the time.'

'And when did that happen?'

'Oh, a long time ago. Must be – I don't know, at least four years, maybe more. They're the best of friends now,' he added gaily, 'so it didn't leave any lasting coolness.' And then it struck him. He faltered. 'I mean – I suppose I should say they *were* the best of friends. Oh dear.' He fumbled out his handkerchief and blew his nose. 'Do you have any idea who did this ghastly thing?' he asked.

'We have some leads to follow up,' he said. Never tell them you haven't the foggiest. 'I can't say more than that at present – you understand.'

'Of course, of course,' Plumptre said obligingly.

Slider rewarded him for his compliance by saying, 'You've been the greatest help to us.

Thank you for coming in,' and Plumptre went away happy in the knowledge that he had done his duty.

When Atherton came back from seeing him out, he found Slider staring at the wall, deep in thought. 'Well,' he said. 'What d'you make of that?'

Slider came to. 'I'm wary of making too much of it,' he said, 'but there's a suggestion of a break in Bygod's life when he moved to Hammersmith. It's odd for a friend – if Plumptre was a friend – not to know anything at all about one's previous life. I suppose,' he added with a sigh, 'we'll have to ask some of his other friends as well, in case Plumptre was just the sort you don't tell things to.'

'Well, at least, if Bygod was a solicitor it'll be easy to follow that up. No next-of-kin is a bummer.'

'We'll have to hope there's something in that document safe, when we get to look at the contents,' Slider said.

Atherton sat on Slider's windowsill, musing, arms folded. Slider, with his keenly-trained professional eye, couldn't help noticing that he appeared to be wearing the same clothes as yesterday. Slider didn't know what, if anything, to make of that, especially as he knew Emily was in the States, covering the election campaign for an article. Before Emily, Atherton had tomcatted so dedicatedly he had been named Posturepedic Man of the Year three years running. Surely the new dog couldn't be up to old tricks? *Not my business*, he told himself firmly.

Atherton stirred at last. 'Am I beginning to see a pattern here?' he asked.

Slider said, 'I've always wondered, what is the point of rhetorical questions?'

Atherton let that opportunity pass. He enumerated on his fingers. 'Lionel Bygod lived alone. Had no girlfriends. Plumptre talked about his "partner".'

'Bridge partner,' Slider reminded him. 'He was clear about that.'

'Doesn't mean he wasn't some other sort of partner as well. Work with me.' He marked off another finger. 'The restaurant bod said he was very helpful to a young male waiter.'

'He was married,' Slider countered with a finger of his own.

'Even if he was, it doesn't necessarily mean anything, as we both know. There are many with rings on their fingers who dance the other way. And in fact, nobody seems to know anything about this putative wife, so we don't know for certain that he ever *was* married.'

'We do now,' Hollis said, appearing in the doorway in time to catch the last exchange. He waved some folded papers. 'Contents of the safe, guv. These were on top – marriage certificate and birth certificate, together in an envelope.'

Slider took them. 'Well, that's clear enough. He married a Miss June Alexandra Bromwich at All Saint's church, Stamford, in 1975. You might see if you can trace her.'

'Right, guv.'

'And the birth certificate ... Oh, look at this.

Father was Sir Ernest Bygod, occupation given as barrister. Address Beaufort Hall, Colleyweston.'

'Beaufort Hall? Sounds like a community centre,' Atherton objected.

'Sounds posh to me,' Hollis countered.

'And where's Colleyweston when it's at home?'

'Lincolnshire,' Slider said. 'Round the back of Burghley where the horse trials are held. Very Shire.' Points to Hollis – posh it was. 'So it sounds as though he came from a moneyed background. He may have had a private income, or had money left him.'

'Strange he should live in a flat above a shop in Shepherd's Bush, then,' Atherton said. 'Even a large flat. Some sort of a kink in the straight line of his personal history, I wouldn't mind betting.' He gave Slider a significant look, which Slider resisted.

'What else is in the document safe?' Slider asked. 'A will would be nice, for the next of kin.'

'No will, guv. It's all just papers, like the housekeeper said. These, his passport, exam certificates and legal qualifications, deeds to the flat, and the rest are financial – share certificates and bonds and that sort o' thing,' said Hollis. 'I've given 'em to Swilley, since she's doing the financial stuff. But there looks to be a lot of 'em. Looks as if he might have been well off.'

'Nothing it would do anyone any good to steal, though,' Slider said. 'Unless, of course, something else *was* in there, and is no longer.'

'Which brings us back to Mrs Kroll,' Atherton

said, 'who was the most likely one to know. And we've only her word for it that he never locked the safe.'

'Check that with Mr Plumptre,' Slider told him. 'Who's looking into his other friends?'

'Nobody yet,' said Atherton.

'Well, put Connolly on to it, and make that one of the questions she asks: what was in the safe, and did he lock it? And who was his next of kin?' he added in a slightly fractious tone. 'Why hasn't anyone come asking for him?'

Gascoyne came in, with McLaren lingering at his shoulder. It was getting crowded in here. 'I've got the first of the fingerprint results, sir. The marks you were interested in on the study door come back without a match.'

'That's disappointing,' Slider said. 'But not unexpected.'

'Marks on the desk were the victim's, and only his, same on the document safe,' Gascoyne went on. 'Housekeeper's are all over the place, as you'd expect, except in the bathroom, so it sounds as if she might have been telling the truth about not wearing gloves.'

'Also disappointing,' said Slider.

'Don't you hate it when people are caught out telling the truth?' Atherton said.

'And the mass of prints up the stairs I've still to go through,' Gascoyne concluded.

McLaren intervened. 'I might have something for you to work on, Phil,' he said, squeezing past to get Slider's attention. 'I been looking into the Krolls, like you asked, put 'em into Crimint.' This was the Met's intelligence data base. 'The old man's come up flagged all over the place.' He grinned happily. 'Must be the only crooked Polish builder in London. No criminal record – yet – but he's been tugged plenty of times.' He spread out some sheets on Slider's desk. 'This is him, Jacek "Jack" Kroll. Lives Eastman Road, Acton Vale – got a yard behind his house backs on to Acton Park Industrial Estate. Got a son, Mark, age nineteen, works with him. No previous.'

'Is that the one that lives at home?' Slider asked.

'Yeah. Doesn't stop him claiming social security, though. Older son, Stefan, twenty-six, he does have a record, possession and handling stolen goods and a lot o' driving offences, going back to joyriding age twelve. Nothing on the daughter, Judy, twenty-four. She's on welfare an' all, got two kids, living with a bloke in Birmingham, according to Terry Cleaver at Ealing.' Acton came under the Ealing Borough command.

'So what has Jack Kroll been up to?' Atherton asked for them all.

'They've tugged him several times on suspicion of illegal dumping,' said McLaren. 'Dun't sound like much, but it can be big business. Also he's a bit too close to a bloke that owns a scrap metal yard, who they think is behind a load o' lead thefts in West London, going all the way out to Hounslow. Cleaver says he thinks Kroll is shifting the stuff on his lorry, may even be knocking it off under cover of doing building jobs.'

'Well, he certainly sounds tasty,' Slider agreed. 'None of that gives a connection to Lionel Bygod, however.'

'Except his wife,' said Atherton. 'Anything on her?'

'No, she's clean,' said McLaren, 'but Acton's been keeping an eye on her, anyway. She's seen hanging around with the female her son Stefan lives with, by the name of Mirela, or Mary, Dudnic. This Dudnic's got form as long as your arm for drugs and prostitution, and she's coming up in court on a charge of dealing next month.'

Slider twiddled his pen thoughtfully. 'All very nice, but what motive does that suggest for killing Bygod?'

'We don't know,' Atherton said reasonably, 'that something valuable *wasn't* stolen from the safe. By someone who didn't have to break in and who knew the safe would be unlocked – or maybe knew where the key was kept.'

'If she was going to rob him, why would she wait ten years to do it?' Slider asked.

'Some sudden need,' Atherton said.

'Well, it's pure speculation,' Slider said, 'but given that she did have the key, it's worth having a closer look at them. Trouble is, we don't have an exact time of death, so we don't know when they need an alibi for. Still, check out what they were doing for the whole of that day. Are Kroll's fingerprints on record?' McLaren nodded. 'Right then,' he said to Gascoyne, 'check if any of the unidentified ones in the house are his. And check for the son Stefan and Mary Dudnic as well. We've no particular reason for suspecting them but it's best to clear as you go, otherwise this sort of thing is apt to come back and bite you later.'

The crowd drifted away. Atherton was last out. He said, 'On the basis that the stupidest answer is usually right in these cases, you'd have to put your money on Mrs Kroll and her key. But I'd still like to know more about the mysteriously reticent, strangely out of his place ex-solicitor.'

'Go to, with my blessing,' Slider said. 'I can't join you in hoping for complications – a solid case against the prime suspect would be a joy – but he certainly seems to have been an oddball.'

'Fortunately, one with an odd name,' said Atherton, 'so it ought to be easy enough to find stuff on him.'

He was almost out of the door when Slider called, 'You might look in his address book for the Nina who called him and left messages.'

'According to Mrs Kroll,' Atherton qualified gloomily.

FIVE

Driving Miss Crazy

Molly Shepherd lived in Overstone Road – just a stone's throw from Bygod's place, Connolly noted – but she taught at a school in South Ealing, and Connolly sought her out there.

It was a plain, dull, 1970s' building, three storeys high with enormous picture windows, the liberal educationists' reaction to the high, narrow windows of the Victorian school buildings that everyone had been educated in until the Second World War. The Victorians had assumed that if children could see out, they wouldn't concentrate on their lessons. The liberal educationists thought that demanding concentration from children amounted to cruel and unusual punishment.

Classes were in session when Connolly arrived, and the building was quiet. She stepped in gingerly, her nostrils quivering at the hated smell. Why did schools everywhere smell the same, she wondered – kind of rubbery. A youth with his hair a mad, waxed ziggurat, his tie at half mast and his trousers apparently falling down, hove into view, lounging along the corridor. He stopped dead at the sight of Connolly and looked furtive, but she hailed him cheerily before he could leg it, and asked him where she could find Mrs Shepherd.

'Dunno,' he said, staring at her, eyes blank, mouth ajar, as if he had evolved from a fish. 'She ain't my teacher,' he added after some thought. 'You a parent?'

'Do I look like a parent?' Connolly said exasperatedly. He shrugged, as if it were a mystery beyond his grasp. 'Where's the head teacher's office, so?'

He pointed, and shuffled off, his duty to the world discharged. Connolly watched him go, and her police instinct coupled with her taxpayer's outrage drove her to call to him. 'Hey!'

He looked back apprehensively.

'Why aren't you in class?'

'Goin' a' toylit,' he mumbled. His hand strayed guiltily of its own accord towards the shirt pocket hidden under his pullover. She remembered the whiff of tobacco she had caught from him and concluded he was sneaking off for a fly fag, the gom.

'Education's wasted on the likes o' you,' she said, turning away. It was a better world when they were allowed to send them down mines and up chimneys.

Given her aversion to hanging around schools, it was a piece of luck that Mrs Shepherd was not in a class, but on a free period, and even greater luck that she was alone in the staff room, marking work, when Connolly tracked her down. She seemed to be in her fifties, a neat, brisk woman with a well-controlled figure, firm face, and rather nice wavy brown hair that looked as if it belonged on someone else, too soft and loose and inviting for this professional pedagogue.

'I've just put some coffee on,' she said cordially. 'Won't be a minute. Sit down. Which one of them is it? My money's on Kelly Watson. We've already got a sweep going on whether she gets pregnant or expelled first.'

Connolly sat and told her why she was here. Her face changed.

'Oh, God, yes, Lionel,' she said. 'Such a terrible thing! It's hard to believe it. Have you any idea who did it?'

'How well did you know him?' Connolly countered this unhelpful opening.

'Oh, I've known him for years – what is it? – nine or ten, anyway – though I'm not sure one ever really *knew* Lionel, if you know what I mean. He was a very private person.'

'How did you meet him?' Connolly asked, settling back into the armchair. The staffroom was catastrophically untidy, with books and stacks of exercise books everywhere; dirty coffee mugs; newspapers; personal belongings stuffed in bags of various types from plastic carrier to canvas sport; bits of clothing; bits of equipment on their way from one class to another; and, messily pinned on peg boards all round the walls, notices and appeals and leaflets and timetables in profusion. It was all horribly reminiscent. Connolly sat, the most miserable of captives, trying not to allow her eyes to wander towards the freedom beyond the big window. Outside there was sunshine and gently waving treetops. Inside, the smell of bodies, and the coffee machine, hawking and spitting like an elderly chain-smoker.

'It was at a planning meeting, actually – I was part of a group protesting about a development in Brook Green, and he'd just joined the local Residents' Association, which was representing one of the neighbours. We happened to be sitting next to each other, and after the meeting a bunch of us went off for a drink. He and I took to each other and we were friends from then on.'

'What was he like? As a person?'

'Oh, lovely, a lovely man!' she said with enthusiasm. 'Gentle, rather shy, which was odd when you think he was a solicitor. Very intelligent, educated of course. Just the *best* company. He knew so much about everything, you could never run out of things to talk about – and I don't mean he was a bore, either. He listened as well as talked. Everybody loved Lionel.'

The door opened and a dreadlocked female child stuck its head in. 'Please, miss, Mrs Gandapur says—'

Mrs Shepherd's face snapped into ferocious denial. 'No!' she bellowed.

The child blenched. 'But, miss—'

'Out!'

The head was withdrawn, and she resumed her pleasant mien. 'What were we saying?'

Connolly had been at school herself within living memory, and in Dublin at that. She adjusted smoothly. 'Did you and him have a romantic relationship?'

'Oh, goodness, no, nothing like that. He was

just a dear friend. He was such a kind man – he'd do anything for you.'

'He was pretty well off, wasn't he?'

'I think so,' she said, offhandedly. 'He didn't flash it about, but he always seemed to have plenty – and I bet some of those paintings in his flat are worth a bob or two. He was generous with it. When a group of us went out, often he'd just quietly pay the whole bill. If you said anything, he'd say, "From each according to his means." I don't think money meant much to him, actually.'

'Is that why he lived in that flat?'

Mrs Shepherd raised her eyebrows.

'I mean, it's not a posh sort o' kip, is it – a flat over a shop?'

'Oh, that was Lionel all over. He was an odd creature in many ways. Didn't have a car, for instance – said living in London, he had no use for it. Went everywhere in taxis – must have cost him a fortune in the end, probably would have been cheaper to run a car. But he wasn't keen on modern machines.'

'No computer?' Connolly suggested.

Mrs Shepherd smiled. 'That's right – how does anyone live without a computer, these days? He hated the social media. He could do a very good piece – funny, but you knew he meant it – about young people who never spoke to another human being face to face. He said Twitter and Facebook ruined people's lives – well, we all have to cope with that problem,' she added with a frown, 'we teachers. Internet bullying, "sexting", terrible lies being spread about people, obscene pictures posted on YouTube, kids driven to suicide. Well, I don't need to tell you. Funny, we used to think Lionel was behind the times when these things first came out and he condemned them,' she added with a sigh, 'but I wonder now if he wasn't ahead of the times after all. He saw the dangers before we did.'

The door opened again. A pallid, spotty youth said, 'Please, miss, is Mr Sullivan here?'

The bellow returned. 'Does it look as if he's here, you half-witted object? *Get out*!' The door closed. 'It's like Piccadilly Circus in here this morning,' she said in a normal voice. She got up and fetched the coffee.

When she was settled again, Connolly picked up the thread. 'But his kitchen and bathroom are fierce modern, full o' gadgets.'

'Yes, funny that, isn't it? But I suppose he liked his comfort, and he did love to cook. Very good at it, too,' she added, almost wistfully.

No more din-dins at Lionel's, Connolly thought. 'Did you ever meet his wife?' she tried.

'No. I heard from someone that he had been married once, or they *thought* he had been married, but he never mentioned a wife. In fact, he never said anything about his past, or his family, his career before he retired, anything like that.'

'Did you ever meet any of his friends from before he came to Hammersmith?'

'Never a one. Strange, don't you think? That's what I meant, about wondering whether you ever really knew him.'

'Did he have any lady friends while you knew

him? Romantic friends, I mean.'

'Not that I know of. Actually, I've always sort of subconsciously wondered if he was gay.'

'How come?'

'Oh, nothing tangible. Just the lack of lady friends, as you put it, and something about him as a person – you know, the bachelor life, the quaintness, the antiques, the nice clothes, fond of cooking, knew all about wines. Epicene – is that the word?'

It could be the word for all Connolly knew. She thought about Atherton – there was something of that about him, especially the cooking and the clothes. But he wasn't gay – far from it. If mattress surfing was an Olympic event, he could have represented Britain. No reason old Lionel should have been gay either. Love a God, could a man not own a spatula without his credentials being questioned?

'Anything else?' she asked.

Mrs Shepherd thought about it. 'He was terribly fond of the theatre. And very knowledgeable. He must have seen every play ever written. Loved his Shakespeare, even the ones nobody reads any more – you know, *Coriolanus* and so on. Loved Tom Stoppard, too, for the wordplay. He used to go a lot, I do know that. And he organized trips to the theatre for groups of his friends. I've been several times. He usually ended up paying for that, too.'

'Why would that make him gay?' Connolly asked, still processing *curry o' l'anus*. What the feck was that?

'Oh, it doesn't, I didn't mean that. But from

the way he talked, he seemed to know quite a lot of actors personally, as well as the plays, so I put him down as a bit of a luvvie. It was just another piece of the jigsaw, you know.'

Somewhere a bell rang. Mrs Shepherd made getting-up movements and said, 'The hordes are about to descend on us. And I've got playground duty, God help me.'

'Just one more question,' Connolly said, wondering what it should be. She didn't feel she'd got much further, but there seemed no way in to this man's life. 'Do you know one of Lionel's friends called Nina?'

'Nina? No, no I don't think so.' She paused in thought. 'No, I don't think I've ever met a Nina. Who is she?'

'Apparently she telephoned him now and then, left a message with his housekeeper.'

'Oh! The sinister Mrs Danvers,' said Mrs Shepherd, with half a smile.

'I think the name is Kroll, Mrs Kroll,' Connolly corrected her.

'I know, dear, it's a reference,' said Mrs Shepherd. 'I shouldn't take too much notice of what Mrs Kroll says, if I were you. I don't think she's very reliable. Several times when I've rung up and Lionel's been out, I've left messages which she hasn't passed on. And sometimes she's simply refused to take a message. Lionel lets her have all too much rope, in my opinion. She's the sort who takes advantage.'

The door opened, and a knot of adults shot in as if expelled from the corridor like peas from a pea-shooter. 'Tea!' cried the front runner desperately. 'Haven't you put the kettle on, Molly? What have you been *doing*?'

Connolly made her escape so that the Shepherd could explain herself any way she liked. *Calling a detective constable 'dear', the cheeky skanger*! she thought as she made her way down the corridors against the flow and bedlam of youthful humanity. It was like one of those nightmares where you can't make any progress towards your goal. She suppressed a panicky feeling that she'd never get out.

Slider sent Atherton for brains and McLaren for muscle on the Krolls Quest – it did sound a bit Dragons and Dungeons, that. Atherton was slightly offended at the idea that he might need McLaren, but Slider said he didn't know what he might get into, and he didn't want him suddenly having to send for back-up. McLaren did not look hefty, like Fathom, or powerful, like Gascoyne, but he had a whippy strength, was fast and hard and, since he possessed no imagination, fearless.

Getting into the car beside him, Atherton winced and said, 'For God's sake!'

'What?' McLaren protested, wounded.

'You had curry again last night.'

'Why shouldn't I?'

'It can't be good for you to have curry every single night. There's madras sauce coming out of your pores.'

McLaren started the engine. 'Leave me alone.'

'I swear, next time I get in a car with you I'm bringing a canary in a cage.'

'I liked it when you and Norma were always fighting,' he said. 'At least I got a bit of peace.'

'I liked it when you were going out with whatsername. Pam, was it?'

'Jackie,' he corrected sulkily. She had dumped him, but he liked to believe he had dumped her because her programme of improving him – clothes, haircut, diet – had got on his wick in the end. She'd even made him have a manicure, for Chrissakes!

'Ah yes, the ineffable Jackie,' Atherton said.

'What're you talking about, effable?' McLaren asked suspiciously. It sounded rude to him.

'But at least for a while she had a good effect on your personal grooming regime,' Atherton said. 'Your nose hairs are back with a vengeance. You look as if you've been sniffing Growmore!'

'And you're about as much fun as Joan Crawford with PMT,' he countered.

'That's pretty good,' Atherton said generously. 'I never knew you could do quick repartee.'

'I can think on my feet,' McLaren protested.

'Well, I've seen you count on them,' he agreed.

The Krolls' house was at the end of a short turning off the main road. It was detached, but that didn't make it grand: it was small, Victorian yellow brick and slate roof, and about the size of a gatekeeper's cottage.

Behind it was a small yard and a separate brick building that looked as though it had been a stable with hayloft above. You still found places like these in the untouched parts of some outer London villages, probably purpose-built in the late nineteenth century for a local tradesman, a greengrocer, say, with a pony-and-cart round.

There was a sign on the windowless side of the house, a large wooden board with battered edges, which had been painted with the words KROLL & SONS BUILDERS. The paint had cracked like the mud of a dried-up pool and was coming off in large flakes, revealing some other wording underneath. The Krolls had painted over an existing sign without doing the base work properly, which was not, Atherton noted, a very good advertisement for the business. The front garden of the house had been roughly tarmacked over and sported a motley collection of pallets, scaffold boards, broken boxes, a cement mixer that had been left caked in cement, and some other junk including a supermarket trolley with its wheels missing. And in the back yard, the original stable building had been joined by several rough sheds, cobbled together out of old doors and corrugated iron.

'Well, here's a man who cares about appearances,' Atherton commented.

Behind the yard, the backs of the warehouses on the industrial estate reared up, and the road was a dead end, with a high metal fence and more warehouses beyond. McLaren, out of native caution, turned the car and parked facing back down the road.

Kroll's high-side van – they had got the description and reg number from the Crimint database, along with his photo – was not in sight, though there was a dark-blue-and-rust coloured combo van, with no wheels, up on blocks directly in front of the house, and a beat-up Ford Focus parked in such a way as to prevent the van's doors being opened. The street was quiet when they got out – only the whine of a forklift truck from over the end fence arguing with the trill of an equally unseen robin. The house had the air of being empty. Atherton went ahead and both knocked and rang, while McLaren stood at the gate, keeping an eye on the road.

'No-one in,' Atherton said at last, at exactly the moment when a shadow appeared behind the frosted glass pane, and the door was slowly opened.

'No need to keep ringing bell like that! You think we're deaf?'

It was a small, old woman in a black dress with iron-grey hair pulled back into a bun, like any peasant grandmother from any country in Europe. She had left her teeth out so the lower half of her face had collapsed together, but her dark eyes sparked with vigorous anger. She looked like a bulldog that'd swallowed a wasp.

'What do you want?' she went on without waiting for Atherton to speak. She reached into the pocket of her dress and brought out a set of dentures which she inserted, smacking her lips, the better to articulate her hostility. 'My grandson Marek is asleep upstairs. If you wake him he will be angry. You want my son, you have to come back later.'

There had been no mention in the intelligence that Kroll had his mother living with him. 'We're CID officers,' Atherton said. 'Detectives,' he added for clarity's sake, showing his warrant card.

The little lady bristled. 'Why you don't leave us alone? Jacek has done nothing! *No*thing! We come here from Poland to get away from persecution, Nazis knocking on the door in middle of the night.'

Atherton recognized a line when he met one. To remember the Nazis she would have had to be well in her eighties and she looked a good ten or fifteen years short of that.

'Nobody's accusing anyone of anything,' he said soothingly. 'We just want some information. Can we come in, Mrs Kroll?'

'Not Kroll – Adamski,' she said.

Atherton recalibrated quickly. Records had their Mrs Kroll's maiden name as Adams. Anglicizing was common among long-term settlers. This must be Angela's mother, not Jack's.

The old lady examined both the warrant cards carefully, and then scrutinized their faces before stepping back to let them in. And she still added, in warning, to prove herself not alone and helpless, 'Marek is asleep upstairs. He will hear if you start anything.'

She led them down a dark passage of closed doors towards the back of the house. It felt cold, despite the warm day outside, and there was a smell of stale cigarettes and male sweat and, under that, the sharp, sour smell of mould. She led them into the kitchen, which Atherton noted had not been refitted since the eighties. The lino tiles on the floor were worn and chipped, the unit doors were all on the slant as their cheap hinges sagged; there were dirty dishes in the sink and the gas stove was crusted in spillings. Either the business was not doing well, or the Krolls had found something else entirely to spend their money on.

Mrs Adamski sat herself at the Formica-topped table, fumbled a pack of cigarettes out of a pocket and lit one. She waved it at the other chairs around the table. Atherton sat; McLaren remained standing in the kitchen doorway. 'So, what you want to ask?'

'Your daughter worked as housekeeper to a man called Lionel Bygod,' Atherton said.

Mrs Adamski wagged the cigarette in assent.

'I expect you will have heard that he was killed on Tuesday.'

'Nothing to do with us,' she said quickly. 'Why you come here asking questions? We don't know nothing.'

'It's purely a matter of routine,' Atherton said soothingly. 'We have to establish where everybody was at the time.'

'Everybody working all day,' Mrs Adamski snapped. 'What you think?'

'Your daughter doesn't work all day, only mornings. What time did she come home on Tuesday?'

A shrug. 'Three o'clock, maybe. Like always. Then she change and go over The King's Arms.'

Atherton knew it: a pub just across the main road from here, which had been prettified recently to make it look like an old coaching inn – though as it featured live entertainment and big screen TV sports, the effect was only skin deep.

'She went for a drink?'

'She work there!' Mrs Adamski said indignantly. 'Evenings, five to eleven.'

'I see,' Atherton said, making a note. Even given that her job for Lionel Bygod was not tiring, for her to want to hold down a second job suggested a need for money that did not sit with Kroll making big money at his nefarious activities, or indeed at the building trade. 'And after eleven?'

'She come home. Go to bed.' A shrug. *What do you expect a working woman to do?*

'Fine,' said Atherton. 'And your son and grandson? Where were they?'

'Out all day on a job. Not come home till half past four. Then I cook supper, then they go to pub seven, half past.'

'The King's Arms?'

A nod.

'And what time did they come back?'

A shrug. 'Half past eleven maybe. And go to bed. That is all.'

Not by a long chalk, Atherton thought. 'The job they were out on all day – where is that?'

'I don't know. They don't tell me.' Now the anger was back. 'I don't know what they do. Angelika work, work, and for what? For nothing! Pennies! Jacek should take care of her. That's what Polish men do, they take care of their women and children. She should not have to do these jobs. Working in a pub! That where she is now – so soon Mr Bygod dies, she gets more hours at King's Arms. And what does *he* do all day? *Swinia leniwy*! There is never any money, only what Angelika brings. She should not have married him!'

Atherton could make a guess at *swinia*, anyway. 'It must be very hard for you,' he said, 'seeing her neglected like that.'

Mrs Adamski bloomed under the sympathy. 'Very hard for mother,' she confirmed. 'Her father was not that sort of man. I *never* go to work – he would have thought it shame on him. He had pride. Jacek has no pride. And always the rows between them, the shouting, on and on. I say to him, you have no right to say *anything* to Angelika, until you bring home money. He say to me, you don't understand, but I understand very well when a man does not do his duty.'

'What does he think you don't understand?'

'Oh, he say he work very hard, but the money does not come. The bad men take it from him. He say he has bills to pay, debts. Ha!' A mirthless laugh.

'What bad men are these?' Atherton asked. He slipped it in as casually as possible, but still Mrs Adamski took alarm.

'I don't know. I talk too much. I am foolish old woman. There are no bad men.'

McLaren made a sound of warning, and Atherton glanced past him to see a scrawny, bed-draggled figure come slopping along the passage from the foot of the stairs. It was wearing track-suit bottoms and a sleeveless vest, none too clean. Its feet were bare, it was unshaven, and its too-long hair was a mess, not improved by the slow scratching that accompanied the dragging walk. It appeared not so much to have descended from the apes as to have been overtaken by them.

'What's going on?' he said in a plain Acton accent. 'Gran? You all right? Who're *you*?' He addressed the last to Atherton, but reaching the door he finally spotted McLaren, who had been hidden from him, and alarm belatedly tensed all his muscles. 'Who the fuck are you?' he asked in definite fright.

'Ten o'clock in the morning, already he is awake!' Mrs Adamski said witheringly. 'My grandson, Marek. Another lazy pig who lies in bed all day while his *mother* works.' She managed to inject a superb amount of scorn into 'mother'.

'I told you, Gran, it's not Marek, it's Mark,' the lad said sulkily. 'Who are you people?'

'The police, Marek,' Mrs Adamski said with heavy irony. 'They have come to wake you up gently so you should not lie in bed all day and maybe hurt your back.'

'Fuck, Gran, you don't talk to the police!'

This elicited a stream of furious Polish aimed at the lad, who showed no sign of understanding any of it. He rubbed one bare, dirty foot over the other, looking from Atherton to McLaren nervously. When the old woman stopped, he said, 'Me dad's out, and me mum. Me gran don't know nothing. Me mum won't half be mad if you upset her.'

McLaren caught his attention. 'Where's your dad?' he asked in the tone that brooked no prevarication.

'He's out – at a job,' he added just in time.

'Where?'

'Out Hanwell.'

'This is the job you've been helping him on?'

'Yeah.' Reluctantly dragged out.

'We'd like to have a word with him. What's the address?'

Alarm. 'He might not be there. I mean, he might have to go and get stuff. Materials. Or something.'

'I think you need to talk to us,' Atherton intervened firmly.

McLaren caught the ball and said, 'Come and sit in the car – no need to upset your gran. We've got a few questions to ask.'

'No! I don't have to. I'm not going!'

Atherton got up and stepped close, masking him from his grandmother with his body. He said quietly, 'I can smell the weed on you. What have you got in your pocket?' Mark's hand made the automatic, guilty movement. Dope, Atherton thought – in both senses. 'I can bust you for possession, we can toss your room and see what else you've got up there. Cuff you and take you away. How will your gran like that? Or you can sit in the car nicely and answer some questions. We're investigating a murder. This is serious stuff, Mark. You don't want to mess us about.'

He caved. McLaren led him out, while Atherton took a moment to soothe the old woman.

'Where you take him?' she demanded fearfully.

'Nowhere. Just outside to talk. Don't worry. You can have him back in a minute.'

Spirit flared. 'You keep him! I don't want lazy pig. Every day he breaks his mother's heart!'

SIX

Repaint and Thin No More

Connolly came into Slider's office, where he was talking to Hollis.

'Guv, I've got something,' she said with a smile so bright Slider could feel the skin of his face turning brown.

'Let me have it,' he said.

'Sure God, you're going to love this!' she obliged. 'It's the answer to all the questions about your man.' She had been on the computer all morning, and now proudly displayed the results. 'He was a solicitor right enough. He'd a practice in Islington, specialized in criminal defence. Worked with this big-shot barrister called Wickham Williams QC.'

'I've heard of him,' Slider said.

'Have you, so?' said Connolly. 'Well, he'd a name for defending bad lots, and apparently your man Bygod was the solicitor behind him.'

'Ah,' said Slider, 'so he could well have had criminals coming up his stairs in Shepherd's Bush.'

'Maybe chummy was a disgruntled client he didn't manage to get off,' said Hollis.

'Wait'll I tell ya,' Connolly said impatiently.

'He was involved in this big case in 1996, defending a man called Noel Roxwell. Seems this Roxwell had been questioned a couple o' times for hanging around school playgrounds and talking to the kids. This time it was alleged he followed a girl called Kim North, age fourteen, on to a bus, got off at the same stop and caught her in an alley where he indecently assaulted her. According to the police report he kissed her and put his hand on her breast and made certain suggestions, before she ran away.'

'Doesn't sound like a very big case,' Slider said.

'I haven't got to it yet, boss,' Connolly said. 'The North kid told her mammy, and the peelers came and nicked him, and when the word got around, this other girl in the same class, Debbie Crondace, came forward and said he done the same to her, only he'd gone all the way, done the nasty with her up against the wall, without her consent. So then it was all over the papers. Roxwell went to Lionel Bygod, who got him Wickham Williams to defend him.'

'I think I remember hearing something about that case,' Slider said. 'Roxwell. Crondace. The names ring a bell.'

Connolly nodded. 'O' course, your man's previous counted against him, and the press was hostile. There was a big paedophile scare going on at the time. It looked like Roxwell was a goner. But Wickham Williams pulled the evidence apart, and apparently Roxwell was good in the box and the girl wasn't, and anyway, however it was, he got him off. So then there was a big fuss in the papers, and a campaign led by the Crondace kid's da to get the acquittal overturned. He went after Wickham Williams and our Mr Bygod – Crondace did – and the papers loved it, splashed it as the nobs' conspiracy against poor working folk, and all that class o' caper. Asking why any decent person would defend a pervert like Roxwell.'

'I'm sure that went down well in the Inns of Court,' Slider said.

'It got worse,' Connolly assured him. 'The story spread that Bygod and Wickham Williams were kiddy-fiddlers themselves, part of a big circle, including Roxwell, that looked out for each other's backs. One remark Crondace made went viral – whatever the equivalent was in them days when they hadn't the social media. He said QC meant Queer Customer. O' course, something like that was jam for the press.'

'Why didn't they sue?' Slider asked.

'Well, boss, it happened that the silk dropped dead suddenly in the middle of all the fuss. Nothing wrong about it – apparently he'd had an undiagnosed heart condition, and maybe the strain brought it on. So Bygod was left alone to face the music. And instead of suing, he went to ground. Gave up his practice, sold his house, and disappeared.'

Swilley had come in to listen. 'Interesting,' she said. 'So there was something sinister about him after all?'

'You automatically assume he was guilty?' Slider said. 'A nice case of "give a dog a bad name and hang him".'

'If he wasn't guilty, why did he run? Why didn't he sue? If a solicitor can't sue, who can? Atherton said there was a pattern emerging.'

'That was about him being a homosexual,' Connolly objected.

'Paedophiles often are,' Hollis said. 'Or at least, they're not particular one way or the other. Boys or girls, it's all the same.'

'It would certainly provide a motive for his murder,' Slider said thoughtfully, 'if he was reviled for getting a guilty man off.'

'Right,' Connolly began eagerly.

'If,' Slider interrupted, 'there was any evidence that anyone had been after him in the intervening sixteen years.'

'Well, we don't know, do we, boss?' Connolly said. 'He went to ground. Maybe they'd only just found him.'

'It's something to look into. I think I'll have a word with Jonny Care at Islington, see if I can get any more information on the Roxwell case. I'd like to know if there really was any substance in the accusations against Bygod – if he'd come to anyone's attention before that.' Care was the Islington DI he had worked with over the Ben Corley murder.

'Anyway, it gives a reason for the break in his life, doesn't it, boss?' Connolly said. 'Why his current friends never met anyone he knew before.'

'And why he was no longer married,' Swilley said. 'Even if he was innocent, it'd be hard for a marriage to survive that sort of trauma.'

Slider nodded. 'The trouble with accusations

of that sort is that, even if they're untrue, a taint always lingers. The old "there's no smoke without fire" argument.' He sighed. 'We can talk all we like about justice, but a malicious accusation can never be wholly wiped clean.'

'Cheer up, guv,' Swilley said. 'Maybe he was guilty – think of that!'

'Oh, how you comfort me,' said Slider.

Gascoyne came in. 'Got one!' he said jubilantly. 'One of the fingermarks on the stair rail matches with Jack Kroll. So he's definitely been in the house.'

Slider felt a surge of relief. Proper evidence at last! 'Right. Radio that through to Atherton and McLaren straight away. No reason he shouldn't have visited, but if he denies he's ever been there, they can put him on the back foot.'

'Should they bring him in, guv?' Gascoyne asked.

'I leave that to Atherton. He'll know if he seems like a dodgy customer.'

Mark Kroll was about as hard to break as a slice of Madeira cake. Once outside, McLaren patted him down before putting him in the car, and the tin in his pocket that he had not wanted them to find turned out to contain a spliff, a small piece of foil-wrapped resin, and a book of matches.

'Enough to nick you on, mate,' McLaren said. 'If you want us to forget about it, you better cooperate.'

That was when he crumbled.

Now he sat in the back seat of their car, savaging a cigarette and his fingernails alternately, his left knee jiggling the well-known dance of shame, and confessed with only the gentlest of prods that the job in Hanwell they should have been doing had been abandoned because they could not afford to buy the materials. The householder had given them a substantial deposit, but that was all gone. Now she was ringing them all the time, asking when they'd be back to finish, and threatening to sue them.

'Me and Dad stay out of the way all day. Dad's had to change his mobile and he's told Gran not to answer the phone. If they start coming round the house, I dunno what we'll do.'

'So you weren't at the job in Hanwell on Tuesday?' Atherton said.

'No, I told you. We can't even buy a can o' paint. Got no credit anywhere any more.'

'So where were you?'

'We went out in the morning, Dad and me, like usual, so's Gran'd think we was going to the job. He doesn't want her to know. She gets mad about the money – him not having any, I mean. Him and Mum had a terrible row the night before. I could hear 'em yelling at each other, and then Gran woke up and she went and joined in. I put the pillow over me head and stopped quiet.'

'What was the row about?'

'Like I said. It's always the same – money. I don't know exactly – a lot of it was in Polish. They always end up yelling in Polish when they get into it.'

'So, tell me about Tuesday,' Atherton said. 'Every detail.'

He looked puzzled, but complied. 'Well, we left about half seven, had breakfast at this caff up West Ealing, Ruby's in Argyll Road. Spun it out long as we could. Then Dad leaves me and goes off in the van.'

'Where?'

'I dunno. He never said.'

'And where did you go?'

'I went and sat in the park a bit, had a fag, read the paper. I didn't have me wheels, see.'

'Is that your Focus?' McLaren indicated the rust bucket at the kerb.

'Yeah, but I couldn't come home to get it, case Gran saw me. Can't afford the petrol, anyway. So I was stuck, wasn't I? So I went down the snooker club, down Northfields Avenue, and stopped there all day.'

'How did you manage without any money?'

'I got some mates hang out there. They paid for the tables, and I bummed some fags off 'em. Dad picked me up about four o'clock on the Uxbridge Road, and we went home.'

McLaren got a call on his Airwave and got out of the car to take it. He beckoned Atherton out.

'One of the fingerprints on the stair rail has come back to old man Kroll,' he said. 'So it's starting to look tasty.'

Through the car window they could see Mark watching them with mad, frightened eyes from under his mess of hair. 'I wonder how much he knows,' Atherton said. 'I wouldn't trust him with important secrets if he was my son.'

'Nah,' said McLaren from the depth of his copper's instinct. 'He's a dipstick. That's why the old man went off and left him.'

They got back in. Atherton said, 'So you didn't see your dad all day on Tuesday? Do you know where he was?'

'No, he never said.' The boy was sweating now, and the smell of marijuana came out of his pores like curry out of McLaren's.

'Have you ever been to the place your mum works – Mr Bygod's flat?'

'No,' he said with a simple bewilderment that sounded genuine.

'Has your dad?'

'No,' he said. 'I don't think so. Why would he? Look, I haven't done nothing. Can I go now? I gotter go to the toilet.'

Atherton shook his head. 'Where's your dad now?'

'I dunno!'

'Guess,' he suggested, with menace.

Mark evidently tried. The effort made him look miserable. 'Maybe some pub. Or down the betting shop. He goes there a lot.'

'He's got a gambling habit, your dad?' McLaren said.

He nodded, and said dolefully, 'Bloody right!' Little bits of misery came spurting out of him under the pressure like leaks in a hosepipe. 'They row about it all the time.'

'Your mum and dad?

'She said if he didn't stop betting she'd kill him.'

'Is that why there's no money?' Atherton asked.

'It's worse 'n that.'

'What's your dad got into?' McLaren urged.

'I can't tell you! Me dad'd kill me.'

'You're in enough trouble already, chap,' McLaren said. 'Don't make it worse for yourself. What d'you think your mum and gran will say if you get nicked?'

The knee jiggled, the eyes flitted, the hands fidgeted madly as he lost his mellow; and the mellow – or a long history of mellows – had already robbed him of his wits. He needed someone to tell him what to do. He wasn't capable of thinking anything out for himself.

'Who are these bad men your gran told us about?' Atherton tried. 'Are they after your dad?'

He looked so scared they knew they were on to something.

'Look,' he cried, 'my dad's a good man. He's never done nothing wrong.'

'What about the illegal fly-tipping?' McLaren put in. 'And the stolen lead? And cheating that woman out of her deposit.'

'It's not his fault! He's into them for thousands. You don't get it! They said they'd break his knees if he didn't get the money. Then he'd never be able to work again. He's a good man, my dad! It's them you ought to be going after.'

'Oh, we will, don't you worry,' Atherton said. 'But you've got to help us. Tell us what you know about them.'

'I *can't*,' he wailed. 'Dad'd kill me. And they'd go after me if I talked. You don't know what they're like. You got to help my dad – you *got* to.' He started to cry. 'Mum don't understand.

She thinks he's mad to go on gambling, but it's the only way to get that sort of money. But he never wins enough,' he wept. 'He keeps on trying, but it's never enough.'

A fairly clear picture was emerging, Atherton thought. A runnel of snot was hanging from the snivelling youth's nose and he handed him a tissue, waited until he'd cleaned up, and said firmly, 'Tell me.'

The Roxwell business had been before Jonny Care's time, but he put Slider on to one Gerald Hawes who had been a detective sergeant on the case. Hawes had retired from the Met and was living out in Greenford where he worked free-lance as a carpenter, making bespoke furniture and built-in cupboards.

'It was always a hobby of mine,' he told Slider. 'I love wood. Now I can indulge myself all day long, and earn a crust at the same time. Come through to my workshop. We can talk privately there.'

The house was a modern one on a new estate, with picture windows and an open plan layout intended to give a sense of space and dignity to a basically cramped and cheap design. They passed by the open door to the lounge where a stout, grey-haired woman was sitting watching daytime television. 'The wife,' Hawes said briefly, but didn't offer to introduce Slider; nor did the wife turn her head from the quiz show that was absorbing her.

Hawes was a cheerful, overweight but bouncy man with thinning hair and glasses. Behind the lenses he still had copper's eyes: any other copper – and probably any career criminal – would have made him immediately. He led the way into a large extension that had been built on behind the garage and fitted out into a workshop with every facility, well-lit, spacious, and smelling deliciously of wood shavings and varnish. It was not without creature comforts – an armchair, a table bearing an electric kettle and toaster-oven, a small fridge, a radio quietly playing Classic FM.

'I sit in here a lot,' he said, noting Slider's cataloguing of the scene. 'Pat's always got the telly on – drives me mad. I read and listen to the wireless in here, do the crossword, and we meet up at bedtime for cocoa.' It was said jokingly, but Slider read an old, accustomed hurt under the lightness of tone. Policemen's marriages were always strained. The wife, so much alone at home, living with the knowledge that the Job meant more to her man than she did, generally turned either to anger or indifference, or found a more sympathetic mate. That's why the divorce rate was so high; but it seemed the Haweses had found an accommodation of sorts.

'So,' Hawes said, 'that old Roxwell case has come alive again, has it?' He walked over to a large rocking-horse that was evidently under construction, and picked up a piece of glass-paper. 'Make yourself comfy. Mind if I carry on with this while we talk? It's meant for one of the grandkids, but it's taking me so long, she'll be on her A levels before I get it finished.'

Slider waved assent, and sat down in the arm

chair. Hawes began rhythmically and lovingly rubbing at the horse's neck.

'You didn't sound surprised that I was asking about the Roxwell case,' Slider said.

'Well, no. It was a nasty business, and there were always question marks about it. What's your interest, if I may ask?'

'The defence solicitor, Bygod.'

'Oh, really? Has he been getting into trouble? You know, I never truly believed he was a nonce. You know how you get a feeling for people. But when he disappeared, I had to wonder. No smoke without fire, and all that sort of thing. What's he been up to?'

'He's dead,' Slider said. 'Murdered.'

The rubbing hand stopped, and Hawes looked up. 'Oh,' he said, with a world of meaning. He pondered. 'Well, there were threats against him, as I expect you know. But it was all a long time ago.'

'Tell me about it, will you? Everything, from the beginning.'

'There was no doubt Roxwell was hanging around the school playground. He said he just liked watching the children play – and of course, twenty years earlier nobody would have thought twice about it. But we'd all had to get a lot more suspicious by that time, and one of the mothers complained so of course we had to give him a tug. Then we found he'd been a scout master once and had to give it up when some of the parents heard things about him. No charges were ever made, but once you're on the radar...' He shrugged. 'As far as the original charge went, the Kim North business, he denied he'd been following her. He said he was going home to his mother, and it's true she lived in that direction. She's dead now – his mum. Never got over it, all the nastiness. Anyway, he said he was just walking in the same direction as Kim, and when they got down the alley she turned and waited for him. *She* said she asked him why he was following her. *He* said she asked him for a cigarette. *She* said he offered her one. They apparently got talking while they smoked. Roxwell said she flirted with him, and said, "I'll give you a kiss if you give me the rest of the packet." Kim said he just suddenly lunged at her, grabbed her tit and kissed her against her will.'

'So he didn't deny he had touched her?'

'He denied he touched her tit, but he admitted straight away he kissed her, only he said she'd initiated it. Well, they always do. Fancy a cuppa? Put the kettle on, will you. It's filled, just switch it on.' Slider got up to comply, and Hawes went on. 'Well, you pays your money and you takes your pick. Probably it was a bit of one and a bit of the other. There's no doubt Kim was a well-developed young lady, and not backward in coming forward. Anyway, he said when he kissed her she grabbed the packet of fags out of his hand and ran off laughing. *She* said she managed to escape his 'orrible tentacles and ran home in terror.'

'But she was under age,' Slider said. The mugs and teabags were on a shelf above the table, and he got two mugs down and went about making the tea.

'Oh yes, she was only fourteen, so of course whether she wanted it or not was academic. Soon as he admitted it, he was in trouble, especially with the previous complaint against him from up the school, and the scout troop. All the same, I'm guessing he'd've got off with a suspended, seeing as it was his first offence, and there was no violence done. But that's when it all got nasty. Because the Crondace girl and her mother came in and said that he'd raped her down the same alley days earlier. Oh, ta.'

He put down his tools, took the mug from Slider, and leaned against his work bench.

'Debbie Crondace,' Slider said. 'What was she like?'

'Another one like Kim North, only more so. Big, bold and busty, fourteen going on thirty-five. They say it's all the hormones in the chicken that makes 'em develop so young. Her mother was a real hard case – a mouthy cow, all "I know my rights" and "Who are you looking at?" Straight off *EastEnders*. You know the sort. Kind of made you sorry for the girl – up to a point.'

'There was a father in the picture, too, I believe?' Slider asked.

'Yes. Derek Crondace. He was a market trader. Had a pitch in the Chapel Market, down the Angel, mostly selling cheap clothes. Big ugly bugger with a foul mouth, the sort who likes to settle arguments with his fists, and he was a "Nobody insults my wife but me" sort. He went after Roxwell like a pit bull. But he had a lot of native wit. He wasn't stupid by a long streak. The first thing he did was to involve the tabloids.'

'Did they pay him?'

Hawes gave him a wide-eyed, innocent look. 'Now what do you think? I couldn't prove it to you, but he bought himself a new car just about that time, and Mrs C sprouted a lot of gold jewellery.'

'So how did Roxwell get to instruct Bygod? And how could he afford a top silk like Wickham Williams? Did he have money?'

'No, he lived with his mum in a flat and worked as a librarian. Hadn't a bean, but he was just over the limit for legal aid. No, it was Bygod approached him, offered his services pro bono, and negotiated Wickham Williams for a reduced fee which he paid himself – Bygod did.'

Slider's eyebrows went up. 'I can see where the idea came from that they were all in it together.'

'It was nuts for Crondace,' Hawes agreed. 'Bygod said he was convinced of Roxwell's innocence, said he was being set up by the Crondaces, and that the furore in the press meant he would never have a fair trial. Well, between them they pulled out all the stops and got Roxwell off, which was quite a feat in the prevailing atmosphere. The evidence against Roxwell was only Debbie's word and the admitted assault on Kim North. There was no material evidence. Debbie said she'd been too scared to tell her parents at the time it happened – and knowing her parents I wouldn't blame her – so there was no rape kit or anything of the sort. When she finally went to the police two days later, there were bruises on her wrists, but Roxwell had notably small hands and they didn't match. Prosecution made what they could of claiming bruising spreads as it ages, but defence brought their own expert to say it didn't. And what she knew about Roxwell could have been accounted for by the fact that she and Kim were best mates. In the end, the jury decided there wasn't enough evidence, and acquitted him. More tea?'

'No, I'm fine, thanks,' Slider said, deep in thought.

Hawes heaved himself up. 'I'll get on with my horse, if you don't mind.'

He resumed his rubbing, and Slider said, 'So what happened to Roxwell afterwards?'

'Well, the press attention turned more on Bygod and Wickham Williams after the trial, but he still came in for a lot of nastiness. Windows broken. Parcels of shit through the letter box. Name calling in the street. He stuck it out for a bit, until someone put a petrol-soaked rag through his letterbox one night. He managed to put the fire out, but his old mum had a heart attack from the shock – she'd not been well since the first Kim North business – and she died in hospital two days later. There was nothing to keep Roxwell after that so he upped sticks and went to Spain, and as far as I know he never came back.'

'Do you think he was innocent?'

Hawes hesitated. 'I don't know. It's always hard to say in cases like those, when it's one person's word against another. And in the bad old days, women who came forward were routinely not believed and given a hard time, and that was wrong. Maybe we've swung too far the other way now, I don't know. But I must say I liked Roxwell. He seemed a genuine chap, mild, polite, kind to his mother – the sort that always get the shit kicked out of 'em. And the papers always go after the easy targets. Why should someone be crapped upon from a great height, just because he's not married, wears specs and doesn't swear like a footballer with Tourette's?'

'On the other hand,' Slider said.

Hawes gave a rueful smile. 'Yes, on the other hand, coming across as nice doesn't mean you are. Well, like I said, you pays your money. Anyway, Bygod certainly believed he was innocent, and he put his money where his mouth was.'

'Yes – Bygod. What did you make of him?'

'Bit of a rum bird, I thought. I didn't get him. Why'd he pick on this case among all the others to back? – except for the press campaigning against Roxwell, and he had a bee in his bonnet about the press. He certainly paid for it. The tabloids turned their attention on him, innuendo was rife, his life was made a misery, his wife left him, his practice went down the tubes. Then old man Crondace started stalking him and issuing death threats for getting his precious daughter's attacker off scot free, and brought out this story about the paedophile ring. Set up a vigilante group – torchlit marches, complete with placards. Gave us a few interesting nights, I can tell you.'

'Why didn't Bygod sue him?'

Hawes shrugged. 'I don't know. Maybe he was just too miserable.'

'A *solicitor*?'

'It's just a guess. You'd have to ask him. Oh, you can't, can you? Well, we had to pull Crondace in over the death threats and the marches, and I went to see Bygod at the time, to tell him what we'd done, and to tell him to get in contact with us if any more threats were issued. And he seemed very low then. Absent in thought, you know, and not very interested in what Crondace might or might not do. Acted like he was depressed – and who could blame him? Shortly after that he closed his office and left his house, moved to Hackney. Didn't tell anyone where he was going, but Crondace managed to find him again – we'd been keeping an eye on our Del for unrelated reasons, which was how we knew. Bygod did another flit, and he must have done a good one, because that was it as far as we were concerned. We never heard of him again. So he was in Shepherd's Bush, was he?'

'The last eleven years. But not practising law – as far as we know, he'd retired.'

'And now he's dead,' Hawes said thoughtfully, pausing in his rubbing to push his glasses back up his nose. 'Interesting. How'd they do it?'

'Bashed on the back of the head while he was sitting at his desk. Several violent blows.'

Hawes nodded. 'Frenzied attack, eh? Well, I suppose your mind might legitimately turn to Delboy Crondace, because he did love thumping and bashing. And some of his vigilante pals were even more unpleasant – stupid as well as violent, which is always a nasty combination. One of them tried to set fire to an innocent man's house because he'd heard he was a paediatrician. We had a lot of fun with that, I can tell you.'

'I can imagine.'

'But it was a long time ago,' Hawes said. 'Sixteen years. Would Crondace carry on a vendetta that long? Or his chums? Unless Bygod had been up to something else.'

'There's no suggestion he was up to anything, but of course if he was, he'd be careful, and it would take some ferreting out. But if Crondace really believed Roxwell had raped his daughter – if the hurt went deep enough...'

Hawes nodded. 'Well,' he said, 'all I can say is, if you go after Crondace, be careful. He was a nasty piece of work then, and he'd only be – what? – fifty-five, fifty-six now, so he's still in the prime of life. He could take you with one hand tied behind his back.'

'I'm not the stuff heroes are made of,' Slider said with a grin. 'I was thinking of going after the mother.'

SEVEN

The Dog it was That Dyed

'He got *away*?' Slider said.

Atherton refused to look cowed. 'The pub was packed. Kroll spotted me over the heads the same moment I spotted him, and he was nearer the door. By the time I'd extricated myself he was gone.'

Slider turned his gaze on McLaren, who at least lifted his hands in regret. 'The Red Lion, guv. Three doors, two of us. He must've come out round the corner. I dunno how he made us, though.'

'Maybe he didn't,' said Slider. 'Maybe any strange man catching his eye across a crowded room was enough to put fear in his heels.' He brooded. 'Well, we'll have to find him, that's obvious.'

'Should we bring Mrs K in?' McLaren asked hopefully.

'Not yet,' Slider said. 'He might go home if she's not disturbed, and we can get him there. Meanwhile, I'd better talk to Mr Porson. We'll need an alert out on him, and some more bodies.'

* * *

'What do you mean, he got away?' Porson demanded, his brows rushing together like wartime lovers at Waterloo station.

'I'm not sure it was anyone's fault,' Slider said, and explained Kroll's situation. He had started gambling some years ago with an illegal bookmaking cartel called the Chang brothers, who despite their name were not Chinese but from the Baloch region of Pakistan. In the days when he had been illegally fly-tipping (and possibly other activities Mark either didn't know about or wouldn't admit) he'd had plenty of money to gamble, and he lost freely, so the Changs had been willing to let him run up a substantial debt when his ponies didn't pony up. But a couple of tugs from the friendly local constabulary had shut off Kroll's quick sources of income, and the only way he could think of to raise enough to get the Changs off his back, or rather off his knees, was to keep betting through more conventional channels. Of course, like every gambler needing to win to pay his debts, he only amassed more debts. The 'one big win' that was to pay for all remained elusive, and he was now at the end of his tether and on the Changs' immediate 'to do' list.

'So now he's in more of a flap than a flag in a gale,' Slider concluded. 'I suppose someone looking at him was enough to trigger his flight mode, without stopping to wonder who they were.'

'Can't say I blame him,' Porson said. 'The guilty flee when all men pursueth, like the poet says. Well, you'd better work with Acton on this one – they know the ground. Tell 'em everything. They might be willing to help run down Kroll if it helps 'em nail the Changs. Set a thief to catch a monkey.'

'I'm hoping he'll go back home, sir,' Slider said, 'which is why we're not pulling in Mrs Kroll.'

'Right. And you say it's a cul-de-sac? So you can keep a watch without making it obvious. Put someone on it who doesn't stick out like a sore head.'

'Mackay's good,' Slider said. 'And one of the uniforms – Coffey – he's a bright lad. We can put him into plain clothes.'

'Whatever you want.'

'And we'd better keep an eye on Mrs Kroll, both in case she bolts, and in case she leads us to him. Or he might go to his other son, Stefan. I suppose we ought to have the daughter's house in Birmingham watched as well, in case he goes there.'

Porson nodded. He was thinking. 'This makes him a bit tastier, doesn't it? Desperate for money, knows his wife's boss is well off.'

'And that he's a philanthropist,' Slider added.

Porson shrugged. 'I wasn't thinking that so much. I mean, can you ask a philanthropist to fund your gambling debts?'

'If he's fond enough of your wife and it'll help you turn over a new leaf, maybe,' Slider said.

'Hmph. Maybe. What I was thinking is, wifie's got the key, and she lets him know when the boss is going to be out so they can rifle the place and nick – well, whatever's nickable.' He forestalled

Slider's objection. 'We don't know that he didn't keep a bundle of readies somewhere. Old-fashioned bloke who doesn't like modern technology is just the kind to pay for everything in cash. Then the boss comes back unexpectedly and there's nothing for it but to whack him.'

'But in that case why did the boss obligingly sit down with his back to Kroll? And why was he writing a cheque?'

'Oh, all right!' Porson said grumpily. 'Have it your way. The visit was while Bygod was at home, the Krolls appealed to his better nature and he agreed to help.'

'But then why kill him?'

Porson's eyes gleamed with triumph. 'Because the help he was offering wasn't enough, and there was a bigger prize somewhere in the house. There was no sign of disturbance because Mrs Kroll knew exactly what it was and where it was. She could put her hand straight on it.'

Slider sighed. 'It's a possible scenario, but how the hell would we prove it?'

'Catch Kroll first. Once you've got him, reel 'em both in and one or other will crack.'

'What we have to do,' Slider said, 'is establish exactly when Mrs Kroll arrived and left, and whether Mr Kroll was there on that day. We know from the fingermark he was there some time, but it could have been an earlier occasion. If we can fix his van in the area on the Tuesday ... Put McLaren on it.'

'Right, guv,' said Hollis, adding another note to those about who was going to be watching what and whom.

'But we can't just hang around waiting for Kroll to turn up,' Atherton objected.

'Is that your guilt speaking?' said Slider. 'I agree. I think we should have a good look at the Crondaces, particularly the father. He's the only person we actually *know* issued threats against Bygod. Get on and trace them – father, mother and Debbie – and we can have a chat with them, see what they've been up to. Carry on with the other things we were doing. And meanwhile—'

'Meanwhile?' Atherton urged. 'That was an interesting pause.'

'Meanwhile –' Slider came back from his thoughts – 'I don't see any harm in paying a little visit to the ex-wife, see if she has any light to shed on our mystery man. See if you can track her down, will you?'

It turned out not to be too difficult to find Mrs Bygod, who was still using his name, at least professionally: she had a dog-grooming business. She was living on the edge of Chipping Barnet, a leafy spot to the north of Finchley where golf courses roam free as God intended, and breed and flourish in the verdant Hertfordshire pastureland. Slider claimed the privilege of rank to get out of the office for a while and breathe the fresh air.

According to the land registry, the house was owned by one Philip Buckland, presumably her new husband. It was called Field End, which sounded leafy, but it was actually a large, modern bungalow, disappointingly right on the

Barnet Road, the A411, which was busy and noisy. Still, Slider supposed, it was better for business not to be tucked away where passing trade could not take note of your existence. It did at least back on to open countryside – or in this case, open golf course, which in Hertfordshire amounted to much the same thing.

The bungalow was showing its age: the original wood-framed windows were in dire need of painting, the chimney needed repointing, and there were several slipped tiles among those on the roof. The wide front garden of the bungalow had been surfaced to make parking space, but it was cracking round the edges, and weeds were beginning to establish bridgeheads on it.

A sturdy signpost against the front wall announced JUNE BYGOD PET GROOMING CLIPPING DYING SHOW SERVICES, and a phone number. It, too, could do with repainting, Slider noted. A minivan, with the same words painted on its sides under a depiction of a show-cut poodle with its hair dyed pink and a pink bow on its head, was parked on the tarmac to one side, and on the other was a large black Range Rover with sheep bars on the front – a real Chelsea Tractor. Slider pulled up alongside it.

A dog started barking when he rang the doorbell, and since the door was glazed with reeded glass, he could see it prance into view from somewhere in the back of the house. When the door was opened it flung itself on him – a grey standard poodle with a suspiciously blue tinge to the grey of its coat, wearing a blue collar stuck with large imitation sapphires. It was as tall as a man when it stood on its hind legs, as it was only too happy to prove. It put its front feet joyously on Slider's shoulders, bent on proving its Gallic credentials by French-kissing him.

'It's all right, he won't hurt you,' a voice trilled. 'He's only being friendly.'

Slider liked dogs, but he had no need of a saliva sample at this stage of the investigation. He pushed the poodle down firmly with a hand on its chest, projecting mastery, and it sat, gazing up at him adoringly. Atherton had the same sort of effect on women, he remembered, a trifle wistfully.

'Down, Buffy, down,' its owner commanded redundantly. 'There, you see? He likes you.'

June Bygod was small and well-corseted, firm curves embraced by a two-piece Jersey suit in beige with blue trim. She had a tight, smoothly pink face, professionally made up, expensively styled wavy hair, light brown with blonde highlights, and a good deal of gold costume jewellery. She was smiling a professional smile, with a hint of teeth that were either capped or amazingly regular for her age, which he knew from the marriage certificate to be sixty. Under the make-up, he thought her face missed being attractive by some distance, but in day-to-day business transactions you would never realize it. Probably she had never been pretty, and had learned to make the best of things.

He got out his warrant card. 'I'm Detective Inspector Slider of the Shepherd's Bush CID,' he said.

The Shepherd's Bush bit did not seem to mean

anything to her. 'Oh yes?' she said brightly. 'Is it about a dog?'

'I'm afraid I have some bad news, madam,' Slider said. 'May I come in?'

She blinked, and her mouth sagged into disappointed lines that seemed more natural than the smile. 'Oh,' she said, slightly crossly. 'I thought you were a customer. Oh well, come in, then.' She stepped back to let him in and shut the door. 'Come through.' The poodle pranced ahead of them, and she led the way through a narrow, parqueted hall to a sitting room at the back, with sliding French windows the whole width giving a view on to a very dull garden – lawn in the middle and shrubs round the edge – with a chicken-wired dog run and kennels at the end, and beyond them the verdant pastoral idyll of the ninth hole, 180 yards, dog leg right, par three.

The wallpaper was ambitiously patterned, as was the carpet: together they gave the same effect as when you rub your eyes too hard with the heels of your hands. The overstuffed three-piece suite and fake fireplace, glittery chandeliers and onyx-topped coffee-table reminded him of his ex-wife's new home with her second husband, Ernie Newman, except that Irene's stuff was all brand new, and this was old and somewhat worn. There was a strong smell of dog and a fainter one of cigarettes. The former was explained by the presence of an elderly dachshund and a greasy-looking Yorkshire terrier, curled up together on a rug on the sofa, the latter baring its teeth and emitting a low, rattling snarl.

The cigarettes – since Mrs B did not herself smell of them – suggested Mr Buckland smoked.

'So what's all this about?' she asked. 'Please sit down.' She waved him to an armchair facing the window. He sat, and the poodle immediately plonked itself in front of him, offering utter devotion if he felt inclined that way. 'He seems to have taking a liking to you. Does he bother you?'

'No, I like dogs,' he said. Buffy, who evidently spoke human, responded by putting one paw on his knee. He removed it, gently but firmly. This relationship was going no further.

June Bygod, or Buckland, whatever she was now, sat on the sofa facing him, and thought from the direction of his eyes that he was looking out of the window over her shoulder. 'Lovely view, isn't it? We get the occasional golf ball coming in – one broke the bathroom window last year – but it's a small price to pay for a vista like that on to open country.' She said this without irony. She spoke with exaggerated refinement, like an early Mrs Thatcher, as if she were disguising a country accent with too much RP. Cruelty to vowel sounds, Slider thought. 'So, how can I help you? Shepherd's Bush, did you say? I don't know anyone from Shepherd's Bush.' A little laugh. 'Oh, except my ex-husband Lionel, but he's Hammersmith, really. Anyway, I'm sure he hasn't broken any laws. He's not the type.'

She hadn't heard, then? Well, thanks to the cottaging MP's frailty, it hadn't made the national dailies. 'I'm very sorry to have to tell you that he's dead,' Slider said.

She looked at him alertly, head a little tilted, questioning frown. 'Dead? When?'

'He died on Tuesday. I'm afraid I have to inform you that he was murdered.'

You got a lot of reactions in the Job, but he wasn't really expecting this one. She smiled. The smile was quickly removed, and she said, 'Oh dear, I don't mean to – of course, murder's no smiling matter. But if you knew Lionel, you'd know how ridiculous that sounds. You must have got the wrong name somehow. Really, you've made a mistake. I mean, who on earth would ever want to murder Lionel?'

'It's no mistake. As to who would want to murder him – I was hoping you might be able to help me with that.'

'What on earth do you mean?' She seemed slightly affronted.

He responded to the urgent poodle eyes by gently scratching the curly poll as he answered. 'Do you know of anyone who might have wanted to do him harm?'

'No, of course not,' she said, at once and firmly.

'When did you last see him?'

'Oh, I really can't remember. Ages ago. I haven't had anything to do with Lionel for years, not since we split up. We exchange Christmas cards, and that's about it. I don't know anything about his life now. We went our separate ways and that was that.'

'That was because of the court case, wasn't it? The Roxwell case.'

She frowned. 'Oh, you know about that, do you? Well, it wasn't so much the case as all the unpleasantness afterwards. The newspapers, and the reporters hanging around outside all the time. The terrible things they said.' The strained RP was slipping, and she sounded more like a middle-class midlander now. 'It wasn't possible to have a normal life any more. That dreadful man, Derek Crondace—' She paused. 'You don't think it was him who killed Lionel, do you? He threatened him most dreadfully at the time. It was one of the reasons I left. I saw no reason why I should be put in the firing line when I had nothing to do with any of it.'

'It's one of the possibilities we're looking into,' Slider said in the mildest possible way. He didn't want her getting off on that. 'You say you haven't had any contact with him, other than Christmas cards? Did you part on bad terms, then?'

'Oh,' she said with a throwaway gesture, 'not that, so much. I don't think it was possible to be on bad terms with Lionel. He was the world's mildest man – everyone took advantage of him. No, it wasn't a bitter parting, I don't mean that, but it was all over between us and there was no sense in pretending otherwise. I felt he'd ruined my life through his ridiculous crusade, and I wanted out. I wasn't prepared to suffer alongside him while he rode out on his white horse, in his shining armour, especially when I didn't agree with it.'

'By crusade, you mean—?'

'Defending undefendable criminals. Like that

dreadful Roxwell man. He was so obviously guilty, he ought to have gone to prison for what he did, but Lionel got him off – and *used his own money to do it*! And let us in for all that dreadful – unpleasantness.' She seemed dissatisfied with the word. 'I can't describe to you what it was like,' she went on in a low voice. 'All those horrible accusations. And then of course one started to wonder – well, whether there was anything in it.'

'And was there?'

She hesitated, looking in his direction, but through him. 'I don't know,' she said at last. 'I'd never suspected anything like that before. He seemed normal enough to me. A bit milk-and-water, maybe. A bit over-polite, if you know what I mean. Sometimes a woman likes a little bit of, you know, the cave man to come out in her husband.' She gave a coyly roguish smile that made Slider blench inwardly. 'But of course I didn't know where he was every hour of the day. And his practice meant he mixed with some pretty strange people. And why did he take up for Roxwell if he didn't have some special sympathy for him? You had to ask. It did make me wonder whether he was just *too much* of a gentleman, if you get my drift. Well, once you start having doubts...' She shrugged. 'You can't just dismiss them.' She paused a moment. 'Has he been getting up to anything like that in Shepherd's Bush?'

'We have no information to suggest he has.' He changed direction. 'How did you first meet him?'

'My father was a solicitor, in Stamford, and Lionel did his training there. We met and fell in love – he was very handsome, tall, distinguished-looking. His father was a barrister, you know, and I always thought Lionel was wasted as a solicitor. He should have gone to the bar instead. He'd have looked so wonderful in the robes, in court. But he always said he was happier as a back-room boy. No ambition, that was his problem.' She shrugged. 'Anyway, we married, and Daddy made him a partner, and when Daddy retired he bought the practice. But he wanted to do more criminal work, so he sold it, we moved to London, and he set up there.'

'How did you like moving to London?'

'Oh, I was very happy. What girl wouldn't want to swap a place like Stamford for the big city? But of course as he got more successful we saw less and less of each other. Splitting up in the end wasn't such a big step,' she remarked, 'because we were already pretty much living separate lives.'

'He had a particular interest in the theatre, I believe?'

She looked slightly cross. 'Oh, he was mad about it. Went to see all the plays. It got to be a bone of contention, if truth be told, because, well, I like the theatre as much as anyone – I've seen *Phantom* twice – but all that Shakespeare and stuff, people droning on and on and not the faintest idea what they're talking about...! I tried to be interested at first, for his sake, and a nice musical's one thing, but as to being bored stiff night after night – it's not to be borne. And the seats are so uncomfortable! But Lionel got the bug at Oxford when he was doing his law degree. He was in the Drama Society, so I suppose he fancied himself a bit of an expert.'

'He acted in OUDS?'

'He actually wanted to be an actor at one time, but apparently his father didn't approve, made him to go into law. But whether he'd have been any good ... He didn't do the acting at Oxford, you see, he did the backstage stuff – stage manager and lighting and so on. They always want people for that, because most people want to be on the stage, so anyone who's willing to do the boring stuff is very popular. And of course a lot of those Oxford people went on to be professional actors, so he knew them personally, and when he went to a play he could go back-stage and schmooze with them.'

'Didn't you find that exciting?' Slider asked. 'Meeting the celebrities?'

She sniffed. 'It's not like they were film stars. Well, he did do a production with Richard Burton and Elizabeth Taylor once at the Oxford Playhouse, but I never got to meet *them*. Gyles Brandreth, yes – oh, and he knew that Diana Quick from back then. But that was about the best of it. Not exactly earth-shaking. And any-way, there's nothing glamorous about the back-stage of a London theatre. Dirty and dark and cramped. And there's mice everywhere! And of course it was him they wanted to talk to, not me. I'd end up squashed in a corner longing for a gin and tonic while they talked rubbish about the play that I didn't understand one word in three of. So, no,' she ended with elaborate irony, 'I didn't find it exciting. I was happy for him to go without me.'

Slider was getting a pretty clear picture of the marriage and the difficulties thereof – highbrow, modest, gentlemanly Lionel and his lowbrow, impatient, scornful bride who wanted him to be more macho in the bedroom and in his profession – but he wasn't sure it was getting him any closer to who killed him. And however modest and retiring he was, he must have been tough enough in his professional life, because he was in criminal law, and it was the solicitor who met the clients face to face, not the barrister.

'How did he meet Mr Wickham Williams?' he asked on the back of that thought.

She made a moue. 'Oh, that was one of his theatre contacts again. Hugo was another theatre nut, like Lionel. He'd been at Oxford as well, and they could talk about it for hours. Bored everybody stiff at dinner parties.'

'So they were friends as well as colleagues?'

'Oh yes. I never really got on with Magda, though – Hugo's wife. She was a barrister too, and I found her very cold, and a dreadful snob. At Hugo's funeral the seating arrangements were just an insult – she had Lionel in the second row, just behind the family, while I was stuck way back. She said afterwards it was because Lionel was doing a reading so he had to be at the front but there wasn't room for partners as well, and she apologized, but I could see the way she looked at me. She thought I wasn't good enough for them because I didn't go to university.'

There were certainly some old resentments there, Slider thought. This was a woman who knew how to hold a grudge. He imagined the Bygods' married life being one long series of pointed silences, tight lips and plates being slammed down on tables.

'One thing I meant to ask you was about next of kin,' Slider reminded himself. 'Were there any children?'

'No,' she said, sharply, in the sort of tone that said this was a topic best not explored.

Slider drew breath to ask the next question when the dog jumped up and started to bark, prancing towards the door. Outside there was the sound of a vehicle arriving, its door slamming, and a moment later the front door was opened and a man's voice bellowed, 'June? Juney!'

'In here,' she trilled.

'Didn't that parcel arrive?' the cross voice went on, coming closer. 'Didn't you ring about it like I told you?'

The dog frisked back in, and hot on his tail came a very tall, lean man with wiry grey hair, pale blue eyes, and the raw complexion of a man who works outside but subscribes to the 'real men don't moisturize' school of grooming. He was wearing smartly fitting jeans, a chambray shirt with the sleeves rolled up to the elbow, displaying strong, brown forearms, and desert boots. He seemed to be in his late fifties and his face gave the impression of being good-looking, until you examined it more closely and discovered the nose was too small and the mouth rather pink and petulant. It didn't help, of course, that he was scowling furiously.

'If I don't get it today the whole job's going down the pan,' he began angrily as soon as he reached the door. 'I *told* you to ring me if it—' He stopped as he saw Slider, and his face registered uncertainty mingled with an incipient ingratiation as he wondered if he were a client.

Slider, who had risen politely, looked towards June for an introduction. Her lips were tightly closed and her eyes sparkled with something that boded her mate no good – the sort of something that said *must you show me up in front of visitors*? 'This is Phil, Phil Buckland,' she said. 'Detective Inspector—?' She'd forgotten the name.

'Slider.' They shook hands. Buckland's was large, knuckly and hard as a plank. He evidently worked with them. 'Mr Buckland,' he said, managing to get a faint question mark on to it.

'I only use Lionel's name for my business,' she added quickly. 'I started it up when we first split up, before I met Phil, and the customers knew it, so it made sense not to change.'

'What can we do for you, Inspector?' Buckland asked, swallowing his irritation with an effort. He managed a golf-social, nineteenth hole sort of smile. 'Don't tell me June's not been paying her parking fines again?' He turned the smile on her with a hint of menace in it. It looked as though the parking fines were an old bone of contention.

'It's nothing to do with parking,' she snapped.

'Speeding, then. I told her not to paint that pink poodle on the van,' he offered Slider merrily. 'Makes it too conspicuous.'

'Phil,' she said warningly. 'It's nothing like that. It's serious. Lionel's been killed.'

'Killed? What do you mean, killed? In a road accident, you mean?'

'No, I'm afraid he's been murdered,' Slider said.

Buckland looked from one to the other, seeming puzzled. 'Well, June doesn't know anything about that,' he said at last. 'She's not seen him in years. And I've never even met the man. What are you asking her about it for?'

'For one thing,' Slider said, 'we don't know who the next of kin is. You were saying there were no children?' he said to June.

'No,' she said. 'And his parents are both long gone. He hadn't any brothers or sisters, either. I suppose I'm the nearest thing he had to family,' she concluded with a nervous laugh.

'You were no family,' Buckland said roughly.

Slider thought how sad it was to end one's life so thoroughly repudiated. He tried one last tack. 'I believe he was quite well off,' he said. 'I don't suppose you'd know who he would have left everything to?'

'Well, no,' June said. 'Of course, before we split up, he'd left everything to me, but that was a long time ago – what, sixteen years, now? I'm sure he must have made new arrangements since then. Knowing Lionel,' she added, 'he probably left everything to charity. If there was anything left. I don't think he'd worked in years, and he was always giving it away.' This last had an accusatory tone.

'Is there anything else we can help you with, Inspector?' Buckland asked briskly, with more than a hint of hoping there wouldn't be. Outside the sun was declining and it was nearing the hour when a working man required his dinner on the table. With possibly a drink beforehand, as it was Friday and the start of the weekend.

'I can't think of anything at the moment,' Slider said, leaving space for a return visit if necessary. 'Thank you for your help.'

The three of them saw him out, Buffy much the most sorry to see him go. Buckland yanked the dog back in and shut the front door so fast that Slider almost lost a buttock.

On the tarmac outside there was another, much larger, high-side van, white, with bold black letters on the sides and back that read:

BARNET MULTIBELT LTD
MATERIALS HANDLING SOLUTIONS
INSTALLATION AND MAINTENANCE

Well, Slider thought, getting back into his car, you couldn't get more industrial and manly than conveyor belts, could you? June Bromwich-as-was, having taken a wrong turning with the epicurean Bygod, had finally got her caveman in the bedroom.

EIGHT

Marital Arts

Slider rang his old friend Pauline Smithers at Scotland Yard. She had done hard years in the former SO5 Child Protection unit, pursuing a vicious child pornography ring, the sort of job that burns you out, and from which you have to go into convalescence. Hence she was now in charge of the missing persons section of the Homicide unit. Following the rule that Met Police initials have to be changed every two years, it was called SD1 – SDs being the newer, sexier versions of SOs.

She was also now a Detective Chief Superintendent, though she and Slider had started at the same time and had been at Hendon together. The difference in their career trajectories had upset his first wife, Irene, no end.

'Bill! Good to hear from you again.'

'How are the missing persons?' he asked.

'It's "missing persons and abductions with danger of the taking of life",' she corrected him sternly.

'Having fun?'

She caved. 'After child pornography, it's the equivalent of a stay in a cottage hospital,' she admitted. 'I've got a good team – all old-fashioned coppers, no lightweights or prima donnas. I think there's a sort of ox-bow effect going on, where the weighty, experienced and human candidates get washed into my corner and deposited, while the frolickers float merrily by on the main stream.'

'I'm glad to hear it,' Slider said. Like him, she had never been happy with the politics in the Job. Unlike him, she had concealed her dislike better and learned to work round it. But of course, being a woman and headed for the stars had meant she was never able to marry. She had a very expensive riverside flat on the Isle of Dogs and a Siamese cat.

'What can I do for you?' she said. 'You only phone me up when you want something.'

'That's cruel. How often do you phone me?'

'True. Well, what is it?'

'I wondered if you knew anything about Lionel Bygod from your former incarnation in SO5.'

'That name sounds familiar. Context?'

'He was the defence solicitor in the Noel Roxwell case.'

'Oh, I remember that vaguely. It wasn't one of ours, but I remember reading about it in the papers. Refresh me.'

Slider gave her an outline of the case. 'What I want to know is whether there was any grain of truth in the accusations against Bygod, and whether he's been up to anything similar since then.'

'Well, it's not my bailiwick now, of course, but

I can ask around for you. Why do you think he *has* been involved in it?'

'He's turned up dead – murdered – and I'm wondering if there's a revenge or vigilante element in it. He seems to have been a secretive sort of bloke – nobody knows much about him.'

'And you think he may have been secretive for a reason,' she finished for him. 'All right, since it's you asking, I'll see what I can find out. I wouldn't do it for just anyone, you know.'

'I know. I love you, Pauly.'

'Ha! If only! Famous words, Bill Slider – never backed up by any action, I note.'

'Why don't you come over to my place for dinner some time?' he invited. And realizing that 'some time', in the context of an invitation, is as good as 'never', he added cordially, 'What about this evening?'

'This is your place with your wife, is it? And child, and dear old dad?'

'They'll all be there,' he said, with a grin to himself. They had always played the game between them that she was hopelessly in love with him. There had, in fact, been a certain *tendresse* at one stage in their lives, but he had been too diffident to pursue it, and events had drawn them apart.

'I'll pass, then, thanks,' she said, and added: 'As a matter of fact, I'm seeing someone these days.'

'Really? I'm glad to hear it. Who is he? Not another SO headcase, I hope?' She had once gone out with a DCS in the drugs unit of SO7 who had brought her close to suicide.

'We're not all headbangers,' she objected. 'He's in SD6.' This was the Economic and Specialist Crime Command. 'Cheque and Plastic Crime Unit. A nice steady nine-to-five job, no midnight stake-outs or high-speed car chases. He's normal, Bill.'

'Is it serious?'

She didn't answer that. 'I like him,' she said instead. 'His name's Bernard and he's nice and funny and I like him.'

He smiled to himself. 'Well, if you won't come to dinner, we must get together for a drink after work one evening.'

'You always say that, and we never do it.'

'This time we will. I'll ring you.'

'You always say that, too.'

'Well, I don't see that it gets us any further,' Atherton said when Slider recounted his visit to the Bucklands.

'More suspicions on your side of the argument,' Slider pointed out.

'That Bygod was a little light on his feet? In his ex-wife's opinion? But where does *that* get us?'

'I don't know. Clear as you go, that's my motto. Found the Crondaces yet?'

'Yep. And since they're now in three different locations, I think I did pretty well. You'll have to decide which you want to lean on.'

'Yes, but not now. Time to go home. Why don't you come over to supper tonight? Joanna's not working. Come home with me – I don't like thinking of you alone all evening.'

'I have to go and feed the cats,' Atherton said neutrally.

'Well, come on from there,' Slider said cordially.

'Thanks, but I have plans,' Atherton said. Slider waited a receptive moment, but Atherton did not elaborate. He wasn't usually secretive about his after-work life, not with Slider, who was friend as well as boss. But as boss, Slider could not press him. With a mental shrug, he had to leave it at that.

'That's twice in the course of half an hour I've been turned down,' he said instead. 'I'm beginning to feel rejected.'

'Who else turned you down?' Atherton asked.

'Pauline Smithers. She's going out with a man called Bernard.'

'But I bet she'll be thinking of you,' Atherton reassured him.

Joanna was at home, but Dad wasn't – Friday night was his bridge night. 'Not that it makes any difference,' Joanna said. 'All the same people go to the bridge club as the Scrabble club. It's the over sixties pickup centre of Chiswick. He gives me a sly smile and won't answer when I ask what goes on there. I'm thinking Sodom and Gomorrah.'

'More likely Schweppes and Gordons,' Slider corrected. 'I asked Atherton back to supper tonight.'

'Oh, good,' Joanna said. 'I can stretch the chicken. What time's he coming?'

'He isn't. He turned me down. Said he had

plans.'

'"Had plans"?' she queried. 'That's a bit American of him. What plans?'

'He didn't say.'

'Didn't or wouldn't?'

'I suspect it was "wouldn't".'

Joanna regarded him a moment. 'You aren't thinking ... Oh, come on, Bill! Just because Emily's away, you can't think he's—'

'Riding the carnal carousel? I hope not. But she's been away a lot lately,' he said unhappily.

'But he loves her.'

'He does,' Slider agreed. 'But he's not used to going without. Satan finds mischief for idle hands to do. And other bodily parts.'

'Don't go there.'

'And I get the feeling just lately that they've been quarrelling a lot.' He looked at Joanna. 'Has she said anything about it?'

Joanna paused. 'I was going to say "no", but ... She did say they had a disagreement about something. I didn't think it was important – I mean, who doesn't disagree from time to time? But if you think...' She brooded.

'Well?' he prompted eventually. She looked up. 'What did they disagree about? Or is it girly stuff you can't tell me?' He held up his hands quickly. 'Don't tell me anything sticky. I have to work with this man. In fact, you probably shouldn't tell me anyway. None of my business.'

'It's nothing like that,' she said, amused by his sensibilities. 'It's just she wants them to move into her father's old flat, and he doesn't want to leave his house. She was afraid he had issues –

sorry, horrible word – about their living together but, as I pointed out, they practically do live together anyway, only it's at his place. But the flat is much bigger and the parking is easier, and it's easier for her to get to Heathrow from there, so it seems sensible to move. She doesn't understand why he's resisting.'

'It's a big step,' Slider said. 'He'd be giving up his independence.'

'Oh, rubbish! Why do men always regard relationships as a trap set by female praying mantises?'

'It's not a matter of relationships,' Slider said. 'The house is his. The flat's hers. He'd be living in her house. That's just a fact.'

'Well, they could work out the finances,' Joanna said reasonably. 'Anyway, I don't even know if it was a serious disagreement, so I don't know why I'm talking.'

'No, and they'll sort it out for themselves in any case,' Slider said. 'As I said, it's none of my business. Subject closed.'

Joanna stepped close, took his face in her hands, and kissed him.

'What was that for?' he asked when she released him.

'For being a nice man, and caring about Jim's welfare.'

'I did say "subject closed",' he reminded her.

'I'll worm it all out of him next time we're together,' she promised. 'Invite him again, another night. When's Emily coming back?'

'Not sure. Next week some time, I think.'

'Plenty of time, then,' she said, turning back to

the cooking. 'Do you want potatoes as well, or just veg?'

Plenty of time to get into trouble, Slider thought. That was the problem.

Slider's instinct was right, and Kroll did come crawling home; not under cover of darkness, though, but halfway through the morning with the air of a weary dog after one of those marathon cross-country treks that always get in the soft pages of newspapers.

Mrs Kroll hadn't gone to work that morning, which had made it easier for the surveillance teams, so all four of them were inside when the word was given for the teams to move in.

'Kroll came quietly,' Hollis reported to Slider. 'I think he were too knackered to care any more, but Mrs Kroll blew a fuse. Went for Mackay tooth and nail. Took two of 'em to hold her down, so they've nicked her for assaulting a police officer.'

'That's good,' Slider said. It was always better to have something solid to detain people on.

'The old lady went shouty-crackers an' all,' Hollis reported with amusement, 'but she did it in Polish so nobody knew who she was shouting at.'

'Please tell me they didn't bring her in as well,' Slider said.

'No, guv. And they left the lad, Mark, to look after her. Didn't want to leave her all alone, given her age an' everything.'

'That's all right. We've got everything out of him already,' Atherton said. 'He's a sucked lemon.'

'He won't leave his gran, anyway,' McLaren said. 'They're shit hot on family, that lot. So we can always pick him up again later if need be. He's taking her over to the other son's house, Stefan, to stay for a bit.'

A team of four, led by Swilley, was now turning over the Krolls' house.

'What's he said so far – Kroll?' Slider asked.

'Nothing, guv.'

'Nothing – as in...?'

'Not a dicky,' Hollis said. 'Mouth tight shut. Wouldn't even confirm his name. Asked if he wanted a phone call – nothing. Asked if he wanted a brief – nothing. He's sitting there like a pillar o' salt – hoping it'll all go away, maybe.'

'Hmm,' said Slider. It was a good ploy if you could keep it up. Most people couldn't. Sooner or later they had to blab. But Kroll was probably exhausted, which would make it easier for him. 'Well, let's give him some grub and let him rest. Once his mind gets working again he'll see the position he's in. What about Mrs K?'

'Still mad as a wet cat,' Hollis said. 'Can't shut her up.'

'We'll have a go at her, then,' Slider said. Talking was good. The more the better. Things you wanted to hear came out with the torrent you didn't, like bits of debris carried along on flood water.

Mrs Kroll was evidently an adherent of the 'best form of defence is attack' school. As soon as Slider appeared she fired her opening salvo.

'What the hell is this all about? What're you lot going after us for? We've not done anything. Frightening my poor mother to death – if anything happens to her, I'm holding you responsible. You've got no right dragging us away and locking us up like this. What is this, communist Russia? Where's my husband? Hasn't he got enough on his plate without you lot harassing him? You got no right to arrest me. You can't keep me here. I'm going to sue the lot of you!'

And so on. Slider sat down opposite her, with Swilley taking her place standing off to one side, and let her run herself down. When she drew breath he said, 'You assaulted a police officer, so we *did* have the right to arrest you, and we *can* keep you here. And you know perfectly well why your husband is here. This is a serious matter, Mrs Kroll, so let's drop the histrionics and talk seriously about it.'

Her nostrils flared. 'You're not talking about Mr Bygod, I hope? You're not going to try to pin that on us? We had nothing to do with it. Why the hell should I wish the old geezer any harm? I'm out of a job because he's dead, and it was a good job, let me tell you. Why would I want to put him out of the way?'

'Because you are in deep trouble and desperate for money. And Mr Bygod had money. When it comes to your lives or his...' He shrugged. 'Your husband comes first.'

If her nostrils flared any more they'd be in danger of sucking the whole room inside out. Her eyes narrowed with fury, and she yelled, 'That stupid, useless, brainless moron! I could kill him for what he's done to us. How many times have I told him, *begged* him to stop? But no, he's got to go back for more! "It'll be all right, it'll be all right!" Well it's not all right! But will he listen? No, he likes banging his head on a brick wall. Wish to God he'd knocked his brains out, the useless bastard! I'd be well rid of him!'

From this Slider gathered it was not Mr Bygod she was yelling about. 'Your husband has a gambling problem,' he said mildly, to keep her going.

'Oh, you *think* so?' she demanded with heavy irony. 'He's spent every penny we had, can't buy so much as a bag of cement because he owes money everywhere, the Changs are after him – and I don't mean to give him a friendly hug. He can't go to work, can't show his face anywhere, but he still spent all day yesterday putting money on horses, and you say he's got a gambling problem. *You think so?*'

The last sentence rose to a scream which strained her throat so much that she broke into a paroxysm of coughing. Slider pushed a glass of water and a box of tissues towards her, and eventually she managed to stop, blew her nose, sipped some water, and then sat back, exhausted, looking at him with a flat expression.

'The Changs are not people you want on your backs,' he said. 'I know about them.' In fact, the knowledge was new – he'd just had a crash course over the phone from DI Fromonde at Ealing – but there was no need to tell her that. 'They depend on their reputation for violence to make their fortune, so they're not the sorts to forgive a debt.'

'You think I don't know that?' she said grimly. 'Why don't you lot do something about them, instead of persecuting their victims like us? You bastards always go after the easy targets. You're all the same.'

Slider said, 'Believe me, I have some sympathy with you. You were in a terrible bind. The only way out was to get the money, and get it right away. But who did you know who had that sort of cash? Only Lionel Bygod.'

She turned her face away. 'Oh, give it a rest,' she said wearily. 'I didn't kill him.'

'Even if you didn't strike the blow, even if it was your husband who did the actual killing, you're still just as guilty. You were the one with the key, you planned it, you were there. I'm quite sure you're the brains of the family.'

'You got *that* right,' she muttered, still staring at the wall, her profile to Slider. She looked pale, drawn, and somehow doomed. He thought of Bygod's beaten head to harden himself against her.

'Your only hope is to cooperate,' he concluded. 'Get your mitigating circumstances taken into account. But the clock's ticking on that. The time to speak up is now.'

She turned back to him. 'I told you, he went out about half eleven and that's the last I saw of him. He didn't come home before I left at two. And my husband's never even been to the house. You got nothing on us.'

'Your husband's never been to the house?'

Slider asked, feeling the quickening of relief. 'What not even once – to pick you up from work, or something like that?'

'He's never been to the house,' she said with ironic emphasis. 'What d'you want, me to draw you a picture?' Slider didn't answer, only regarded her gravely, and suddenly she grew nervous. 'What you looking at me like that for?'

'I wanted to see what you looked like when you told a lie,' he said.

She reddened. 'Don't you call me a liar! Who the hell d'you think you are?'

Slider stood up. 'I'm going to give you a little time to think about it. Your one hope is to tell the truth.'

'You've got nothing on me!' she shouting, standing up, fists against the table top. 'You got nothing!'

'Think about it,' he said quietly, and went out, with Swilley behind him.

Out in the corridor, Swilley said, 'She's good. Sounds very convincing.'

'Good job we know she's lying. All the same, I'd like a bit more to take with me next time I go in. More leverage.'

'Boss,' Swilley said, 'it occurs to me that if they did get what they wanted at the flat, they'd have paid off the Changs by now. But don't you think she still seems genuinely scared of them?'

'Many suggestions come to mind,' Slider said. 'That they couldn't find whatever it was they wanted. That they got something but it wasn't enough, that the Changs have upped the interest. That she's only pretending to be scared. Or that she's scared, but not of the Changs any more.'

'Scared of facing a murder charge, you mean?' Swilley contemplated the idea. 'I wonder which is worse – a spell in prison or the Changs? Hard one to call.'

At the end of the corridor they met Mackay, with an interesting bruise coming up on his cheekbone where a wild flail of Mrs Kroll's had found its mark. He had already been well teased by the uniforms on his woman-handling skills.

'How is Mr Kroll?' Slider asked.

'Still staying shtum,' Mackay answered. 'Can't get a peep out of him – won't even have a cup of tea, and when did you ever meet a Polish builder who wasn't ready for a cuppa?'

'We'll let him soak a bit longer,' Slider said, 'while you people upstairs get me some evidence on his movements on Tuesday.'

'Yes, guv,' Mackay said. They turned for the stairs together. 'Can I get you a cup of tea?' he offered.

'Thanks. While we wait for the Krolls to soften up to the right degree, we'd better have a look at a Crondace.'

'Which one?' Swilley asked.

'All of them,' Slider decided.

NINE

Parent Rap

Once a client of the state, always a client of the state, so the saying went. The Crondace family, who had lived at public expense in a council dwelling in Islington at the time of the Roxwell case, now occupied three separate ones. Debbie, now aged thirty, had been displaced sideways into Hoxton, to a council maisonette with her three children by different fathers. Her mother had gone even further east, to a flat in Haggerston in a new block, built where the council had knocked down an eighteenth-century terrace in a fit of egalitarian frivolity.

Mr Crondace had gone the furthest, to a flat in an old LCC block on the edge of Stratford Marsh, under the thundering shadow of the East Cross Route Blackwall Tunnel approach, with a delightful view over the industrial canal to the abandoned gasworks. Nudge him just a bit harder, Slider thought, and they could have set him down next to the sewage treatment works at Creekmouth – which would have been poetic justice since he had arrogated to himself the right to clear up what he saw as nasty smells.

Mackay and Coffey did the long haul out to

Stratford; Atherton and Connolly went first to Haggerston, where they found Mrs Crondace at home. She was a big woman, both tall and broad, with meaty arms and a face like clarified dripping. She was also chronically, terminally indignant – which at least meant she was glad to see them, being brim-full of a spleen that really, *really* needed an audience.

The one-bedroom flat was neat and tidy, and though cheaply furnished even had some touches of finery to it: a fancy mirror – the shape reminded Atherton vaguely of the Isle of Wight – with seashells stuck round the edge, and a framed reproduction of the green Chinese lady. A budgie in a cage on a stand by the window chirped regularly but at long intervals, its head tilted in a listening pose between whiles, as if it was carrying on a conversation, the other half of which was audible only to itself.

But there was a sourish, stale smell about the flat which, unlike most odours, grew more unpleasant the longer you were exposed to it. Atherton noted that though Mrs Crondace's hair was tidily, even severely, scraped back into a bun, it was dirty, and concluded the smell was coming from her.

'Wot you raking all that up again for?' she demanded stridently, when he conveyed the reason for their visit. 'Roxwell? Has he come back, the dirty nonce? I tell you, if he has, I'm going after him, you c'n say what you like. He ruined my Debbie, and he got away with it, the dirty little bastard.'

'He was proved innocent in a court of law,'

Atherton said, to tempt her out.

She was duly provoked. 'Don't give me that! He was guilty all right. He was let off after his paedo pals done their stuff, all them fag lawyers – and that judge was one of 'em an' all. Don't tell *me*! I can spot 'em a mile away. Justice? Don't talk to me about justice! There's no justice in this country. It's all "who you know", the old boy network, you scratch my back and I'll scratch yours. That Bygod – he was behind it all. You could tell from the namby-pamby way he talked he was one of them. Well, we scotched him good and proper, Del and me. He couldn't show his face again by the time we'd finished.'

'Sure, your husband did a grand job o' that,' Connolly said admiringly. Atherton saw what she was up to and left the talking to her.

Mrs Crondace glared at them indignantly. 'That useless git? It was me had to put the backbone in him! He'd have give up if I hadn't shoved a rocket up his arse. Lazy sod was all "oh, we can't do anything about it, the likes of us"!' She imitated a ludicrous whine. 'He'd have gone off down the boozer with his market pals and that'd've bin that. Sooner be swilling pints than standing up for his own daughter. Well, not while I got breath in my body. That Wickham whatever his name was, the barrister, he copped out, dying like that, but we fixed that Bygod once and for all. But that Roxwell got away in the end. Went abroad somewhere. If he comes back...' She pounded one fist into the other palm with slow menace.

'Now, I'm asking meself,' Connolly said, 'did

you not let Mr Bygod off a bit light, the way it was? I mean, he still had his health and strength. He could set up somewhere else and start carrying on the same way all over again.'

She scowled. 'He wouldn't dare. He knew we was watching him, Del and me. 'F he stuck his head up agen, we'd a blown it off.'

'So you knew where he went, then, after he left Islington?'

'We got our spies,' Mrs Crondace said. 'There's a lot o' good people out there as don't like that sort. A 'ole network's keeping an eye out for the likes of him.'

'So where did he go, then? Mr Bygod?'

She became suspicious. 'Wot you asking me for? You lost 'im? Cuh! Find 'im your bloody self! Don't ask me to do your job for you.'

Connolly smiled encouragingly. 'Well, you kind o' did that already, didn't you?'

'Wot you talking about? Did what?'

'Did the law's job. He's had his head bashed in, hasn't he?'

'What, Bygod?' A slow smile spread across the wide, lard-pale face. 'Blimey, that's the best news I've heard in years! I knew somebody'd do for him in the end.'

'We were kind of thinking it was you and Derek we should thank. You've saved us all a mort o' trouble.'

'Not me,' she said with complete unconcern. 'I'm saving myself for that Roxwell, if he ever shows his dirty face again.'

'So, it was your husband, then?'

'What, Del? He's not my husband any more,

that lazy sod. I divorced him. Neither use nor ornament, he wasn't. He give up his stall 'cos he said he had a bad back. I give him bad back! I said you can go out to work or you can get out. I'm not wearing myself out waiting on you hand and foot. Bad back my eye! Wasn't so bad he couldn't go down the pub with his mates, was it? So I chucked him out and the council give him his own place, out Stratford.'

'You keep in touch with him, then?'

'See him now and agen,' she admitted, eyeing them cautiously. 'So you're saying Bygod's been done in? Well, whoever done it done a public service, that's all I got to say.'

'Did Del not discuss it with you?' Connolly asked innocently.

Atherton's phone rang and he stepped out into the hall to take the call.

Mrs Crondace stared vaguely after him, then answered Connolly. 'He did not. If it *was* him. I'd a' thought he was too fond of sitting on his arse, but good for him if he did! He never stopped talking about it, that I do know. Thought the world of our Debbie, he did. Never forgave them creepy lawyers.'

Atherton came back in and said, 'Sorry about that. Mrs Crondace, when did you last see Derek?'

The lapse into more policeman-like speech seemed to alert her, though not alarm her. 'Haven't seen him in weeks,' she said promptly. 'Talked to him on the phone a coupla times.'

'When was the last time?'

'I dunno. Sat'd'y last, maybe. Or the Frid'y.

Not since.'

'Any idea where he might go if he's not at home?'

'Looked in all the boozers, have you?' she enquired ironically.

'I mean, if he was away for longer than that. A week, maybe.'

'No idea,' she said indifferently. 'Wot, not at 'ome, is he? Well, he had a brother in Hackney – but he died last year, back-end. I s'pose he might still have a few mates in Chapel Market, but whether they'd give him house room's another question.' She snorted. 'Maybe he's gone to Spain to look for that Noel Roxwell. Finish the job.'

'So you're thinking he did do away with Lionel Bygod, then?' Connolly tried, casually.

Mrs Crondace gave her a ripely sardonic look. 'Don't ask *me*. That's your job, innit? You're the bloody p'lice. You figger it out.'

'If we find out that you do know something about it but haven't told us—' Atherton began, but she interrupted him, unmoved.

'Oh sod off,' she said, without rancour. 'Don't gimme that old toffee. You can't threaten me. What Del does is his own business – I ain't responsible. And if you'd put that Roxwell away the first time round, like you should've, other people wouldn't have to clear up the mess after you, would they?'

The budgie chirped, stretched its wings, shuffled two steps along its perch, and resumed its listening stance.

'For the record,' Atherton said, 'where were

you on Tuesday?'

'Tuesd'y?' She pondered. 'Oh yeah. Morning the sheropadist come, I had me feet done. Afternoon I went down the bingo, the Mecca down Hackney Road, stopped there till about nine o'clock and come home. Is that when he got done, then, that old Bygod, Tuesd'y?'

'Did anyone see you at the bingo?'

Her eyes gleamed with amusement. 'No, I was all on me own,' she said with ripe sarcasm. 'It's a bingo hall. What, you think I was the only one down there?'

'Anyone in particular who can vouch for you?'

'That's for you to find out,' she said. 'I'm not doing your job for you.'

The budgie chirped. It had a listless, imprisoned sound to it that Atherton disliked. Also the smell in the flat seemed to be coating the back of his throat. He thanked Mrs Crondace for her help, and took his and Connolly's leave.

Outside he said, 'That was Coffey on the phone. It looks as though Crondace has done a runner. A neighbour says he hasn't been around since last weekend.'

'So it could 'a' been him, then?'

'What did you think of Madame Defarge?' he asked, with a nod towards the flat.

'I think she was full of shit,' Connolly said. 'I wouldn't believe a word the owl bitch said. If she said rain was wet I'd go out and check.'

'But what about the murder?'

'If Crondace did it, she was in on it. Probably wouldn't be there in person, though. She'd watch her own back. And she seemed powerful pleased with her alibi, didn't she?'

'Yes,' Atherton said, 'though that may just be because it'll be a bugger to follow up. I think she relishes giving the police trouble.'

'So now we've got to find Crondace?' Connolly asked. 'Mary 'n' Joseph, that's going to be another needle in a haystack.'

'At least,' Atherton said. 'Come on, let's go and see the daughter. Maybe she'll know where her dad is, if he really thought the world of her.'

'Why wouldn't he? Three kids by different fathers. Sure, she must be a charmer to attract so much love.'

Debbie Crondace was still living under the name of Debbie Crondace, so presumably hadn't married any of the happy authors of her pregnancies. Atherton expected to find her a younger version of her mother, invigorated by the same spite and self-righteousness, but in fact she seemed merely lethargic. Her children were all at school, so either she had had no recent sexual liaisons, or she had at last worked out how to use contraception.

They found her at home in a three-bedroom purpose-built maisonette of minuscule proportions. It still sported the original developer's plain white walls and cheap beige carpeting throughout, both of which were much marked and stained. A glimpse through the open doors showed bedrooms hysterically cluttered with things heaped on beds and overflowing on to floors: clothes, plastic toys, comics, sports goods, food debris. The tiny kitchen was full of unwashed dishes and everything that would no longer fit in the bedrooms. All her children were boys, and the pervading odour in the house was of male sweat, trainers and cigarettes, but it was somehow less creepy and more bearable than the insidious reek in her mother's flat, which Atherton had mentally put down as the smell of malice.

The sitting room, which was about nine by twelve, contained only a much-abused three-piece suite and a vast flat-screen television. What else indeed did it need? To this room it was that Debbie led the way after she had opened the door and stared at them open-mouthed for long enough. Presumably it was where she had been when they rang, judging by the automatic way she resumed her place on the sofa facing the screen; and judging by the ample dent into which she slotted her behind, it was where she spent most of her days.

There was an American confessions show on, with a strap-line along the bottom of the screen that said I SLEPT WITH MY DAUGHTER'S BOYFRIEND. There were three assorted women flanking the host who all had curiously plastic-looking faces, and a whooping audience.

'Could we turn the television off, please?' Atherton asked.

After an appreciable pause to process the request, Debbie switched it off with the remote, and then automatically reached for the packet of cigarettes in her cardigan pocket. She was wearing sweat pants, a T-shirt and a baggy brown cable-knit cardigan that reached almost to her knees. She was quite short – about five-four – but so wide it made her look shorter. The early-sprouting bosoms noted in the reports of the fourteen-year-old Debbie had spread into vast udders, and her buttocks and belly had come out in sympathy. You could have drawn her with a pair of compasses. In her doughy face there was still the hint that she might once have been puggily pretty, but her eyes were dull and her thick brown hair was unkempt. For whatever reason, she had obviously given up.

She gave them no help by asking anything, sitting like a pudding and waiting for them to open the conversation. Her lack of curiosity suggested that visits from the police were not unknown, yet Atherton would have thought she'd have wanted to know if it was something to do with one of her three boys – or at least, which one. But she sat and smoked and stared at the screen as if it was still on. Could apathy go any further?

He glanced promptingly at Connolly, who was evidently thinking the same thing, for she said, 'Do you not want to know why we're here, Debbie?'

Debbie shrugged.

'You get that many visits from the police, is that what it is?'

'Me mum phoned,' she said. 'Said you'd prob'ly be coming round.'

'And did she say what it's about?'

'That s'licitor, Mr Bygod. She said he'd been done in.'

'Right, so. And what do you know about that?'

Now there was a sideways flit of the eyes – reaction at last! 'I don't know nuffing about it. Why you asking me?'

'Sure, you were a central player in the whole business. He let you down, getting that Noel Roxwell off. Made your ma and da mad as hell. You must have hated him like fire,' Connolly suggested.

'That was Mum and Dad,' she said. 'They was the ones made all the fuss.'

'So you weren't upset by what he did to you?' Connolly asked.

'Look,' she said – the opening word to many a gaping lie, many an imprudent confession. The fat of her face seemed to tense slightly.

Connolly flicked a look at Atherton, who nodded to her, so she went on in her most comradely, inviting tone. 'Is there something you want to tell me, Debbie? I think there is, isn't there?'

'Look,' she said again. She darted a glancing, fearful look at Atherton and then back to Connolly. Atherton effaced himself into wallpaper; Connolly managed somehow to emit motherliness.

'Go on. Tell me what happened.'

'Look, I didn't know it'd go that far,' Debbie said weakly. 'I didn't mean it to happen like it did.'

Connolly said soothingly, 'Ah, sure I know you didn't. T'wasn't really your fault, was it?'

'No, it wun't,' she cried plaintively. 'It was Mum. She made me. And then Dad got all upset and – well, I, like, couldn't stop them. You don't know what she's like – Mum.'

'I've an idea,' Connolly sympathized. 'Haven't I just met her?'

'And Dad – well, when he was mad, and he'd had a drink or two, you wouldn't cross him. He'd even hit Mum. But I never knew anyone would get in trouble, honest I didn't.'

Atherton adjusted his mental template. This was not going to be a confession about the murder – or not immediately. But it might throw light on it. He silently willed both women on.

Debbie's hopeless, hunted eyes were on Connolly, and she smiled kindly and said, 'Tell me all about it, why don't you?'

'I dunno where to start,' Debbie said uncertainly.

'Start from the beginning,' Connolly said. 'From that day when it happened.'

'I only done it for a cigarette,' Debbie said fretfully. 'Kim, she dared me. Mum wouldn't let me smoke, and one time she found a fag I'd bummed off some boy at school in my pocket she belted me, then she told me dad and he belted me. They both smoked like bleedin' chimneys,' she added bitterly. 'All right for them!'

'Tell me about Kim.' Connolly moved her along. 'Kim North, wasn't it?'

'Yeah. She and me was mates at school. Anyway, we'd seen this bloke, whatsisname.'

'Noel Roxwell.'

'Yeah. He went home the same way as Kim and me. So one night, I'd not been in school 'cos I had the curse, and she's on her own, and she waits for him in the alley and says give us a fag. So he says all right. So he does. So they both have a smoke, and they're chatting, like, and then he goes, "I'll give you all the fags you want if you're nice to me." So she says, what, nice like this? And she gives him a kiss. And while he's still kind of thinking about it, she grabs the packet out'f his hand and runs for it.'

Connolly nodded calmly, as if this was all par for the course. 'And how do you know about it? Did she tell you?'

'Yeah, she come straight round my house. She goes, "I got something to tell you," so we goes out for a walk, and she shows me the packet o' fags. So we both have a smoke and she tells me about it, and then she says you should do it too, and I say I don't want to, and she says go on, you'll get fags for it, and kissing him's nothing, it's not like you got to do much. And then she dares me. Well, so I goes, "All right, I will, then."'

She paused, evidently not used to ordering her thoughts into a narrative. Connolly encouraged her. 'Go on. What happened next?'

'Well, Kim, she didn't really smoke properly, not then, and we had three each, one after the other, and she starts feeling sick, so she gives me the packet and goes home. An' I goes home and hides the packet under me mattress. Well, Kim, when she gets home, her mum's all, "Where've you been?" and she feels sick an' that, and she starts crying. And her mum's on at her, so she says this bloke stopped her in the alley and kissed her and touched her up. Well, her mum goes ballistic, and she goes down the p'lice.'

'And what about you? How'd you get involved?'

She frowned, remembering. 'Well, it was the next day, or the one after that, me mum found the fags in me room, and she went mad. I just wanted to stop her, that was all. She kept going on and on. And Kim'd got out of it all right – everybody was on her side now and being nice to her – so, well, I said this bloke had given 'em me, the same bloke as Kim.' She stopped, flushing with guilt.

'You told your mum he'd forced you to have sex,' Connolly suggested gently.

Debbie looked up. 'It wasn't my fault! It was Mum. I only just sort of mentioned something, but she jumped on it, and then it was did he do this and did he do that, and she went on and on, and I just sort of – said yes. Just to shut her up. She wouldn't let go of it. And then she got Dad in and it all sort of—'

'Got out of control,' Connolly suggested.

'Yeah,' she said eagerly, glad of the understanding. 'I never meant it to happen. I never thought anyone'd get in trouble. But once Mum and Dad went down the p'lice I couldn't get out of it. I couldn't say I'd made it up – they'd've killed me. I mean – I couldn't, could I?' Her appeal was desperate and awful. 'It just went on, week after week,' she said, in a low, miserable voice. 'P'lice and social workers and doctors and lawyers. And Mum and Dad, it was like they loved it! They had the neighbours round, and reporters, and everyone making a fuss of 'em, and their pictures in the papers, and Dad was down the pub talking about it, and people coming up to him on his stall in the market. He had the telly filming him one day. And then he started this anti-paedo campaign ... well –' she sighed – 'it was like I'd started something, like some bloody great...'

Her voice trailed off as a choice of simile failed her. Illustrative language wasn't her forté.

But Connolly could imagine perfectly well how a rather dim fourteen year old with forceful parents could be both run over and carried away by a juggernaut she had set in train with no intention but to save herself a telling-off. No, it would have taken a degree of character she plainly hadn't got, to say at any point in the process that she had made it up. Connolly could imagine her being dragged along, silent and miserable, terrified that the majestic forces of the law would pin her down and extract the ghastly confession from her that it was all a lie. Fortunately for her, girls in her position were by then treated with kid gloves and helped in every way possible to assemble their testimony. And with Kim's accusation against Roxwell, and his having already come to the attention of the police, weight of belief would have been on her side.

'I suppose,' she said, 'the doctors examined you?'

Her misery intensified a degree. 'They said it was too late to get anything – like, you know, evidence. But they said I wasn't a virgin.'

There was a brief silence as Connolly contemplated the ramifications of that. Atherton made a gesture that she caught out of the corner of her eye, and she asked, 'Where'd you get the bruises on your wrists?'

'What? Oh, that was Dad. He grabbed me and shook me when Mum told him, called me a slag, but Mum stopped him and said it weren't my fault, and then he went off on one about Roxwell instead.'

'Have you seen your dad lately?' Connolly asked casually. 'Has he been round?'

'He come Sat'd'y before last to take the boys to the Arsenal match. That's the last time.'

'He's fond of your boys?'

She shrugged. 'S'pose. They all like the footy. Mum always hated it, wouldn't have it on. But my kids are mad about it. So he, like, comes here to watch if there's a big match.'

'Have you spoken to him since that Saturday?'

She shook her head. Then belatedly, alarm came to her. 'You're not going to tell 'em, Mum and Dad? About – you know. Me making it up. They'd kill me.'

'We're not going to tell them,' Connolly said.

She subsided, sinking further into her pothole as the spine it had taken her to make the confession dissolved again. Then, but with much less alarm, she asked, 'Will I get into trouble?'

Perjury and perverting the course of justice could get you twenty years. She'd been a juvenile at the time, but there were all the years since when she could have said something. Connolly glanced at Atherton, and he said, 'We've got more important things on hand at the moment.

Has your dad been talking about the old case lately – about Roxwell and Mr Bygod?'

She sniffed. 'He never stops talking about it. It's like it's the only thing that's ever happened to him.'

'So when you last saw him, he was still talking about getting revenge, was he?' Atherton almost held his breath, but she didn't seem to make the connection between his question and the death of Lionel Bygod – or maybe she had forgotten already that that was what they had come about.

'Yeah. He talks big, my dad, but it's all talk. He'd never do anything. Long as he's got his beer and his footy. Mum says it's a wonder the bleedin' sofa ain't grown on to his bum.'

Outside in the fresh air, Connolly breathed deeply and said, 'Talking about her dad growing a sofa on his arse! Love a God, she'd want to cop on to herself.'

'That was her mother talking,' Atherton said. 'I don't think our Debbie would have the wit to think critically about her father. Or about anything at all.'

'You're right, she never even wondered what we'd come round for,' Connolly noted. 'All the same...'

'Yes, all the same,' Atherton agreed. 'Her dad was still obsessed, and now he's missing, and her view that he's all mouth and trousers is probably her mother talking again.'

'And the mother's sharp enough to cover their tracks by saying that, knowing she'd repeat it. So it could be them,' Connolly concluded. 'What now?'

Atherton looked at his watch. 'Lunch,' he proposed.

'Shouldn't we get back?'

'Gather ye rosebuds while ye may. We don't get many perks in this job, but eating out is definitely one of them.'

Connolly gave a glance around. 'Here?' she protested.

'Don't be precious. We're only a stone's throw from Islington, and Upper Street is crammed with nice cafés and restaurants.'

'Are you buying?' Connolly asked.

He looked at her suspiciously. 'This isn't a date,' he said.

'Ah, but I'm smashed broke,' she said. 'And you with the grand sergeant's wages!'

'If this is Irish charm, I should warn you I'm immune.'

'But you could never say no to a female.'

'You've got me there. All right, I'm buying.'

'Ah, you're such a dote,' she exclaimed, beaming. 'And I'm so starved I could eat a nun's arse through the convent gates.'

'I think we might do better than that,' Atherton said gravely.

TEN

Yvonne the Terrible

There had been a steady trickle all morning of people 'coming forward', as the police and media jargon had it, as the news of Bygod's death spread through the community. Unfortunately, no-one had anything useful to offer. They wanted to say that Bygod had been kind to them, had helped them in various ways, was a nice man – 'a real gentleman' was the most common description – and that they wished, rather wistfully, they could do something to help find his killers. It was notable that nobody knew anything about his private life, or his life at all before he came to Hammersmith. It seemed he had kept the secret of his past from everyone.

Slider had been with Mr Porson, and returned to the CID room to find both his teams were back. 'All right, report,' he said, settling himself on the edge of a desk. 'You first,' he said, nodding to Mackay and Coffey.

They told of their abortive visit to Crondace's flat. 'We asked all the neighbours we could find, guv. Nobody's seen him later than last Saturday,' said Mackay.

'This old woman next door had the key so we

went in,' said Coffey. He wrinkled his nose. 'Place is a tip. Filthy. Empty beer cans and take-away boxes everywhere. Dirty clothes. Dirty bed sheets. He's really let himself go.'

'There was a free newspaper lying inside the front door,' Mackay said, 'and the old lady says it comes on a Tuesday morning, so it looks as though the latest he could've been there was Monday night. This other neighbour said he drinks down the Navigation – that's his regular – so we went there.'

Slider knew the area slightly, and with Mackay's description he could imagine it: a dreary place of derelict Victorian warehouses, modern industrial units, shabby lock-ups, breaker's yards, and vacant lots behind graffitied hoardings; the whole much intercut with railway lines, canals and abused rivers. Here and there on the main roads were isolated blocks of flats, sticking up like icebergs from the surrounding sea of bleakness: some former LCC buildings from the 1930s, a few raw-looking, flat-faced low-rises from the 70s; and where the buses stopped, a forlorn shop or two.

The Navigation was a survivor from the age of canals, when the whole area was thriving with workshops, small factories and wharves. Now it stood at the end of a stained concrete approach road, with a wasteland of ragwort, buddleia and car tyres around it. The canal – the River Lea Navigation, after which it had been named – ran behind it, shut off by steel palisade security fencing, though Mackay and Coffey had noticed that two of the upright pales had been removed by vandals, and a beaten path through the weeds showed that the gap was well-used.

The Navi had done its best with bright paint, pub grub and decent beer, and it had its faithful clientele. 'You wouldn't think there was anyone living round there, guv,' Mackay said, 'but I suppose they come out of the woodwork come opening time. Anyway, there was a lot of people in there for a weekday lunchtime. Old boys with caps and roll-ups, old Dorises drinking Mackeson. And a lot of warehousemen and blokes in overalls and working clothes as well.'

So, given the time of day, they had had a pint each and sausage and chips and, thus licensed, got talking to the landlord, Reg Driffield, who knew Derek Crondace.

'He knew him all right!' said Mackay.

Crondace was in there most nights drinking and shooting his mouth off, Driffield said, rolling his eyes as he polished a glass. He was a big drinker all right – big man, great big belly on him, red face like a side o' meat. Used to be a market trader – didn't work now, lived on disability benefit, supposed to have a bad back. Never seemed to bother him, though. Mind you, carrying all that weight in front, you'd be bound to get a twinge or two, eh? Driffield had winked.

Yes, he drank a lot – don't know how he could afford it on benefits – but on the whole he wasn't any trouble. Argumentative, yes, and he could be foul mouthed, but Driffield just told him to put a sock in it if he got too noisy. Mostly he was just a bore, going on and on about that old court case.

What? Oh yes, he talked about that all right.

Didn't hardly talk about anything else! They'd had all the details of it till they were sick of it. Made you feel almost sorry for the feller – Roxwell was his name. Not that Driffield held with nonces – string 'em up, was his view, prison was too good for 'em – but it sounded like Crondace's precious daughter had been a bit of a madam and probably led the bloke on. And Crondace was all mouth about what he was going to do to this bloke if he ever found him again, but to Driffield's mind all mouth was about what it was. The more talk the less action, that was what Driffield had observed in a long lifetime of keeping bar and listening to the old humbugs who grew mushrooms on the same stool night after night.

Yes, Crondace had been in Saturday night. No, he seemed about the same – drinking his pints, boring everyone to death. He'd moaned a bit about his old woman – ex-wife, but like he said you'd never know it the way she still bossed him about. He went on about his grandkids never coming to see him. That was all par for the course. He'd had a bit of a shouting match with somebody about football – also par. There was an Arsenal vee Tottenham match coming up and somebody said they thought Spurs might have a chance. Crondace wouldn't have it, shot his mouth off, Driffield had to shut him up before he got it punched. They were all Arsenal supporters at the Navi, but Driffield wouldn't have any nonsense if someone wanted to put up a contrary view. Free country, wasn't it? It was football, not World War Two.

Say again? Oh yes, Bygod – that was the lawyer in the case. They knew all about him. Well, Crondace was always talking about him, threatening to go and sort him out. Said it was all his fault the nonce had got off. On Saturday – yes, Driffield thought he had been issuing the usual threats, but that wasn't anything out of the ordinary. Mind you, Driffield didn't stand around and listen, did he? In one ear and out the other, as far as Driffield was concerned, or you'd go barmy.

Well, Crondace was there till closing time, and he went off pretty tanked up, bit doddery on his feet and slurring his words a bit, but that was nothing unusual. About a quarter past eleven, time Driffield had got him out of the gents and shoved him out the door.

No, as a matter of fact, and now they came to mention it, he hadn't been in since. He didn't always come in on a Sunday, but most other nights he was there. Practically his second home. Lovely and quiet it had been without him, though the till was probably down, ha ha, because the old bastard could certainly neck a few. Was there something wrong? Not ill, was he? Oh, certainly, of course – if he came in again Driffield would let them know right away. Or if he heard anything. Hoped he wasn't in trouble of any sort.

They had left a card with Reg Driffield, finished their pints, had a chat with one or two of the customers, who'd had nothing really to add that they hadn't already heard, and came away.

'So it does look as though he might have done

a runner, guv,' Mackay concluded.

'Which might mean he did something he had to do a runner for,' Coffey added.

And they looked at Slider hopefully.

Porson drummed his fingers on the desk. He was a tall man and had to lean over to do it because he was standing up – he was hardly ever seen sitting – which made him look as though he was about to launch himself into a forward roll.

'So now you've got Kroll with a money motive, and Crondace with revenge.'

'We haven't exactly got Crondace,' Slider reminded him.

'And Kroll's still not talking?'

'Nothing, sir. I had another go at him, but he just sits and glowers, won't open his lips.'

Porson straightened and paced up and down in front of his window. 'I like the revenge motive better, and Crondace is the only person we know has actually issued threats against the victim.'

'And he *is* missing,' said Slider. He felt like a waiter pushing the dish of the day because they had to get rid of it.

'Yes, well,' said Porson thoughtfully. 'Missing is as missing does. One swallow does not make a meal, you know. There's any number of reasons he might have gone walkies.'

'Yes, sir. Except that he's a creature of habit and it hasn't happened before. I don't think his daughter knows where he is, but the wife – or ex-wife, rather – is a different matter. According to Atherton, she's sly, and a lot sharper than her daughter – probably sharper than Crondace, too.

She's the motivator of the family. If anything's going on, she's in on it, I'd bet on that.'

Porson sighed. It was not a sound an investigating officer liked to hear from his boss. 'Well, we'd better find him,' he said. 'What borough's that, Stratford Marsh? Newham, isn't it?'

'Tower Hamlets, sir. He's just on the boundary.'

'Better. I don't know anyone in Newham. Hamlets is Trevor Oxley. All right, I'll get on to him and see what I can work up. Have to be tactful – can't go in like a bowl in a china shop. Meanwhile, we ought to keep an eye on Mrs Crondace, in case he turns up there, or she leads us to him.'

'And the Krolls, sir?'

'Find anything in the house yet?'

'They're still looking. Nothing so far.'

'Well, we'll keep 'em until the search is done anyway. Although...' In thought, he cracked his knuckles mightily, with a sound like a road roller going over a bag of walnuts. 'I'm wondering if Kroll's not a bit too comfortable. Where he is, the Changs can't get at him. Wonder if you mightn't get more of a rise out of him if you threaten to turn him out on the street.'

'Worth a try, sir,' Slider said.

'It could work,' Atherton said. 'It's Mrs K who's anxious to get home – worrying about her old mum.'

'Why isn't Kroll worrying about her?'

Atherton shrugged. 'Hard to know, when a person won't speak, guv. Maybe he doesn't like her. Or he's in such a funk about himself he can't think about anyone else.'

Connolly came in. 'Boss, I've talked to all the friends of Bygod I can get hold of.' She exhibited a sheaf of paper. 'I can go over all this if you want, but there's nothing new here. It's all what a great guy he was and how much we'll miss him and we don't know a thing about him. Some friends!'

'On the specific points I asked you to check?' Slider enquired.

'They all thought he was well off. Livin' on the pig's back, so he was. But they didn't know about anything in the house that anyone might-'ve wanted to rob. And several of them said the document safe wasn't kept locked. They remembered because they'd mentioned to himself at some time that he'd left the key in, and he'd said it was just papers in there, nothing valuable, and it was just to keep them safe against fire an' flood.'

'It still doesn't mean there *wasn't* anything valuable in there,' Atherton said, 'or in the house. Only that these friends of his didn't know about it. And if I had a safe of any kind, I'd certainly put the idea about that there was nothing in there worth nicking.'

'So what was the point of me asking?' Connolly demanded indignantly.

'It's a very different matter,' he went on, ignoring her, 'for a housekeeper who's in there every day, going into every room, left there alone when the master's out, overhearing his phone calls, maybe looking through his mail. She'd have a level of information not available to all these so-called friends.'

'All of which may be true,' said Slider, 'but it's not evidence.'

Gascoyne put his head in. 'Crondace's fingerprints are on record, sir,' he reported. 'He had his dabs taken when they pulled him in for threatening behaviour.'

'And?' Slider asked.

'No match with anything in Bygod's house.'

Slider got to his feet. 'Negative again! I've got more negatives than a wedding photographer.' He went to his door and looked into the CID room. 'I want evidence. Doesn't anyone have any evidence for me? Come on, I'm buying here. No offering too small.'

At the far end McLaren was at his desk with Fathom behind him, leaning over his shoulder. They both looked up, Fathom straightened, and McLaren removed the end of a Ginster's jumbo sausage roll from his mouth (was there something sinister in McLaren's phallic choice of junk food these days, Slider wondered) and said, 'We got something, guv.'

'At last,' said Slider. 'Come and tell me. No, leave the hostage.'

'Sausage,' McLaren corrected automatically, but he put the greasy love-toy down on his desk, though with a lingering regret. 'We been looking for Kroll's motor,' he reported, as the others gathered round, 'and we got it all right. I been on the ANPR and Jerry's been on the TFL, and we've got his movements on Tuesday about sussed out.'

'Well, give, then,' Atherton urged irritably. 'Never mind the dramatic pauses. We're all hanging on your lips. Well, flakes of pastry are hanging on your lips, actually, but we're right up there among them.'

'Sweet Baby Jesus and the orphans, would y'ever give him a chance?' said Connolly to Atherton; and to McLaren, 'Work away, Maurice. He's narky as arse when he hasn't had his nap.'

McLaren barely blinked, having long ago developed, perforce, a carapace against banter. 'Right,' he said. 'We've got him going west on the Uxbridge Road at the junction with Horn Lane at a quarter to eight, and the same camera coming east just after half past nine. That fits in with his son Mark's statement that they went for breakfast in West Ealing, after which Kroll dumps him and goes off. Then we lose him for a bit—'

'Gloriosky!' Atherton said, rolling his eyes.

McLaren was unmoved. 'But there's a lot o' betting shops along the Uxbridge Road, and Mrs K says he was still trying to get on the ponies on Tuesday, so we reckon he could well have been parked up somewhere while he went in one or more of 'em.'

'OK, where *do* you pick him up again?' Slider asked.

Fathom answered. 'I got him on a TFL control camera, guv, just after ten, waiting to turn right down Askew Road, then five minutes later on Goldhawk Road, turning right down Hammersmith Grove.'

'So he's headed in the right direction,' Connolly said, a little current of excitement in her voice.

Fathom nodded, pleased. 'Yeah. And we reckon he must've cut through the Trussley Road tunnel—'

'Fathom, you absolute moron,' Atherton interrupted, 'never mind the Baedeker tour, get him somewhere we care about!'

Fathom looked wounded. 'I'm coming to it. We got him at the junction of Lena Gardens and Shepherd's Bush Road. There's a TFL camera practically outside Bygod's house.'

'Yes,' said Slider. 'I saw it.'

'He pulls out into the middle of the road to turn down Sterndale, and then he's facing the camera and you can see him in the driving seat.' He looked round them triumphantly. 'He must've gone down Sterndale to park up, because we've got nothing on him for a bit.'

'If he did park in Sterndale Road he might have got a parking ticket,' Swilley offered. 'It's all residents' parking down there, and they're pretty hot on it.'

'Look into that,' Slider said. He saw McLaren had more to say and turned back to him. 'Go on.'

'This is the best bit, guv,' McLaren said. 'There's this gift shop place – Ludlow Hearts and Crafts, it's called.'

'Yes, I remember,' Slider said.

'It's between Sterndale Road and Bygod's flat, and it's got this kind of poncey wooden dressing-table thing in the window with a mirror on it. And Kroll stops in front of it and he looks in the mirror and kind of brushes his hair back, and walks on. The shop's got a security camera pointed at the door, and it's caught it all.'

'I thought you were checking security cameras,' Swilley said. 'How come you didn't get that before?'

'Because I told him to start at two p.m.,' Slider said. 'We had no idea, if you remember, when the murder took place.'

'That's right, guv,' said McLaren, 'and it wasn't until Jerry got the van in the area at twenty past ten that I went back and looked.'

'Was that the time?'

'Ten twenty-two on the CCTV film,' said McLaren. 'And where's he going, if he's not going to Bygod's, where his wife's going to let him in to kill the old boy and rob whatever there is to rob?'

'Yes,' said Slider. 'You've done marvels. Well done, both of you.'

'We got him bang to rights, didn't we, guv?' Fathom said excitedly.

'Yes,' said Slider, wanting to be generous. He knew how tedious it was to go through hours of blurry CCTV footage, how hard to keep your attention honed through it all. And they had certainly caught both Krolls out in the lie that Mr Kroll had never been near the flat. But the time was wrong – wasn't it?

'Get back to work and find when the van moves again, and where it goes. I must go and ring Doc Cameron,' he said.

'Half past ten?' Freddie said thoughtfully. 'That

would make it twenty-four hours from when I saw him. I said twelve to eighteen, didn't I?'

'You did,' Slider confirmed.

'Hmm. Well, you know it's not an exact science. So many factors to take into account. I'd have thought twenty-four was a bit on the generous side, but anything's possible.'

'Possible,' Slider said. 'Can I quote you on that?'

'You sound like a man with a hot tip.'

'Our top suspect's been nailed almost to the door at that time.'

'Oh, I see. Well, it's perfectly possible—'

'*Perfectly* possible, now. Any advance on that?'

'You have to woo me, not force me,' Cameron warned daintily. 'Okay, allowing there may have been some chitty-chatty up there first and the fatal blow may not have been struck until, say eleven thirty or even twelve, and there's not that much difference between twelve and two, and two is more or less two thirty...'

'And it's not an exact science anyway,' Slider concluded for him. 'Thanks, Freddy. I'll take your perfectly possible and see what I can do with it.'

'Can't threaten to let him go now,' Porson said, with a hint of regret.

Slider knew how he felt. Someone who wouldn't talk got right up the constabulary nose.

'Still,' Porson went on, brightening, 'we've got good reason to keep him. All that plus the fingermark inside the house – though it'd be nice if someone actually saw him going in. All those people walking up and down the road all day long, and Kroll's a big bloke, not exactly your shrinking violet in the crannied whatnot – some-one ought to've seen him. Going in or coming out. Coming out'd be nice, looking all sweaty and guilty – he'd have caught the eye, all right. And the woman, too – she'd have come out with him. Two for the price of one.'

'I'm on it, sir,' Slider said. 'But you know that sort of canvass takes time.'

It was a matter of putting the question out to the general public via leaflets, boards and the media, and hoping the right witness both spotted it *and* was willing to come forward. Often those who did know something hesitated to 'get involved'. Or were at work and felt it could wait until the weekend. It took days at best, some-times weeks, before the evidence came in.

Porson nodded. 'But you've got plenty to be going on with. Enough maybe to get a confes-sion, then the rest is case-building. There's no smoke without straw. Those Krolls have got some explaining to do. Go get 'em, laddie. Put the pressure on.'

Jillie Lawrence, one of the uniformed officers on loan, had been given the task of checking Mrs Crondace's alibi. The chiropodist was easy enough, although she faffed a bit at first about disclosing her schedule, because of what she called 'patient confidentiality'.

'I don't want to know what you did,' Lawrence said. 'I only want to know if you were there.'

'It's the Human Rights Act,' the chiropodist blethered. 'I'm not allowed to tell anyone anything about the patients. I could get in trouble,' she added, with frightened fawn's eyes. She was a thin, pretty Indian girl and looked about twelve, Lawrence thought. Is it me, or is everyone getting younger? And the young have no sense of priorities. They live in a little bubble where the worst thing they fear is an elf-an-safety knuckle rap from their supervisor. The wider world only impinged on them through television, which was itself an unreality. News was entertainment. None of it really happened. Only Mrs Gupta, who did your assessment and could write bad things about you, was real.

'You'll get in worse trouble with the law if you don't show it me,' Lawrence said brutally. 'Obstruction of the law could have you inside. Fancy going to prison?'

But Lawrence could see she didn't really believe in prison either. She showed the schedule in the end only because Lawrence's personality was stronger than hers. Lawrence rolled her mental eyes. Modern policing, when it came to young people, was a battle for credibility. At least most older people had proper respect for the law – or anyway, a healthy fear of consequences.

Still, there was no doubt that Mrs Crondace had had her regular treatment on the Tuesday morning, which was only what Lawrence expected because DI Slider had said nobody gave an alibi with that sort of smugness unless it was solid, and she had faith in DI Slider's judgement.

The bingo part of the alibi took longer. She had to ask about who the regular players were, which was practically everybody, then whittle it down to those who always came on a Tuesday, then sift out those who knew who Mrs Crondace was. And nobody really wanted to talk while the calling was going on, in case they missed a line or – God forfend – a jackpot.

At the end of the process she managed to persuade two women to come out of the hall during a brief break and allow her to buy them a cup of tea and a cake in the café.

Mrs Crondace? Yvonne, her name was – they pronounced it *Ee*-von. Oh yes, they said, they knew her. They said it without marked enthusiasm, and after a bit of coaxing Lawrence got them to admit they didn't like her much. She was not very nice.

'Hard,' said Mrs Green.

'Hard as nails,' Mrs Orton elaborated. 'Mind you, she's lucky – always wins something. I could do with a bit of her luck,' she went on wistfully. 'You start to wonder when someone always gets the lucky card.'

'I wouldn't put it past her to've fixed it somehow. Hard, she is,' Mrs Green said.

'And coarse. Ever so coarse. She talks too loud and swears too much. She's not our sort.'

'But was she here last Tuesday?' Lawrence pressed them.

'Oh yes. I came about half past two, and she was already here. And she was still here at six when I left.'

'I came half past five,' said Mrs Green, 'and I

saw her. She left about half past nine – Yvonne did. I remember because I stayed on for the super jackpot, they have that at ten, and I was glad she was going, 'cos she wins too often. I thought I'd have more chance if she was gone.'

'Did you get it, dear?' Mrs Orton asked eagerly.

'Course I didn't. I'd've told you,' said Mrs Green. 'Two numbers short. It was that woman from the estate got it – her with the glasses and the hat. What's her name? Big woman.'

'Maureen, is it? With the hat?'

'No, Marjorie, that's it. You're thinking of Maureen Fisher. She's—'

Lawrence interrupted before they got going. 'Did you have a chance to talk to her at all? Yvonne?'

'You don't come here to talk,' Mrs Green said, casting a longing eye at the door. Numbers could be being called out in there, numbers that would make her fortune and lift her from her old, known life of tedium into a new one of exciting possibilities, foreign holidays and redecorating the lounge.

'I did, in the break, when they were changing the drum,' said Mrs Orton. 'Well, it wasn't so much a matter of talking to her. She does all the talking.'

'And what did she talk about?' Lawrence asked hopefully.

'Oh, I don't know. Some stuff or other.'

'Try and remember. It's important.'

Mrs Orton frowned. 'She was going on about something. What was it? Some court case I think. Her husband was taking someone to court? I know she went on and on about it. I wasn't listening, tell you the truth. She uses too many swear words. I'm not a prude, but I don't like that sort of language. Wait, I know – she said someone had got off, that was it. Her husband had taken someone to court about something, but they'd got off, and she wasn't going to let it go at that.' Mrs Orton looked pleased. 'That's what it was. I remember now.'

Mrs Green was scornful. 'She was always talking about that. That old court case. Bores the ears off you with it.'

'Does she, dear? I've not spoken that much with her. But Tuesday, she was quite vehement about it, that I do know,' said Mrs Orton. 'I remember she said she was going to get him. Looked really grim when she said it, and I thought I wouldn't like to be that person, because she's not a nice woman at all, not really. She said, "My God, I'm going to get him if it's the last thing I do."'

Lawrence leaned forward. 'Did she say "my God" or "Bygod"?'

'I don't know. Does it make any difference? It's the same thing, isn't it?' said Mrs Orton.

'Not entirely,' said Lawrence. 'Bygod is a name, you see. The name of the person she was after.'

Mrs Orton's eyes and mouth became perfectly round. 'Ooh!' she said.

Mrs Green clutched her arm. 'There you are, Peggy, you've gone and got yourself into trouble now. And the eyes-down just started again.

We're going to miss it.'

'I won't keep you much longer,' Lawrence said. 'If you can just think back, and tell me which she said.'

Mrs Orton shook her head. 'Well, I thought she said "my God", because that's what I'd expect to hear. But now I come to think of it, maybe she did say "by God". Yes, I think p'raps she did. Yes, because I thought at the time it was rather an old-fashioned way to speak.' She raised a pink, pleased face to Lawrence. 'Yes, I'm sure of it now. She said "by God".'

'You're quite sure?' Lawrence said.

'As sure as I'm sitting here,' said Mrs Orton, beaming.

ELEVEN

Algorithm and Blues

Mrs Kroll was sticking grimly to her story. 'I told you, I was there my usual time. And my husband was never there. He's never been near the place.'

'But we have the evidence of his van being parked right in the next road,' Slider said patiently. 'We have it on camera.'

A gleam entered her eyes as she thought of something. 'Didn't see him, though, did you? You don't know who was driving it. Maybe it was taken.'

'Then why didn't you report it stolen?'

'Maybe they brought it back. Someone borrowed it without telling him. *I* don't know. That's your job. All I know is he's never been to the house, and that's that.'

'Mrs Kroll, we have his fingermark from inside the house.'

'I don't care,' she said flatly. 'You're lying to try and trick me. Or you put it there yourself. Or you're mistaken. He wasn't there and that's it, and that's all I'm going to say.' And she folded her arms and her lips tightly to emphasize the point.

Illogic, Slider thought, was a powerful defence. If someone simply would not agree that if (a) was so, then (b) must logically follow, it left you out on a limb with your predicates dangling.

Mr Kroll took an entirely different approach. He listened in his customary silence as they laid the damning evidence in front of him, and some thinking seemed to be going on behind those buckled brows. Then he unlatched his lips for the first time since they brought him in, and said, 'I don't care. Charge me if you like. There's nothing you can do to me.'

'How does life imprisonment sound to you?' Atherton asked genially.

'I'm safer in here than out there,' Kroll said. 'You can do what you like.'

Slider quelled Atherton with a minute glance, and stared at Kroll in silence for a long time, long enough for him to begin to fidget a little. Then he said quietly, 'If you go down, your wife goes down too, have you thought of that?'

Kroll looked alarmed for the first time. 'You leave her out of it. She knows nothing.'

'No jury is going to believe that. To begin with, she had the key.'

Since Bygod was at home and probably let the murderer in, this meant little, but Slider was hoping to provoke Kroll into making some comment on the observation that would incriminate him. But Kroll only clenched his considerable jaw and said, 'You leave her alone! She's got nothing to do with it. Keep away from her or I'll—'

'You'll what? You'll kill me?' Slider enquired politely. Kroll's meaty fists were clenched on the table. Slowly they unwound. Slider said, 'You have the right to have a solicitor to represent you, as you've been advised more than once. I think you should have one now.'

'I don't want anyone,' Kroll said, staring at the table, and his tone sounded bitter. 'I won't have one.'

'Get him someone,' Porson said. 'I can smell a complaint coming down the track, and I don't want some human rights lawyer stinking up the case. Get him someone good.'

'David Stevens,' Slider suggested. Stevens was a sleek otter of a man with shiny brown eyes, and suits that made even Atherton whimper. He was so successful, you'd think the firm of Lucifer and Faust had a contract on file with his name signed in suspicious red ink.

Porson nodded in appreciation of the point.

'Steven's'd cover our bottoms all right.' While Slider was contemplating this alluring image, Porson changed tack. 'Mr Wetherspoon likes Crondace,' he said, with a latent sigh. Wetherspoon was their Borough Commander, and a royal pain in the arse which he also regularly liked to hang out to dry. He was the ultimate publicity bunny, never happier than when facing the TV cameras and the frenzied clicking of shutters. He had been chummy with the Home Secretaries of the previous administration, and the change of government had not left him with any sunnier a disposition towards the team at Shepherd's Bush. A golfing, lunching, drinkies-at-Number-Ten media star did not want people on his payroll who looked funny (Porson) or got themselves into trouble by doing the right thing (Slider).

Slider digested the information, and said, 'There's no harm in keeping a second string to our bow, sir.'

'Right,' said Porson gratefully. 'And who knows, Mr Wetherspoon may be right.'

To cheer him up, Slider told him about Mrs Crondace at the bingo hall.

Porson was doubtful. 'Sounds as if Lawrence pushed her into it,' he said. 'Can't rely on that.'

'No, sir. And of course Crondace has no alibi at all, as far as we know. There are certainly tempting things about him – not least that he's missing.'

'Keep after him,' Porson said. 'And keep an eye on her. And I don't see any harm in tossing his flat, if Tower Hamlets'll play ball. I'll ask

Trevor Oxley. If Crondace is that much of a slob, you never know what you might find. Meanwhile –' he turned at the end of his walk and faced Slider – 'get more evidence on the Krolls. Her movements as well as his. And a witness who saw him go in. At least.'

When Slider got back to his room, most of the troops had gone. In the CID room McLaren was doing something on the computer, Atherton was tidying his desk, and Hollis was pottering about, mug of tea in his hand, with the air of a man already in his slippers.

'Where's Mackay? I thought he had night duty,' Slider said.

Hollis said, 'I swapped with him, guv. Some school thing for his kid.'

Unusually noble of him, Slider thought. Nobody liked catching the night shift. Then he remembered Hollis had been having trouble at home – maybe he liked the excuse to stay away. Slider cleared his desk and locked everything, then went back out and said to Atherton, 'I'm whacked. Fancy a drink?'

Atherton looked up. Was there the slightest hesitation before he said, 'Yes, okay'?

'I've been thinking about a pint all afternoon,' Slider said, 'ever since Mackay and Coffey came in wittering about the Navigation.' Connolly came into the room at that moment, on her way back from the loo. 'Are you off?' Slider said. 'Want to come for a pint with us?'

Her eyebrows shot up. 'Janey, that's weird. The minute I came in the room I knew you were going to say that. Do you believe in premonition?'

'No, but I've a queer feeling I'm going to. Are you coming then?'

'Thanks, boss, but I've got a date.'

'Anyone we know?' Atherton asked.

'Kidding me? I wouldn't go out with anyone in the Job. They're all mentallers. I got this one off the Internet.'

'Isn't that a little rash?' Atherton said.

'And isn't that what you may find yourself saying tomorrow morning?' Slider added.

Connolly grinned. 'I'll be careful.'

'See that you are,' said Slider.

'Anyway, I don't put out on the first date. One night of meaningless sex can get in the way of a long-term relationship,' said Connolly.

'I've always relied on it,' said Atherton.

'I got a date as well,' McLaren announced, with a hint of pride.

'Way to go, Maurice,' Atherton said. 'Get back on that horse.'

'Tim, that lives upstairs from me, his girlfriend Maura's got a mate,' McLaren explained, getting up and coming over. 'We're doing a double date. Going down the Green Man.'

'Maurice, Maurice, a blind date?' Atherton said. 'Are you mad?'

'Why not?' McLaren protested. 'Maura says she's a very nice person.'

Atherton groaned, and Hollis, ambling across, said, 'He's right, y'know. It's classic code. "She's got a nice personality" means she's either a size twenty or she's got a face like a beaten tambourine.'

'This Maura's nice looking, is she?' Atherton asked.

'Yeah, she's great,' McLaren said.

'Right. Nice-looking girls always have an ugly friend they're trying to get fixed up. We're talking dog here, Maurice. We're talking Crufts' Best in Show.'

McLaren's jaw set. 'I don't care. I'm going. She's called Natalie. I've always liked that name.'

'And you tell me off for picking horses by the name!' Atherton shook his head.

Hollis switched sides. 'Hang about, though. Maybe he's on to something. You should go, Maurice. You know what they say – ugly girls are more grateful. You could well score.'

Connolly, who had been sorting out her handbag at her desk, made a sound of disgust so loud it would unknot your tie. 'Name a' God, I don't believe you people! Would you listen to yourselves? You sound like somethin' out o' *Mad Men*.'

'Oh, and women aren't interested in sex,' Atherton scoffed.

Connolly gritted her jaw. 'Men just use sex to get what they want.'

'Don't be ridiculous,' Atherton said. 'Sex *is* what they want.'

Slider's phone rang, interrupting the exchange – and not before time, he thought. He caught Atherton's eye and hesitated.

'Ignore it,' Atherton advised. 'Those pints aren't getting drunk, and neither am I.'

'D'you want me to get it, guv?' Hollis offered.

'No, it's all right,' Slider said. 'I'll go. Put your coat on,' he added to Atherton. 'We're out the door in two minutes.'

It was Freddie Cameron on the other end. 'I've finished the post-mortem and microscope analysis,' he said, 'and there's nothing new to add to my verbal conclusions about the death. But one thing has emerged that I thought I'd better tell you about. I don't know if it alters anything, but just in case...'

'I'm on my way out for a drink and then home,' Slider said. 'Couldn't it have waited until tomorrow?'

A slight pause as Freddie looked at the clock. 'Good Lord, is that the time? I had no idea. I must get weaving. Martha and I have a black-tie dinner tonight. Charity thing. Damned waste of an evening – I'd sooner give them a cheque and be done with it, but the memsahib likes putting on a long dress. Only blessing is I don't have to make a speech this time. What was I saying?'

'Something emerged from the post-mortem. I hope not a slavering alien from the abdomen.'

'You have a morbid imagination. But, actually, you're not far wrong. It seems that Bygod had a carcinoma of the lung, with metastases just about everywhere. I'd say he only had a few months to live.'

'Poor bloke,' Slider said, with feeling. Life was always precious, but when you had so little of it left ... 'I thought he looked thin. Would he have known?'

'He probably wasn't feeling in the pink,'

Cameron said drily. 'As to whether he'd had a diagnosis, you'd have to check with his doctor. But given he was an intelligent, educated man, I'd bet he knew the game was up.'

'I see. Well, thanks for telling me.'

'I thought it might change the tenor of some of your questions. Or your thought processes.'

'Yes, you may be right.'

'I'll send the full report over tomorrow but there's nothing else you didn't know. And now I must make a noise like a bee and buzz off.'

Atherton was waiting in the doorway, ready to go. 'What was that about a slavering alien?'

'Bygod had cancer.'

'Oh,' said Atherton. He thought a moment. 'Does that change anything?'

'I don't know,' said Slider.

'Fair enough. Let's get a pint.'

They couldn't use the White Horse across the road because it had Karaoke on Saturday nights, and they had time to reflect as they walked down to the Boscombe on what a strange form of masochism that was. They settled into a corner with pints in front of them, and Slider took a minute to phone Joanna and tell her where he was and what time he'd be home. 'She says d'you want to come to supper?' he relayed.

'Thanks, but I've got something arranged,' Atherton replied.

When he had rung off, Slider took a pull at his pint and, gazing studiously into the middle distance, said, 'Is everything all right with you and Emily?'

'Emily is in America,' Atherton said in a deliberately patient tone.

'I know, but – I just wondered.'

Atherton gave him a sidelong look. 'Is that you delving uncharacteristically into my private life?'

Slider did what any sensible man does when he senses danger: shut up and kept still. After a short pause he was rewarded for his reticence. Atherton said casually, 'She wants me to move in with her.'

'Oh,' said Slider cautiously. 'That's good, isn't it?'

'No, it's not good,' Atherton said with a touch of irritation. 'It's too soon, it's too sudden, it's too absolute.'

'She's practically living at your place already, isn't she?'

'Yes, *she's* at *my* place. A perfectly equable arrangement. Now suddenly she wants me to sell my house and move into her father's flat. That's a whole new game of marbles.'

Slider felt about for a thread to tug. 'But you love her, don't you?' he tried.

'This has nothing to do with love,' Atherton said, in an explaining-the-obvious tone. 'This is economics. *My* house, *my* property, *my* assets, suddenly subsumed into hers.'

You could only admire a man who could use words like 'subsumed' in the course of an emotional diatribe, Slider thought. 'I'm sure you could work out the financial side of it – a fair agreement about who owns what.'

'My freedom,' Atherton said, as if finishing his

previous sentence.

'Ah,' said Slider.

Atherton scowled. 'What does that mean – "Ah"? Are you about to spout some psychological pseudo-wisdom and set me straight?'

'I wouldn't dream of it,' Slider said, and took another long pull. 'Nice pint.'

'Don't "nice pint" me. You started this. You see, this is exactly why we don't discuss personal matters with the people we work with.'

Slider looked at him. 'I get it,' he assured him. 'You're afraid of losing your freedom, it's a big commitment, she's moving too fast and pressurizing you – I get it. Women always want to jump ahead to the end of the story. I suppose they've got hormones and Time's wingéd chariot pressurizing *them*. The nesting instinct versus the tom-cat propensity. Classic mismatch. Nothing to be done about it. Nature has a lot to answer for.'

Now Atherton grinned. 'Nifty footwork, ol' guv of mine! From Jung to Freud to David Attenborough in one lunge, with a splodge of Marvell thrown in for decorative effect.'

'Why so surprised? You always seem to think I'm an ignoramus.'

'I don't. I think you're as clever as a fox with a PhD in foxiness. So what's your advice, then?'

Slider gave him a look of broad innocence. 'None of my business,' he said. 'I wouldn't dream of interfering.'

Atherton looked into the amber depths of his Fuller's Pride. 'I do love her,' he said soberly. 'It's just such a big step. I've been on my own for so long. I need more time.'

Slider let him alone to find the solution himself.

'I suppose I have to talk to her,' Atherton sighed. 'Tell her exactly that.' He grimaced. 'Why do women always want to talk about stuff?'

'They do stuff at GCSE, when we're doing woodwork,' Slider explained kindly.

'I suppose you're working tomorrow?' Joanna said when they sat down to supper – spaghetti with her home-made Bolognese sauce, which was so rich and good even Atherton had asked for the recipe. The secret was chicken livers. Joanna didn't do gourmet, but she was big on tastes. 'When I have a Sunday off for once, it's too much to expect you'll be off too.'

'I'll have to go in,' Slider said. 'I hope not for too long, though. Oh, and Atherton's invited us over for supper tomorrow night, if Dad doesn't mind babysitting. I said I'd check and let him know.'

'Oh, you spoke to him, then?'

'No, we communicated by sign language.'

'Don't be cute. You know what I mean. Did you talk to him about Emily?'

'A bit. Men don't do that heart-to-heart stuff you women go in for.'

'You're treading close to the line with "you women",' she warned him. 'What did he say? Is something up?'

'He feels it's moving too fast, that's all.'

'Well, Emily's not getting any younger.'

'That's what I told him. But no man likes to be

regarded as a stud.' Joanna gave him a snort of ripe disbelief. 'In the breeding sense, I mean. We're not just mobile inseminators, you know – we have feelings,' he said poignantly. 'And when a woman has a child, it largely replaces the man in her affections, so he's breeding his own usurper. That simply goes against logic.'

'I had no idea you were carrying so much resentment,' Joanna said sweetly.

'I don't mean me. I love being married to you, and all it entails. I'm talking about ordinary men.'

'Well, of course, you make perfect sense. But what's the alternative? Jim's old life of lonely promiscuity? That's no way for a rational human being to function.'

'He'll just have to work that out for himself,' Slider said. 'Logically.'

'Oh, you and your logic. As if human relationships were electrical circuits: close this switch and the current goes that way.'

'I think they pretty much are,' Slider said, only partly to tease her. 'Just rather complicated ones.'

'On which subject, how's your case going?'

'We've got two very good suspects – or four, if you count their wives.'

'Well, that's nice. What's wrong with them?'

'Nothing yet. We have to map their movements, which is the boring footwork. Of course, they can't both be guilty.' He paused, brooding.

'What is it?' she asked after a minute.

He came back. 'I was just wondering, what sort of murderer checks his hair in the mirror just before going to do the deed?'

'A vain one,' Joanna said. 'Aren't all murderers vain? It's the ultimate in self-obsession to think you have the right to take someone else's life.'

'You have a point,' said Slider.

When Slider got in the following morning and went to the men's' room, he found Hollis in there, braces over a vest, shaving. His arms were very white, as if he never stripped off. Perhaps if you grew up in Manchester you never developed the habit.

'Hullo!' Slider said. 'You in already? Or didn't you go home?'

Night shift ended at two for the CID – the desks were unmanned then until six.

Hollis hesitated, but meeting Slider's eyes in the mirror said, 'Didn't seem worth it, guv. I put in some time on the computer, tracking the Krolls.'

'Oh. Good work. Come and report to me when you're ready.'

When he came, it was with Fathom and McLaren, the latter bearing a cup and a plate.

'Got you a tea from the canteen, guv,' McLaren said.

'Very kind of you. What's on the plate?'

'Bread pudding. Special this morning.'

'Thanks,' Slider said. The canteen's bread pudding was very good. There was the slightest hesitation as McLaren handed it over which made Slider wonder if he had actually meant it for himself; but it was too late now. 'Atherton in yet?'

'Haven't seen him,' McLaren said cautiously. He looked at Hollis and then away, as if they shared a secret. 'Maybe he's in the bog.'

But he came strolling delicately in at that moment, clutching a take-out Costa coffee. His eyes were pink and he looked to Slider as if he hadn't slept, but Slider tried not to think about that.

'What's going down, dudes?' he enquired ironically.

'Kroll movements,' Slider said. 'You're just in time.'

'Right, guv,' Hollis said. 'Kroll's gone past the gift shop again half eleven Tuesday morning, going the other way, and we've got his van on the move again five minutes later – caught him on the ANPR cameras at Hammersmith Broadway and King Street. Oh, and by the way,' Hollis added, looking pleased, 'he did get a ticket for parking in Sterndale Road, so we've got extra confirmation he was there.'

'That's good,' said Slider. 'So where did he go after King Street?'

'Well, guv,' McLaren said, taking over, 'we got him at the end of Chiswick High Road, the big roundabout there, and then we lost him for a bit, couldn't make out what he was doing.'

'But I found him going north past Boston Manor Station, on their security camera,' Hollis said.

'At the end he turns east on West Ealing Broadway,' McLaren resumed. 'So it looks as if he's going a long way home. Very long way.

Doesn't make any sense.'

'Unless,' Hollis suggested, 'he's done the murder and he's driving round trying to settle his nerves. And if that's what it was, it makes sense of him getting another ticket for parking in Culmington Road, right by the back gate to Walpole Park. Maybe he went and sat in the park brooding about it and wondering what to do.'

'That's a lot of maybes,' Slider said, frowning. 'What time was he ticketed there?'

'That's the odd thing, guv. The warden notes the van's there at half past twelve, and it never moves all afternoon. It was still there at quarter to four. The son, Mark, says the old man picked him up on Uxbridge Road around four, and we've caught the van heading east on Uxbridge Road at a quarter past, so that looks all right. And the old lady, his mother-in-law, said they got home about half past, so unless she's in on it...'

'Which I wouldn't put past her,' McLaren growled.

'So between twelve thirty and four he's away from the van and we don't know where,' Atherton said.

'It doesn't sound good,' Slider said. 'A big hole in the story. Although Mrs Kroll said he was still gambling all day Tuesday, trying to make the Changs' money.'

'We can't take her word for anything,' Atherton said.

'No,' Slider said. 'We'll have to check. There are quite a few betting shops within walking distance of Culmington Road. And pubs.'

'Right, guv,' McLaren said. 'I'm on it.'

'And what about Mrs Kroll?' Slider asked.

'I went through the TFL bus tapes and checked the bus routes she normally takes home,' Fathom said. 'We've got her getting on a 220 at the stop opposite Bygod's flat. She gets off the end of Uxbridge Road, then she catches the 207 all the way home.'

'The times,' Slider urged. He had a bad feeling about this.

'She gets on the 220 at twenty past two and she gets on the 207 at two thirty-seven.'

'And her mother said she was home about three,' Slider said. 'So that looks solid. No holes anywhere.'

'But, guv,' Fathom said, frowning. 'If Kroll, or her and Kroll, did the murder before half past eleven, why did she hang about in the flat till two o'clock?'

'Searching for valuables, maybe,' Hollis offer-ed.

'For two and a half hours?' Atherton said.

'It's possible,' Hollis asserted, but doubtfully. 'She'd been working there ten years. She ought to know where everything was kept by now.'

'Or,' said McLaren, 'she done it by herself in the afternoon.'

'Then what did Kroll go there for?' Fathom objected.

'He goes to ask for dosh to pay off the Changs,' McLaren said. 'Bygod refuses. Kroll goes away. Mrs K gets to thinking about what a mean old bastard he is and finally cracks, whacks him, then pops off home, innocent as you please.'

'Yes,' said Slider thoughtfully. 'Innocent as you please. She'd have to be a cold-hearted killer to pull that off without showing any emotion. And she'd have had blood on her clothes.'

'Covered by an overcoat,' Atherton pointed out.

'There's another possibility, I'm sorry to say,' Slider said. 'Kroll comes back in the afternoon in a different vehicle, or even by public transport, and he does the murder. He's missing for long enough.'

They looked crestfallen, and he sympathized. It was exacting work going through hours of tapes, and having assembled the evidence it was disappointing to have the hole pointed out to them.

Hollis recovered first. 'Right,' he said. 'Betting shops and pubs within walking of Walpole Park. Public transport between there and Bygod's place in the afternoon. And anyone who was on the bus with Mrs K, to see if they can tell what sort of a state she was in.'

'Meanwhile,' Atherton said, 'maybe we can lean on them a bit more, get them to crack, and save ourselves a lot of work.'

Slider's phone rang. He answered it and listened, said, 'Right,' several times, then rang off and stood up. 'Well, aren't we having fun?' he said. 'That was Mr Porson. Trevor Oxley from Tower Hamlets rang. They very kindly tossed Crondace's flat for us, and guess what?'

'Don't tell me,' Atherton said, rolling his eyes.
'Oh, but I will,' Slider said. 'They've found bloodstained clothing.'

TWELVE

Rich Man's World

Mrs Kroll was more impressed than alarmed at the revelation that they had followed her movements all the way home. 'I didn't know you could do that,' she said. 'You see it in those American films about people being chased by the FBI, but I didn't know it happened here.'

'More often than you'd think,' Slider told her. It was a lot harder work than the movies made it look, but he didn't tell her that.

'Well,' she said triumphantly, 'it just proves to you what I said all along. I worked my usual hours and went home. That's what I told you, and now you know it's true. So now you've got to let me go.'

'Not so fast,' Slider said. 'There's the little matter of your husband's visit to the flat, which just happens to take place on the day Mr Bygod was brutally murdered.'

She sat up a bit straighter. 'Now wait a minute—' she began angrily.

'No, you wait a minute,' Slider said, stopping her. 'You've been lying to me about that and I don't care to be lied to, especially by someone who makes a parade of her apparent truthfulness. I *know* he visited the flat, you know it, and what's more he doesn't deny it. So let's stop playing silly games. Because at the moment you both look like being charged with that poor man's murder – and you might like to ask what'll happen to your family on the outside when you two are inside doing life.'

She was on her feet. 'Don't you dare threaten me! I had nothing to do with it!'

'Sit down!'

She sat, reluctantly, but her nostrils were white with suppressed anger. 'I'm a good Catholic,' she said. 'I would never kill another human being – except maybe the Changs if I had the chance. That wouldn't be murder, that'd be pest control.'

'Then what was your husband doing at the flat?'

There was a long silence. Slider felt the calculations filtering through her mind, drip by drip. He said quietly, 'You might want to think about your mother. It's not good at her age to be facing all this worry.'

'She's tough. She can take it.'

'And how long Stefan and his charming companion will make her comfortable and welcome in their house.'

He could see that hit home, but she said, 'Stefan will do his family duty.'

'And Mirela. Is she devoted to your family too?'

She looked up at last, and gave him a long,

bitter stare. 'That girl would sell her own mother for the money to buy drugs, let alone mine. The hours I've spent ... Might as well talk to the brick wall. Look—' Oh, that blessed word, Slider thought. 'All right, Jack did come to the house. We arranged it between us. We didn't know where else to turn. Jack said, "Your boss is loaded, why don't we ask him?" So I agreed. He came up that morning, we put it to Mr Bygod together, asked him for the money to get the Changs off our backs. Jack promised to pay it back as soon as he could get back on his feet. But he wouldn't do it.'

'Mr Bygod refused?'

'He said he couldn't give us money to pay off a gang running an illegal racket. He said we had to go to the police. Jack said how could he tell the police he'd been betting illegally? Mr Bygod said he would defend him free of charge, and if Jack helped put the Changs away he'd get off with a suspended sentence. But he said we had to act quickly. Jack said he'd think about it, and he went away.' Another bitter look. 'For all his book-learning and university degrees, that was the best Mr Bygod could say! If Jack split on the Changs to the police, he'd be dead long before it ever got to court.'

'So Jack went away disappointed and afraid for his life. Mr Bygod had refused to give you any of the masses of money he didn't need and you did. You were both angry and desperate. And later that day Mr Bygod ends up dead.'

'I didn't kill him!' she shouted.

'But Jack did?'

He saw something flicker in her eyes. She *had* left the house at two – but had Jack Kroll come back? Had they communicated somehow? Had they both gone back and done the deed together? She worked at the King's Arms from five to eleven, which made it tight timing, but still possible, and her mother was her only alibi for those two hours. Given that family came first with the Krolls, you couldn't be sure Mama wouldn't lie about it.

'You'd much better tell me now,' he said. 'You know we *will* find out in the end, and then it'll be the worse for you.'

'I've got nothing more to say to you,' she said, and folded her lips down.

Out in the corridor he met David Stevens coming away from Kroll's cell.

'Hello, Bill!' Stevens cried with enormous good humour. His little dark eyes gleamed like those of a merry predator. His suit would have brought Giorgio Armani himself to his knees, his aftershave was so subtle you might believe you'd imagined it, his dark hair was styled to swooning point – though Slider noted with guilty pleasure that it was getting a little thin on top. Man proposes and God disposes.

'So, what do you think of Jack Kroll?' he asked. 'Has he flung himself on your manly bosom and confessed everything?'

Stevens brushed a lapel. 'I think you can see I am unruffled. And I *love* you for bringing me in on this one.'

'Uh-oh,' Slider said.

Stevens beamed. 'Anything he says will have been given under the most severe duress, so even if he confesses the whole thing, I'll have no trouble denying everything on his behalf.'

'We haven't laid a finger on him,' Slider protested.

'Of course not, old chum. You don't have to. With the Chang brothers after his blood and family members on the outside, he's under duress both ways. Whether you keep him in custody or threaten to let him out, you're putting pressure on him, and I can't lose. I think I can even smell the sweet fragrance of a compensation case ambling towards us through the forest of Judges' Rules.'

Slider smiled and shook his head. 'You can't scare me. You're talking to DI Everything-By-The-Book Slider here.'

Stevens roared with laughter. *'You*?' he cried, wiping tears of merriment from his eyes. 'Seriously, do I sense that the case against our friend is a little on the emaciated side, given that you haven't charged him?'

Slider was suddenly suspicious. 'He didn't tell you anything, did he?' he discovered with glee. 'He *said* he didn't want a brief. All you know, you've got from the custody boys. He just sat there in silence.'

'Not a blessed dicky,' Stevens admitted with the frankness that was – occasionally – his saving grace. 'But he will.'

'You old fraud!'

'Careful. That's fighting talk where I come from.'

'Well, we just called you in to cover our bottoms, anyway. It's Mrs K who's the weak link. She really wants to get out, and once we've got the last little bit of evidence on her husband's movements, she'll tell us the whole story.'

'Story it is, as well.' Stevens was suddenly serious. 'I knew Bygod slightly, many years ago. He was a damn fine solicitor. It hurts when one of your own gets taken out. Man to man, I hope you nail him.'

'You don't have to defend him,' Slider mentioned.

Stevens grinned. 'Hey, it's me!'

There was a message on his desk to ring back Pauline Smithers, which he did right away.

'I've asked about your Lionel Bygod, and nothing doing.'

'You mean there's nothing on him?'

'Nada. There was no evidence whatever at the time that he'd been involved in anything – my sources say it was believed the whole thing was a malicious lie, which is certainly what it looked like. And since then, nothing, not in Islington or Hammersmith.'

'So he's clean?' Slider said thoughtfully.

'As a whistle.'

It was a classic case of give a dog a bad name and hang him. He thought of Bygod's own wife – or ex-wife, he should say – saying she suspected him.

There's no smoke without fire. He must have done something. It can't all be coincidence. All those people wouldn't have said what they said if there wasn't some truth to it, would they? Bah, humbug!

'Thanks, Pauly.'

'Just a word of caution, though, Bill. Not everyone comes to official attention, though we think we cast a pretty fine net. Underground means what it says. *On paper* he's as clean as a whistle, but you can't say for hundred per cent certain that he never got up to anything. You can't prove a negative.'

'I wish you hadn't added that bit,' Slider said.

'Just keeping an open mind. Every felon's innocent till he gets caught.'

'So are innocent people.'

'You're getting emotionally involved with this one, aren't you? What am I saying – you always get emotionally involved!'

'They only have us to fight for them, the dead,' Slider said.

She didn't follow that up. 'When are we going out for this drink?'

'Soon,' he said. 'Once I've got this case figured out.'

'And before you get snowed under by the paperwork,' she postulated.

'Deal.'

'Next week sometime, then,' she said with a grin in her voice, 'knowing the way you work.'

'I wish,' said Slider.

Norma came into his office with a mug of tea and a chocolate biscuit wrapped in silver paper. 'Satisfied customer brought us in a box,' she said. 'Mixed chocolate fancy collection. I thought I'd grab one for you before the ravening hordes got the lot.'

'McLaren's found them, then, has he?' Slider queried.

'You know, boss,' Swilley said gravely, 'I'm thinking it's unfair the way we pick on Maurice all the time. Maybe we ought to cut him some slack, lay off the food jokes for a bit.'

'Are you serious?'

She grinned. 'No, of course not. Got to have some pleasures in life.' She became business-like. 'I've gone through the contents of the safe and I've got the financial information on Bygod. Turns out he was pretty well off after all.'

'How well off?'

'He wasn't hurting, I can tell you that. Most of it was in shares and various bonds and investment vehicles. He had one or two ready-access savings accounts, and transferred money from those to his bank account from time to time, and there were incoming dividends and other interest, along with regular sums from an annuity he seems to have taken out twelve years ago – I suppose when all the fuss died down and he was sorting his life out. His utilities and other regular bills were paid by direct debit, there was no mortgage on the flat, and he took out five hundred in cash every week, plus other irregular cash sums. It looks as though day-to-day he paid for things in cash.'

'That fits with what we know about him not liking modern technology and gadgets.'

'Right, boss. Anyway, I've done a rough calculation on the bonds and shares and so on, and it looks as though his assets were worth about two million.'

'That's not bad,' Slider said.

'I wouldn't knock it back,' said Swilley. 'And you can add close to another million for the flat and furniture. Plus there was a life insurance policy for two hundred and fifty thousand.'

'He had cancer,' Slider said.

'He took it out a long time ago,' Swilley said, 'so it would still be valid. So he was sick, was he?'

'Doc Cameron says he probably only had a few months to live.'

'Poor old guy,' Swilley said.

'Who was the beneficiary of the insurance policy?'

'It wasn't written to anyone, so it becomes part of the estate. And we still don't know who the next of kin is. I don't suppose he had a solicitor, being one himself, otherwise we could put out a query through the Law Society.'

'Might be worth doing that anyway. I know he cut himself off from his old life, but there might be some people in the trade he kept up with, or at least who might have an idea who his nearest and dearest were.'

'I don't think he had any,' Swilley said, and sounded dissatisfied. 'Not much use having all that money if you don't have anyone to share it with. And then you get murdered. It's a hard way to go.'

'Is there a nice one?'

'There are nicer,' Swilley said, with truth. 'The other thing, boss, SOCA sent over a mobile phone they found in the pocket of a suit in his bedroom wardrobe. Switched off. Very basic, pay as you go, the sort old people have for emergencies only.'

'I suppose these days you can't be sure of finding a telephone box that works.'

'Right,' Swilley said. 'I've got the call record back, and the calls he made were mostly to his own flat – presumably ringing when he was out to give Mrs Kroll instructions or ask her something. Otherwise theatre box offices and restaurants, minicab companies and cab ranks. But it seems he did give the number to someone. The one number he rang that went to a private person also happened to be the only number that rang him.' She paused dramatically.

'And?' Slider prompted, with anticipation.

Norma smiled happily. 'I think we've found Nina.'

The number Bygod had rung went back to a mobile phone in the name of Anna Klimov, with an address in St John's Wood.

'I Googled the name,' Swilley said. 'It turns out that it's the real name of the actress Diana Chambers.'

Slider was impressed. 'The grand dame of the theatre,' he said. He had seen her on stage often in her younger days – and his – when he had worked Central and before marriage and children had claimed his evenings. She had been gorgeous then – well, she was pretty handsome now – and he had been sufficiently smitten to sit through the whole Oresteia cycle at the Old Vic because she had been starring in it, in flimsy Greek robes. She had a voice that went right to the roots of your hair and massaged your scalp, and eyes like liquid velvet. And though in later years she had done quite a few films, she had remained true to live theatre and always seemed to be in *something* in the West End. Atherton would know what the latest thing was – he still went, while Slider, alas, didn't.

Swilley went on, 'It seems from Google that she went to Oxford and was a star in the OUDS at the same time Bygod was there, so probably that's when they met. She was in that Burton-Taylor production of *Dr Faustus* that Mrs Bygod mentioned, that Bygod helped in.'

'But what makes you think she's Nina?' Slider asked.

'Well, boss, Nina is a pet name for Anna among East Europeans.'

'That's not much to go on.'

'And it says on Google she acted as Nina Klimov right at the beginning of her career, before she got her big break,' Swilley concluded. 'Anyway, she's the only person with his mobile number, so she was obviously special to him.'

'Good enough. We must talk to her.'

'According to Google she's married to actor-director Alistair Head,' Swilley went on.

'I didn't know she was married,' Slider said, and felt a ridiculous pang of disappointment. Now he thought about it, he had heard their names in the same sentence before now. He had actually seen them together in a stage production of *Private Lives* long ago, and they had famously starred as Nicholas and Alexandra in the film *Last Days*.

'Married since 1975 – that's a long time in showbiz,' said Swilley. 'But I found some gossip on Google that they've had their ups and downs. Apparently he's got a bit of a taste for starlets – casting-couch stuff – and she once had an affair with Daly Redmond, maybe to get her own back. There was an incident in the Ivy when he found out, when there was practically a fist-fight – all the gossip magazines covered it. *Tops! Magazine* says Head's very jealous and controlling,' she concluded, 'so if she and Bygod *were* seeing each other it was probably in secret.'

'In that case, we must be careful about how we approach her. Can't go asking her about Bygod if her husband's listening.'

'No, boss,' Swilley said. She raised celestial blue eyes to his with a question. 'If he's the jealous sort *and* has a nasty temper...'

'You mean, if he found out she'd had a long-term affair – *if* it was an affair...'

'It's a possibility,' Swilley concluded.

Atherton was probably even more excited than Slider, and certainly had more information. 'She and Head are doing a revival of their *Antony and Cleopatra* on stage. I saw it the first time round and it was electric then, but of course the real Antony and Cleopatra were mature people by Roman standards, so there's a case for preferring older actors in the parts. It'll be interesting to see how differently they play it this time.'

'Did you know they were married?'

‘Of course I did. How could you not? They’re a famous luvvieland couple, like Judi Dench and Michael Williams. Except that Head’s a director as well so they get double the work.’

‘Happily married?’

‘Well, they’re still together. Head’s known for having a bit of a temper, professionally – probably why he prefers to direct himself. He has everyone who works for him trembling.’

‘Except the nubile ones?’

‘Oh, you’ve heard that, have you? I thought you didn’t know anything about them.’

‘Norma Googled and told me the results.’

‘Well, there’s always lots of temptation in the acting world. Plus long absences, late nights and heightened emotions. But if they’ve lasted thirty-something years together they must have worked out a *modus vivendi*, one would have thought.’

‘This production they’re in now...?’

‘It’s in rehearsal – not due to open until December. Do you want me to find out where they’re rehearsing? It’ll be rooms at this stage, I should think.’

‘Do that,’ Slider said. ‘And find out where she and Head are at this moment. We need to interview her alone. I don’t want to rock her boat if she’s not a suspect.’

‘Fancy old Lionel Bygod knowing Diana Chambers! He really did move in the inner circle after all. And if she’s felt the need to keep it secret all these years, there must have been more than just friendship involved, the old dog.’

‘Let’s not jump to conclusions. She might not

want even an innocent friendship revealed if she has a jealous husband. And we don't know yet that she did keep it secret. I'm just erring on the side of caution.'

'That's a first.' He frowned. 'You said "if" she's not a suspect. Why would she want to kill him?'

'Norma's worked out that he was worth about three million. That's reason enough for a lot of people. I could stand to know what her financial position is.'

'So you want me to go and interview her, I suppose,' Atherton said casually.

Slider was not fooled. 'I'm going myself. I didn't sit through six solid hours of Aeschylus in my youth to give up a chance like this when it's offered. I thought I'd take Norma.'

Atherton was aghast. 'I'm the theatre buff around here. You *have* to take me.'

'Norma was the one who found her out. And she can bring the woman's touch to the interview.'

'You've always said women respond better to men,' Atherton objected. 'And theatre's my milieu. And I can use words like "milieu". The only thing Norma's been to is *Mamma Mia*, and she thought that was dangerously over-intellectual.'

'All right,' Slider yielded, as he'd meant to all along, 'you can come. But you owe me. Tea whenever I want it for a week.'

'For Diana Chambers I'll throw in biscuits as well,' Atherton vowed devoutly.

THIRTEEN

Love Among the Rubens

Chambers and Head lived in Highgate, in a modern house that turned out to be one Slider knew by sight. He had passed it many times over the years, and with his interest in architecture had noticed it because it was one of the few modern buildings he liked. It was set just below the crest of the hill, a simple box that worked because of its perfect Golden Rectangle proportions, a felicitous choice of brick, and elegant landscaping.

Atherton had built up a network of theatre sources, and it didn't take him long to discover that *Antony and Cleopatra* was currently rehearsing in the Workspace studio in Archer Street, but that they didn't rehearse on Sundays. Also that Alistair Head was in New York receiving some kind of theatre award, so the chances were that Diana Chambers would be at home, and alone.

'Piece of luck for us,' Slider remarked as they stood before the door waiting for his ring to be answered. It was a cold, grey day, the gusty wind flicking bits of paper along the pavement, trees shaking the leaves out of their hair. It was very quiet in the street – amazingly so for the centre of London. The house had a feeling of stillness and Slider felt the door would not be opened. When you thought of it, why would anyone ever?

But at last there was a crackle and the entry-phone said in a woman's voice, 'Who is it?'

'Police, ma'am,' Slider said. 'Detective Inspector Slider, Shepherd's Bush, and Detective Sergeant Atherton. May we speak to Miss Chambers, please?' He held up his warrant card to the camera and smiled reassuringly. After a moment of consideration, the inner door opened and a woman stepped into the glazed porch and conducted another inspection of the warrant cards through the glass outer door.

Slider's unruly heart beat a little faster because this was the great lady herself. He said understandingly, 'If you'd like to telephone Shepherd's Bush police station, they will confirm that we have come here to speak to you, and describe us to you.'

Evidently this – or perhaps their unthreatening appearance – was enough for her. She unlocked and opened the door, and stood before them, giving them the Old Money stare that duchesses and grand dames of the theatre alone can master. Footballers' wives never get it.

Slider was surprised she was so tiny. He had always thought of her as tall, and he had not been exposed to enough thesps in the flesh to know, as Atherton could have told him, that most actresses only looked tall because actors were so short. If she had been at university at the same time as Bygod, she must be about the same age, but she looked very good for it, though he tried to tell himself her perfect, dewy skin must be at least partly make-up.

But she did have genuinely beautiful features, thick, shoulder-length waves of chestnut hair, and enormous blue eyes, though close to he could see the fine lines around them and the crêpiness of the deep eyelids. But she was still fabulous; and dressed in beige tailored slacks with a long matching jacket over a delicate white blouse, with a heavy gold neck-chain and ear-rings, she looked ready to go anywhere. The thought that she might have to be dressed-up and ready to be papped at any moment struck him as sad. Who'd be famous? Not him, that was for damn sure.

All this observation happened in an instant, of course. She had had time only to look from one of them to the other.

'Perhaps you think my caution foolish, but the paparazzi will go to any lengths to ambush one,' she said. Oh yes, that was the voice! Smooth as Manuka honey, bathing Slider's heart in consolation.

'Not foolish at all, ma'am – very sensible. May we come in and talk to you?'

'Am I in trouble?' she asked, with a hint of a smile.

'I don't think so,' Slider said. 'But we do have something very particular we'd like to talk to you about.'

'You're being very mysterious. However, I suppose you had better come in,' she said, and stepped back for them to pass her, locking the outer door behind them.

The interior spaces of the house were large and plain, with vistas through open doorways and square arches: very much designer-architectural. It was all parquet floors and muted shades of beige and cream, with a little, extremely beautiful, furniture that looked 1920s, streamlined and elegant, and modern paintings on the walls that Slider guessed were worth a fortune. She led them to the back of the house, and suddenly they were in a double-height room whose outer wall was glazed all the way up, giving a breathtaking view down the rolling green acres of the hill.

She turned to inspect their reaction, which Atherton thought touching – she still wanted it to impress people. He obliged, saying, 'What a fabulous room. The view is amazing. It must be wonderful at night, too, with the lights in the distance.'

'Thank you. It is nice, isn't it?' she said, and he could hear she was pleased. 'Come and sit down and tell me how I can help you.'

She led them to a group of chairs and sofas – beige leather – arranged before the glass wall to get the benefit. Slider noted Sunday newspapers and an empty coffee cup on the low table, suggesting what she had been doing when they rang. The Culture section of the *Sunday Times* was lying on top of the heap open at the theatre reviews. He took a seat, she settled herself opposite him, and Atherton sat on the sofa between them.

The view beckoned his eye insistently, and he

took a moment to satisfy it, taking a long sweeping look over the deep green, the trees, and the grey, misty profile of the city in the distance. Yes, it was stunning, and was of course what the architect had designed the house for, to look out at this astonishing stretch of the pastoral, preserved in the heart of an industrial city. But he would not have liked to live here. When he was home he liked to hole in. Here, when it was dark and you put the lights on, you would be visible and what was outside would be hidden. You would not know who might be looking at you, unseen in the darkness. It made him shiver even to imagine it.

Well, perhaps a great star was so used to living in a goldfish bowl it ceased to matter. You could get used to anything, so they say.

'Well, then,' Diana Chambers said. 'It must be something important to bring you out here on a Sunday.'

Slider got down to business. 'I understand you are a friend of Lionel Bygod.'

Her mouth tightened. 'Why do you understand that?'

'Yours is the only number he called on his mobile phone. And the only number that called his.'

She considered a moment, examining him with hostility. 'He and I are old friends. But I must ask you to keep it to yourselves. My husband is a – difficult man. If he were to find out ... And he will, if you allow it to go any further.'

'I assure you, I have no wish to make your life difficult,' Slider said. 'I am a great admirer of yours, have been for many years. I saw your Oresteia—'

'Good Lord!' she interrupted, suspicion joining hostility. 'Is that what this is about? You're just a common-or-garden celebrity hunter.' She started to rise, and Slider saw ejection in her face, but Atherton interrupted.

'Miss Chambers,' he said sternly, 'we've come to tell you that Lionel Bygod is dead.'

She subsided into her seat, her eyes went from him to Slider, and then she lowered her head with an expression of great sadness. 'I wasn't expecting it so soon,' she said. 'I thought there was still time. I didn't say goodbye.' The large eyes filled with tears. 'My poor Bobo,' she murmured. 'My poor darling.'

She drew out a handkerchief and carefully dabbed the tears away. A star, Slider thought, couldn't even cry with abandon for fear of looking less than lovely. He was getting a sharp lesson in the strains of celebrity here this morning.

She didn't seem very surprised by the news, but then – another lesson to learn – how would you tell with an actor?

Then she looked up at him sharply, handkerchief arrested, the suspicion back. 'Why are you here telling me? It's not the police's job, surely? What's going on?'

He answered with a question of his own. 'You were expecting his death?'

'He told me he had cancer, but he said he had a few months left. He said he would tell me when it was time to say goodbye.'

Atherton spoke, holding her eyes so that Slider

could observe her reaction. 'He didn't die of cancer, Miss Chambers. He was murdered.'

She flinched as though she had been hit. Her lips made the 'm' of 'murdered?' but did not go on. They began to quiver, and she shook her head slowly. 'Oh no. Oh no.'

'I'm afraid it's true.'

'But – how? Who?' She left Atherton's face for Slider's, searching it. 'It can't be true. You mean – someone broke in, something like that? A burglar?'

Slider felt like an executioner. 'There was no break in, no robbery. He was killed deliberately, by someone he knew.'

'That's not possible,' she said. 'No-one would hurt him if they knew him. He was the gentlest man I ever knew. He was *good*, a good man. He never did anyone any harm.' A hope dawned. 'It's a mistake,' she pleaded. 'It wasn't him, it was someone else. You've made a mistake.'

'I'm afraid not,' Slider said.

Now the tears welled over. 'I can't believe it. Oh, my poor Bobo.'

She cried, and Slider waited, staring out through the window. The grey light made everything seem curiously depthless. The tree heads whipped from side to side in emphatic negatives. He watched the wind yank a plastic bag along as though it were on a chain, and waited for the storm to subside.

'Bobo?' he queried.

'It's what we called each other from the beginning, at university. He was Bobo and I was

Nina. My parents called me Nina or Ninette at home. I can't remember now why Lionel was Bobo. Something to do with a gorilla, I think. We were probably drunk at the time – we seemed to have spent a lot of the time at Oxford that way. But it was a happy, harmless drunkenness, just youthful high spirits, really. Anyway, the names stuck.'

He saw her remember again why they were here. It was the way with unexpected death, that you forgot it for a few seconds, only to remember again with renewed shock, fresh every time. 'My poor Bobo! How can he be dead? Who would do such a thing?

'We're hoping for your help about that,' Slider said. 'He seems to have lived a very private life, almost one might say secretive. No-one knew much about him, and nothing about his life before he came to Hammersmith.'

'He cut himself off after that terrible court case. I suppose you know about that?'

Slider nodded.

'He made a new life, simply shed his old life like a skin and had nothing to do with it after that. Except for me. I was the only person he took with him from the old days.' She broke off. 'How come there's been nothing in the press about this? How have you kept it out?'

'We haven't sought any media coverage,' Slider said, 'and Mr Bygod was not a famous or important man, so the main papers haven't picked it up for themselves.'

She looked bitter. 'No, not important or famous – just a dear, lovely, good person. He had such a sweetness about him – I can't describe it. He was worth ten of me or Alastair. But it's us they go after.' She looked appeal at him. 'Can you keep me from being named? Not tell anyone about Bobo and me? I'll help you any way I can, but if Al finds out there'll be a row, and if there's a row it'll be in every paper and magazine and my life will be hell.'

'I've no wish to make your life hell. I've only come to you because so little is known about him, and we hoped you would help fill in some gaps.'

She visibly took hold of herself and said, 'Of course. What do you want to know?'

'Everything,' Slider said. 'From the beginning.'

He had been studying law and she had been studying English literature, and they were at different colleges, so they might never have met. But the OUDS and the Playhouse brought people together from every corner of the University.

'He was so stage-struck, it was funny,' she said. 'Much more than me, really. He'd always wanted to be an actor, and he did take a couple of small parts in the beginning, but there were so many other chaps with much more bombastic personalities that he got edged out. And I think in the end he found more satisfaction in doing the backstage stuff. In any case, his family wanted him to go into the law, and he wasn't one for breaking their hearts for his own ends. He cared too much about other people. I suppose for that reason alone he wouldn't have survived on the stage. You have to be pretty ruthless.' She made a gesture with her hands. 'Tunnel vision.' She looked at Atherton. 'We're not nice people, really.'

'I think that's a generalization,' Atherton said, and she took it as a compliment, and smiled a 'thank you' at him.

'But you have to understand – Lionel was an innocent abroad. He never held grudges; he was a damn sight too understanding to my mind. Even later, when he was a solicitor, there was that complete lack of cynicism about him. Strange, really – and apart from acting, I always thought he could hardly have chosen a worse career than the law. He was utterly truthful, you see, without worrying about the consequences. Having to keep our friendship secret was quite a strain on him.'

She and Lionel fell in love. 'Not quite at first sight,' she said, thinking back, 'but it wasn't long. He was tall and handsome, but as well as all that such a *nice* person. And funny! He was so quiet people often didn't notice, but he said the most devastating things, had me in fits. He was witty, you know – and intelligent. Goodness! He took a First.' She nodded to show they should be impressed. 'And he knew more about literature than I did, by a long chalk. If he hadn't helped me study, and explained everything, I'd never have got my degree. I only got a third. I'm not much of an intellectual. But Lionel had a wonderful brain. And he never minded how much trouble he took, when it was for someone he cared about.'

They were lovers throughout the second and third years of university. But when they graduated, their lives moved apart.

'You know how these things happen. We were both young and getting on with our lives, and we'd both picked careers that needed a lot of concentration. We kept in touch for a little while, but it was too difficult to meet, and so it just, sort of, died. But I thought about him fondly over the years. He was one of my happiest memories.'

'You married,' Slider said to move her along.

'Yes. Funnily enough, Bobo – Lionel and I married in the same year, 1975, though of course I didn't know that until much later. He married the daughter of his practice boss. I married Alastair. I don't think either of us has had a particularly easy time of it. June wasn't exactly a sympathetic choice – I don't think she ever understood or appreciated Lionel. It was easy to mistake his gentleness for weakness – God knows I saw enough people do it at university. And my life with Al has been somewhat stormy, as I'm sure you know.' There was a bitterness to the tone of the last words.

Slider reflected it could not be easy to carry out one's private life under the full glare of publicity. 'I'm afraid I don't read much celebrity gossip,' he said kindly.

She subjected him to a brief inspection to test for sincerity. 'Good for you,' she said. Her eyes flicked to Atherton as if to say, *But I bet you do*. 'Well, Al and I have had a lot of ups and downs, and there've been times when I've been close to chucking it, but we've struggled through somehow. We do have a lot of respect for each other and our careers are interdependent, and – well, there's no-one quite like Al, when it comes down to it. But we were going through a bad patch when I met Lionel again, quite by chance.

'It was at a benefit at the National Gallery, in 1995. Some Old Master painting they were trying to buy for the nation – big naked women and cupids and so on, as I remember. Al and I were celebrity sponsors for all the usual reasons. I turned round and suddenly Lionel was there with June, the four of us face to face with champagne glasses in our hands. Al and I were barely talking to each other at the time, and there was some terrible strain between Lionel and June, I could see that at a glance. But one look at Lionel and the years seemed to peel away, and all I wanted to do was go somewhere quiet with him and talk and talk. We couldn't, of course, with the world looking on. But at the end of the evening I managed to slip him my private number, and – so it began.'

'Your affair,' Slider suggested.

'It was more than that. It was deep, deep love. Passion, too – at least at first. Lionel was what I needed just then, a kind man who adored me and made me feel like a woman again. And he obviously needed me, though he was terribly loyal and would never say anything against June. But I could read between the lines. She just didn't *get* him. She didn't appreciate him. And she was cold. The sort of woman who cuts the legs out from under any man she gets her claws into.'

'How well do you know her?'

'Oh, hardly at all. I only met her once or twice, at functions, but that was enough. I could tell all I needed to from that, and the effect she'd had on Lionel. She was one of those pinched, prudish women who makes everyone feel uncomfortable. There was never any prospect we could have been friends, even without Lionel in the case. I'm amazed Lionel stuck with her so long. But as I said, he was terribly loyal.'

'Did they have any children?' Slider asked.

She frowned. 'I'm not sure. I think they may have had a son who died. Lionel would never talk about his marriage, and he never mentioned any children, but I did once see a photograph in his wallet of a little boy.' Slider and Atherton exchanged a swift glance. There had been no photograph in the wallet when they saw it. 'He didn't want me to see it,' she went on, 'and he shoved it out of sight pretty quickly. I said, "Who's that?" and he said, "No-one. He's not with us any more." And then he changed the subject. So I'm guessing maybe they had a son who died. But it *is* just a guess.'

Or, as Slider had seen in Atherton's eye in that instant, perhaps the boy wasn't related to him at all. Slider didn't like thinking it, but the old 'no smoke without fire' adage was as sticky as chewing-gum on the sole. Or the soul. And there were more little boys than sons in the world. But Slider remembered how June had not wanted to discuss it. Losing a child and not being able to have another would certainly put a strain on a marriage.

'So your affair carried on – for how long?'

'Ever since,' she said. 'After the first year it settled down from great passion to great love and affection. We met as often as our various jobs and lives allowed. It had to be secret, of course – for my sake, even after June left him. But I needed him so much – more than ever as the years passed. Al didn't get any easier, and living in the spotlight gets harder all the time. He was my place to hide, my darling Bobo. I could be Nina again with him, just an ordinary person. Safe. And he needed me after that terrible court case and all the dreadful fuss that followed.'

'Yes, that was in 1996, wasn't it,' Slider said, 'so you were together then.'

'It took its toll of him,' she said. 'I saw the change in him. He began to be old then.'

'Do you believe there was any truth in the accusations?'

'That he was a paedophile? No!' she cried forcefully. 'It was the most malicious nonsense, but it wrecked his life. He had to move twice to shake off that terrible man who was pursuing him.'

'Crondace?'

'That's his name,' she said. 'And he had to give up his practice. Fortunately he had plenty of money. He inherited a lot from his father, so he wasn't dependent on his work – he'd always given generously to charity, and taken *pro bono* cases. Roxwell was one of those. That's where generosity gets you,' she added bitterly. 'And now he's dead.' She had remembered it all over again. She looked at them searchingly. 'Was it something to do with that old case? Was it Crondace? Did he manage to track him down at last?'

'That's one of the things we're considering. But we have to look at all possibilities. Have you seen much of Lionel recently?'

'We met every few weeks, and talked on the telephone often. The last time was – Thursday? Friday? No, Thursday. We had lunch.'

'At an Italian restaurant?'

'How do you know? Oh—' She cancelled that with a movement of her hand. 'Silly question.'

'Was it your usual place to meet?'

'No, it was the first time we'd eaten on his home turf. We usually met somewhere in the West End when we went out to eat together, or sometimes we'd drive out into the country, if I had enough time.'

'I didn't think he had a car,' said Slider.

'He didn't, he said it wasn't worth keeping one in London, but he could drive all right. When he needed one, he rented one, for the day or longer, from Melbury Cars in Kensington High Street. He had an account there. Otherwise, he took taxis.'

'So, on this occasion when you met at the Piazza,' Slider prompted, 'did he seem different in any way?'

'It's when he told me about the cancer,' she said. 'We had our usual lovely time, chatting and laughing about old times and catching up on each other's lives. Then he got serious. He held my hand across the table and told me—' She broke off until she had control again. 'He said he wanted me to know that he was going to change his will, and he was leaving me a substantial sum.'

'How substantial?' Atherton asked.

'He didn't say. He just said "substantial". I told him I didn't want it, I just wanted him. And he said, "I won't be around for much longer. And I want you to have enough so that whatever happens, you'll be all right."'

'What did he mean, "whatever happens"?' Atherton asked.

'If I had to leave Al, or if I couldn't work any more. They were things we'd talked about on other occasions. He'd always said if anything like that happened, I could come to him.'

'Had you never talked about your getting a divorce?' Slider asked.

She shrugged. 'Oh, we'd talked about it, idly. But it would have been too messy. The publicity would have been horrendous! My career is dependant on Al's, and vice versa. And he wouldn't have taken it well.'

'He has quite a temper, your husband,' Atherton suggested casually.

Not casually enough. Her eyes widened. 'You can't be thinking – oh, good God! Tell me this is not all about suspecting Al?'

'We have to consider all possibilities.'

'It isn't a possibility. To begin with, he doesn't know about Lionel.'

'You're sure about that?'

'Look, he has a temper, but he never conceals it. Everything comes pouring out of him. If he'd found out he'd have come straight to me, there'd have been a furious row. That's what happened after – well, someone else. He gave me a black eye – I couldn't work for a week. The whole world knew – which is why I was always so careful to keep Bobo secret. But Al wouldn't have plotted in secret and carried out a murder. He's just not like that.'

Slider changed the subject. 'Lionel said he was leaving you a substantial sum. Do you know how it was left before? Or who else he meant to inherit?'

'Not a clue,' she said indifferently. 'Knowing Lionel, it was probably left to charity. That would be like him.' She frowned. 'You do seem to harp on about the money.'

'We haven't yet established who his next of kin is. And of course, money is often a motive for murder.'

She nodded, her eyes full of sorrow. 'I can't believe he's dead, that someone deliberately killed him. The kindest, gentlest of men. He was my best friend, as well as my love.' Her hands folded themselves together in her lap, as if she had taken her friend's hand. In the gesture was all the loneliness of death – the unendurable, unavoidable fact that you would never see him and touch him again.

It had started raining outside, and a gust blew a handful of drops against the glass with a sound like mouse feet pattering.

'I'm very sorry for your loss,' Slider said.

She smiled painfully, but there was sweetness in it. 'I'm just glad I had the chance to know him,' she said quietly. 'But I shall miss him so much.'

* * *

The rain was still scattered and blowy as they scuttled for the car, not having set in yet, but there was a black cloud heading for them with intent.

As he got in on his side, Atherton said, 'Sixteen years she's been doing the nasty with old Lionel, and she still thinks her husband hasn't a clue?'

'It's possible,' Slider said, turning the key.

'But how likely? I think we need to look into their finances. Three million is not to be sneezed at, and she knew about it – or that there *was* money, anyway. Why didn't you ask her where they both were on Tuesday?'

'They're famous people. There are other ways we can find out. I don't want to put her on alert if she did have something to do with it. But I don't believe she did. She really loved him.'

'She's an *actress*,' Atherton pointed out.

'Even so,' Slider insisted. 'You've only got to look at the difference between her understanding of him, and wife June's lack of.'

'Well, but the bad-tempered, jealous, violent Alistair Head...?'

'Now you're running two hares – inheritance and jealousy.'

'Same hare,' Atherton said. 'Diana lets slip about the money, Alastair needs it and wants revenge at the same time. Bump off the old man, satisfy the Old Adam, come into the cash.'

'You're assuming he didn't know Bygod was dying anyway.'

'Even if he did, he might need the money

quickly – couldn't wait for nature to take its course.'

'Take a pull on the reins,' Slider advised. 'We have no evidence of any sort against Head.'

'I know. I'm just thinking aloud. Anyway, if it was a planned murder, wouldn't Head be intelligent enough to wear gloves? And to bring his own weapon with him?'

'You don't know how intelligent Head is. Being clever in your field doesn't make you clever in another. And a man losing his temper doesn't tend to think things out clearly.'

'Now you're being perverse,' said Atherton.

'Just thinking aloud,' Slider said.

FOURTEEN

Kissing Presumed Fed

Slider Senior was quite serene about being left to hold down the fort. It turned out he was going to do a bit of entertaining himself. 'Lydia's coming round for supper.'

'You were quick off the mark,' Slider said. 'We only asked you this morning.'

'I was seeing her anyway,' Mr Slider said. 'What, d'you think I don't have a social life outside this house?'

'I'm all too aware you have a very active one,'

Slider said. 'I'm only grateful you fit us in.'

'I was going to cook for her in my flat,' Mr Slider explained, 'but I don't mind moving it up here. So there's no "fitting in" about it.'

'Well, I'm still grateful. Help yourself to anything – you know that. What are you cooking?'

'I've made a nice steak and kidney pie, so I've only got to hot it up and do the veg.'

Slider thought steak and kidney pie rather heavy for romance, but he said, 'There's a bottle of Hermitage in the rack that'd go well with that.'

Mr Slider grinned. 'Already got my eye on it. I'll replace it, o' course.'

'No, you won't. It's the least I can do.'

The wind had dropped and it was a little warmer, warm enough for a slight fog. It made haloes of the street lamps and half-sucked wine gums of the traffic lights. In the car, Joanna said, 'It's nice to get out for a change. I don't know how much longer I'm going to be able to wear this dress.'

'You look lovely,' he said, easing out on to Chiswick High Road.

'You didn't even look!'

'Well, I know you do, anyway.'

'Did I tell you Georgina rang today?' Georgina was the assistant to Tony Whittam, the orchestra's fixer. 'She said there's a mini-tour coming up in December – four days in Germany. Wanted to know if I was good for it.'

'What did you say?'

'I said yes, of course. The baby's not due till

March.' Out of the corner of his eye he saw her shrug. 'And I sit on the inside of the desk so no-one'll see me.'

'I'm sure no-one's concerned about your appearance,' he said.

'I hope you're not concerned about anything,' she said, with just a little sharpness. She had always resented having to juggle home and career in the way a man never had to. She knew it was illogical to mind something that couldn't be changed, but still she minded it. So she didn't want him telling her she ought to be taking it easy and turning down work.

He went for lightness. 'Me? I have nothing to say about anything. Empty as air, my head.'

'Yeah,' she said with broad irony. 'This thing with your dad and Lydia,' she began.

'Darling, there's no point worrying about that. He has his life to live and we have ours.'

'But it looks as if it's getting serious. When he brought George back from his walk today he had a jeweller's bag in his hand.'

'That *is* serious. I don't like George wasting money on jewellery. He's not two yet.'

'Don't be an ass. What if he's going to propose to her tonight?'

'Well, what if he is? I approve of marriage. Everyone ought to be married.' He glanced sideways at her. 'Stop worrying. Everything will come out all right.'

'How will it?'

He smiled. 'I don't know. It's a mystery.'

At Atherton's house – a bijou little Victorian

two-up-two-down – they had only been inside long enough to get out of their coats, and the cats were still racing round the room like Evel Knievel doing the wall-of-death, when there was a prolonged and rampant ringing at the door bell which sent them into fresh excesses. Atherton thrust the coats back at Slider and went to open it, and there was Emily, fog jewels in her hair, laptop in one hand and flight bag in the other, her suitcase on the ground behind her. Joanna thought how glamorous she looked, in a beautiful calf-length wool coat, long boots, a big muffler round her neck – very much the international business traveller. Slider thought she looked tired, but her grin was pure pleased-to-be-home.

'What the hell?' Atherton said as she flung herself into his arms. 'I wasn't expecting you.' He hugged and released her. 'What if I'd got another woman here?' he said sternly.

'You have,' Joanna reminded him. 'Hello, Emily. Good trip?'

'Yes, thanks. I got all the interviews I need, and suddenly I'd had enough, just wanted to be back, so I changed my flight.'

'I'd have come and fetched you from the airport if I'd known,' Atherton said.

'I got a taxi. I saw Bill and Joanna going in as we turned the corner. God, it's good to be back!'

'Have you eaten yet?'

'Not for centuries. What is that wonderful smell?'

'I'm doing *boeuf en croute,*' Atherton said.

'What's known as "casing the joint",' Slider

explained.

She laughed. 'Now I know I'm home! Oh, those cats!' Tig, who had run up the door curtain, launched himself through the air and landed on Emily's shoulder. Vash was rubbing his face lovingly against her boot. 'What I want first is a giant gin and tonic. No-one makes them like you,' she added to Atherton.

She unpicked the cats and removed her coat. Slider said, 'I'll take it,' and went with all three coats to the rack in the tiny back lobby, and returned to find Emily and Atherton locked in a passionate kiss. He thought of Kate's inevitable eye-rolling comment, 'Get a room!' but held it back. He caught Joanna's eye, and smiled. *You see, it's all right*, he projected. She smiled back, and shrugged.

The kiss broke at last. Their arms still round each other, Emily said, 'I missed you *so* much. I'm sorry if I've been a bore about moving into the flat. I know you love your house.'

'I've missed you too,' Atherton said. 'And I know you've got logic on your side. We'll talk about it.'

That seemed to be enough. They broke apart, and Atherton said, 'Drinks!' and disappeared into the kitchen. Emily called after him, 'Need any help with anything?'

'No, thanks,' his voice came back.

Emily smiled in satisfaction. Gourmet chef that he was, he didn't like anyone else in his kitchen when he was creating a meal. 'I knew he'd say that,' she said, sinking into an armchair. 'He cooks as good as he kisses.'

'I'll take your word for half of that statement,' Slider said.

'So, tell me about this new case of yours,' Emily said over dinner.

Atherton and Slider told her between them.

'Diana Chambers!' Emily said. 'Oh, I *love* her. You actually met her? What's she like in real life?'

'About the same,' Atherton said.

Emily made a face. 'I'll ask someone sensible.' She turned to Slider. 'What's she like?'

'Tiny. Beautiful,' Slider said.

'And she had a long, long affair with this bloke and no-one ever knew? He must have been something special.'

'Well, from all we can gather about him, he was,' Slider said. 'Everyone liked him.'

'Apart from the Alf Garnett family,' Emily said. 'What was their name again?'

'Crondace,' Atherton supplied.

'That's it. And you say he's done a runner, the male Crondace? So it looks like him.'

'We don't know that he even knew where Bygod had gone,' Slider said. 'We're a long way from any conclusions yet. A lot of footwork still to do.'

'Apart from that old court case,' Joanna said, 'the money looks the best bet, given that the victim was so nice.'

'Maybe he wasn't,' Atherton said. 'He went to a lot of trouble to shrug off his old life and hide himself from everyone who had known him. Have some more beef?' His hands hovered over the serving dish.

'I couldn't,' Joanna said. 'It's delicious, but I'm stuffed.'

'I could manage a morsel,' Slider said.

'Morsel!' Emily said. 'I love the way you talk. Where I've just been, they'd have said, "Yeah, hit me!"'

'Going back to Bygod,' Joanna said, frowning in thought as she watched Atherton's hands carving and lifting and spooning, 'you haven't found a will?'

'Maybe he hadn't got round to making one yet,' Emily said. 'It's a thing people keep putting off.'

'He *was* a solicitor,' Atherton reminded her.

'Still, intimations of mortality and all that. And he wasn't expecting to pop off for a while yet.'

'But then,' Joanna said, 'where's the old one?'

'Lodged somewhere we haven't found yet,' Atherton said. 'Maybe the next of kin we haven't traced yet has it in a drawer.' He handed the plate to Slider. 'Have the last of the mashed potatoes, to soak up the gravy.'

'Thanks, I will.'

There was a silence for a moment.

Joanna, looking at Slider, broke it. 'The really odd thing – or at least, how it comes across to me, the way you've told it – is that cheque. He sat down to write a cheque in the presence of the murderer.'

'It isn't odd if the murderer is Mrs Kroll,' Slider said. 'He's just doing his normal work, she's pottering about behind him. The cheque needn't be anything to do with her.'

'But that doesn't work with anyone else,' Joanna said. 'If it was anyone else, the cheque must be something to do with them, or why was he writing it at that particular moment? Which is why I asked about the will.'

'I'm not with you,' said Atherton.

'Because,' Joanna said, 'who wouldn't bother to wait for the cheque? Someone who was going to get the money anyway.'

There was a brief silence while they thought about it, then Atherton said, 'Well, the Krolls are still the best bet. They're desperate for money and we know they were there.'

'But then there's the Crondaces,' Emily said. 'And what about the jealous, violent Alistair Head? The press would love that one.'

'That's why they mustn't find out *anything*,' Slider said, laying down his knife and fork, 'until and unless we have some reason to suspect him.'

'Hey, it's me,' Emily said, offended. 'I don't talk.'

'Pay no attention. He's smitten,' Atherton said. 'Diana the huntress has bayed and netted him. Pudding?'

'You made *pudding*?' Emily was impressed.

'I had guests,' he said with dignity, standing up and reaching for the plates. 'It's just a simple lemon tart.'

'God, your lemon tart!' Emily swooned. 'Will you marry me?'

'Get in line,' Slider and Joanna said at the same instant, looked at each other, and laughed.

* * *

Dad was alone when they got back, greeted them with a calm and perhaps rather sleepy smile, said goodnight and took himself off to his own flat.

'It's like waiting for the other shoe to drop,' Joanna said when he'd gone. 'Do you think anything happened?'

'He'd have told us, surely, if it did,' said Slider, helping her out of her coat.

'I don't think it can have. I mean, she's obviously gone. We're quite early. I thought she'd still be here.'

Slider smiled. 'What makes you think she isn't still here?'

'But – what? Oh, you mean she might be waiting for him down in his flat.' Joanna was enlightened. 'I never thought of that.'

'That's why I'm the detective,' Slider said. 'And you are just the beautiful, desirable woman.'

Joanna considered that for a moment, and then said, 'What do you mean, "just"?'

On Monday morning a fine, steady rain was falling from a zinc-coloured, featureless sky. Roads glistened, traffic swished, leaves gave up and plummeted suicidally to be splattered dead on the pavements.

Slider was in early, came into the CID room shaking off his coat and found McLaren there alone. 'Are you the first?' he asked.

''Cept for Hollis,' McLaren answered. 'He's in the bog having a shave.'

'Again? He was shaving in there the other day.'

'I think he's sleeping here,' McLaren said. 'You know his old lady chucked him out?'

'No, I didn't. I knew they were having problems.'

'She's got a new fancy man. Technician down the King Edward Hospital. He's better off without her,' he added sourly. McLaren's wife had done much the same thing, Slider remembered: junked him for a newer model, one who'd be around more. It was Police Wife Syndrome. So often they ended up wanting someone with a nine-to-five job. Happened to musicians, too, as Slider knew from Joanna's stories.

But McLaren's dumping was ancient history. Slider remembered the much-vaunted blind date. 'How did your date go, anyway? With – Natalie, was it?'

McLaren's face took on a look of dumb bliss. 'It was great, guv. She's really, really nice – just like Maura said.'

'Got a nice personality, has she?' Slider asked, straight-faced.

McLaren looked defensive. 'Yeah, well, she has. She's a nice person. But she's not a dog. I mean, she's not some supermodel, but she's perfectly all right looking. Anyway, we're going out again.'

'You hit it off, then?'

'Yeah, she's a laugh. We had a great time. Likes her pint. Plays darts, an' all.'

'Well, I'm pleased for you,' Slider said, heading for his own room now he'd done his duty.

But McLaren followed, and lingered in the doorway. Slider looked up. 'Yes, I'll have a cup of tea, if that's what you're going to ask,' he tried.

'Oh – righto.' Still McLaren lingered. 'Guv,' he began with uncharacteristic hesitancy. 'When I took Natalie home – she lives down Twyford Avenue.'

'Well, that's handy for you,' Slider said, perplexed. Twyford Avenue was in Acton, ten minutes from the station, but why was McLaren telling him?

'Yeah. But as we went past the North China, I see Jim Atherton come out.' The North China was a Chinese restaurant on Uxbridge Road popular with coppers.

'Oh?' said Slider. 'Well, a man must eat.' That was the evening Atherton had said he had plans: he had turned down an invitation to eat *chez Slider*.

'He had a woman with him,' McLaren said awkwardly. 'I know her – seen her before. She's that solicitor from Kintie and Abrams, did the defence for Graham Hunter. Tall skinny bird – a looker. Jane Kellock, her name is.'

'Yes, I remember her,' Slider said. That was the Melanie Hunter case, some months back. He became brisk. 'Well, why are you telling me?'

McLaren stared at his feet and fidgeted. 'I just thought—'

'Probably you didn't,' Slider interrupted. 'It's none of my business and it's none of yours. Just get me a cup of tea, will you? And say nothing about this to anyone. I don't like gossip in my firm.'

McLaren went away, and Slider tried to put the

unwelcome piece of information out of his mind, but it didn't want to go. He remembered Jane Kellock – yes, she was a looker all right. Tall, slim, gorgeous. And a dresser. They had met a few times on the circuit in the course of the job. He remembered how well she and Atherton had got on together at a meeting they'd had, the three of them, concerning the Hunter case. And Atherton had always had a weakness for solicitors – when it came to 'legal briefs' he was always wanting to get into them rather than out of them.

Kintie and Abrams had their offices in Acton High Street – the North China was a short walk from there. Slider remembered those times recently, while Emily was away, when Atherton had come in looking as if he hadn't been home...

Damn it, Slider stopped himself angrily, he was not going to think about it! He had enough on his plate with Lionel Bygod and the various suspects, without getting entangled in his people's private lives. He wished he hadn't asked McLaren about his date now. Set a bad precedent. And now here was Hollis coming in, freshly shaven and damp about the hairline. He didn't want to know about that, either, but he couldn't help remembering that Hollis's wife was called Anne-Marie, she was Irish, and that she was diminutive and over-lively with a tendency to go off in company unexpectedly like an unstable blonde firework. It had always been hard to picture her and the self-effacing, gawky-looking Hollis together.

Sometimes a trained memory could be a curse.

'Guv,' Hollis began.

Slider interrupted him, afraid of some fresh hell of revelation. 'Kroll's movements. And Crondace's. That's what we've got to get on with, pronto.'

'Right, guv.' Hollis looked slightly surprised at being told to suck eggs, but carried on gamely. 'They just rang up from the shop to say Mr Wetherspoon's in the building. Thought you might like to be warned.'

It was unnerving to know the Commander was on the loose and might appear at any moment. Slider couldn't concentrate on the work in front of him, and his mind, unhitched from the shafts of duty, would keep wandering off and browsing along the grass verge of speculation about Atherton's private life.

He was glad when Paxman rang up from the front desk to say someone had come in with information about Bygod.

'Taxi driver,' Paxman said. 'Sounds all right – could be useful. Want me to send him up?'

'No, I'll come down,' Slider said. He could be fairly sure he wouldn't stumble into Wetherspoon down there. He felt like a sitting duck here at his desk.

The taxi driver had a shaven head and a clipped but vigorous beard, so he looked as if he had his head on upside down. He was waiting in the shop, and stood politely as Slider appeared and invited him to come through: a short-coupled, stocky man – ideal taxi-driver physique – with small neat features and noticing blue eyes.

‘Michael Mansard. Mike,’ he introduced himself. ‘I’d have come in before only I didn’t know the old man was dead. They’re saying murdered – is that right?’

Slider led him into the cleanest of the interview rooms and gestured him to sit down. ‘Who’s saying?’

‘Oh, word gets round – eventually,’ he said with a shrug. ‘Someone drove past and saw the police tape and someone else read something in the local paper and put two and two together. Then when I found it was the address I’d picked up a fare *and* the same day, I reckoned I’d better come and tell someone, in case it was important.’

‘If it was the same day, it’s probably very important,’ Slider said. ‘Tell me in your own words exactly what you did.’

‘Well,’ said Mansard, settling himself, ‘it was Tuesday last week. I drive for Monty’s – you know?’

‘I know,’ said Slider. Monty’s Radio Metrocabs was a Shepherd’s Bush institution. The garage was under the railway arches on the other side of Goldhawk Road, and though the eponymous Monty had died several years back, finally succumbing to overweight, cigars and terrifying blood pressure, his widow Rita and mistress Gloria continued to run the business as if he was still there. Rumour had it that his last cigar was still resting in an ashtray in the Portakabin from which they operated the radio side of it. They had always been the best of friends, united by an exasperated affection for Monty and disappointment over their children. Each of them had borne Monty a son, neither of whom had any interest in the business – or, indeed, even in getting out of bed in the morning.

'Right,' said Mansard. 'Well, I was on my way back from Ealing – I'd done the airport and got a back fare as far as Northfields – when Gloria comes on, telling me to pick up this fare in Shepherd's Bush Road and take him to Soho. Name of Bygod. He's used our garage before. I'd not driven him, but I'd heard of him – he was a good tipper, and that always gets about, you know?'

'I imagine so.'

'So I goes to the address, rings the doorbell – one of them intercom jobs – and the old geezer comes straight down. Tall, skinny bloke, three-piece suit, nice weasel over it – cashmere, I reckon.'

'What time was that?' Slider asked.

'Eleven forty-five, near as I can say. Well, I open the door for him, seeing as he's obviously a gent, and he thanks me nicely – ever such a nice old boy, lovely voice, like an actor – and asks me to take him to La Florida in Wardour Street. So I did. Traffic was pretty average, so I gets him there about quart' past twelve. He pays cash and gives me a nice tip, so I says, "Would you like me to book you in to get picked up later?" Well, rather us than some cruiser, that's what I reckon. But he says, "Thank you, but I don't know how long I'll be." So I says, "Just give a ring then, if you want us," and he goes in and that's that.'

'You actually saw him go into the restaurant?'

Mansard looked a little abashed at his own softness. 'Well, he was an old boy – didn't look all that well, if you ask me – so I waited to see him safe inside. I reckoned he was meeting someone, and once he was inside they'd take care of him. And that's the last I saw of him.'

Slider pondered. 'You say he didn't look well?'

'He was very thin, and not what I'd call a good colour. But he was pretty old,' he added with a shrug.

'What was his mood like? Could you tell if he was happy, sad, worried – anything?'

'I didn't see that much of him to say, really. He was very polite, and gents like that don't show their feelings much. Maybe he was a bit serious, like he'd got something on his mind,' he added doubtfully. 'I'm not sure I could swear to it.'

'Well, thank you,' Slider said. 'You've been very helpful. I only wish you'd come in sooner.'

'Didn't know, did I?' Mansard said, standing up. 'Gloria'll confirm the times and the address, if you need it. I asked her about him 'fore I come in, but he never rang again that day to get picked up, so he must have picked up a cab on the street to come home.'

'Thanks,' said Slider. 'I'll have a word with her, just to double check, but I'm sure you have all the details right.'

'I'm really sorry somebody done the old boy in,' Mansard said in valediction. 'He was a real gent.'

'So I believe,' said Slider, brow creased in thought.

'So that lets Mrs Kroll out,' said Hollis, leaning against the whiteboard. 'She was telling the truth. Bygod went out quarter to twelve. She's left the house at half past two, and she's covered after that.'

'Unless he came back before she left,' Swilley said.

'Not likely,' said Connolly. 'Go all that way to lunch and back by half two? What class of a lunch would that be?'

'A cancelled one, perhaps,' Slider said. 'If the person he was meeting didn't turn up, he might have waited half an hour and then come home. But we can easily find that out. It does look rather as though Mrs Kroll is in the clear. But we know Bygod did come home at some point, and we know he was probably dead by seven because he didn't answer the door and there were no lights on when Plumptre called. Which leaves a couple of hours when Mr Kroll could have come back to the house. So he's not out of it yet.'

'McLaren and Mackay are still trying to track his movements,' Hollis said.

'I'll get on to the restaurant,' Swilley said. 'I wonder who Bygod was meeting? There was nothing in his diary.'

'Try and get a description from the restaurant,' Slider said.

Soho again. He wondered briefly about Diana Chambers. She had said she and Bygod usually met at restaurants in town, and her play was rehearsing in Archer Street, also in Soho. Had she met him on Tuesday and not told Slider about it? Or Head – presumably he was attending the rehearsals as well. He could have followed her, seen who she was meeting, gone after Bygod later at home. Or they could both be in it, for the money ... He so much didn't want Chambers to be mixed up in the death that he half *had* to suspect her to compensate for his bias.

With plenty of new material to think about he had forgotten about Wetherspoon. Heading unwarily for the washroom, he walked right into him in the corridor.

'Ah, Slider,' said the great man. Wetherspoon was a tall and curiously bulky man with a square, chalky-pink face and wiry grey hair like a superior kind of pan scourer. He carried his head high like a horse the better to look down on people from under his eyelids. He looked at Slider now with the expression of a man who has just found old egg yolk between the tines of his fork.

'And where are you off to?' he asked with a kind of grim jollity. Slider didn't think it was a question he should answer. Wetherspoon examined him from above. 'Not getting on very well with this case, are you?'

'I think we're making progress, sir,' Slider said.

'Do you? You think that, do you? And what is this miraculous progress? Mr Porson doesn't seem to know about it.'

'We're following up several lines of enquiry,' Slider said doggedly. 'Tracing various people's movements. It all takes time.' He felt like a fool for saying it, because it was like saying rain was wet, but if Wetherspoon chose to play this sort of power game there was nothing he could do about it.

'Well, time is of the essence, isn't it?' Wetherspoon enquired rhetorically. 'Once a business like this gets away from you, you're playing catch-up. You need to stay ahead of the game.'

And there'll be more readings from the Book of Clichés at the same time next week, Slider announced inside his head.

'There's going to be a lot of interest in this case,' Wetherspoon went on, 'once the connection is made with the Roxwell business.' *Oh, you've discovered who Bygod was, have you?* Slider thought. 'I can see the press making a big splash with it. I can't have us appearing to be caught on the hop, looking as if we don't know who we're dealing with. I'm going to pre-empt the press, let them know we're on the ball.'

'You're going public?' Slider exclaimed in alarm.

Wetherspoon's lips curved in a superbly contemptuous smile. 'Don't worry, *you* won't be called upon to face the cameras. I'm afraid the days of the amateur are over. I'll do it myself from the publicity suite at Hammersmith, a full media briefing, press and TV.'

God, you love all that stuff, don't you? Slider thought.

'It's just a pity,' Wetherspoon said with a sigh,

‘there isn’t a grieving widow or next of kin. Those tearful close-ups, trembling lips and so on, are the best thing for making witnesses come forward. But we’ll manage somehow.’

‘Sir, I wish you wouldn’t do that,’ Slider said.

‘Oh, really? And why is that?’

Slider was thinking about Diana Chambers. Once the press were interested in Bygod, how long before they got hold of her name? It was so easy to leak, and generally so untraceable. Journalists hung around incognito in pubs listening, or rang weak characters in the Job with offers they couldn’t refuse. The only way to stop it was not to start it.

But of course he couldn’t say that to Wetherspoon. He reached almost at random for a reason. ‘We haven’t traced the next of kin yet, sir. It wouldn’t be right for them to find out that way.’

Wetherspoon frowned. ‘Perhaps it’s just the way to make them come forward,’ he said, but less certainly. People sued for post-traumatic stress at the drop of a hat these days.

‘A few more days, sir.’ Slider pressed his foot on the doubt pedal. ‘Once we’ve located the next of kin...’

‘Ha-hm!’ Wetherspoon cleared his throat non-committally, and struck off in another direction. ‘Crondace – what have you done about Crondace?’ he barked, changing the subject.

‘We’re trying to trace him at this end, sir, and Tower Hamlets are working from the other end. It’s difficult, though. He didn’t have a car, so the ANPR is no use. We’re having to do it the hard way.'

'Aha!' Wetherspoon said triumphantly. 'That's exactly the sort of scenario where going public can help. And I'm liking Crondace for it, I'm liking him very much. That court case, the miscarriage of justice burning in his gut, the long search, the violent revenge at the end of it. It all makes sense.'

What it all made was a story Wetherspoon could imagine himself telling to the assembled media, hushed and hanging on his every word. And at the golf club afterwards. And whatever other places the demigods of the Job hung out and displayed their baboon bottoms to each other – *my case is flashier than yours*. He wanted Slider to get Crondace for him, that was it.

Slider saw a chink of light in the tunnel. 'I think it would be counter-productive to go public on Crondace just yet, sir. We need to keep him off his guard, not send him underground. We're watching the wife and we think she may lead us to him, if she's not tipped off. She's got a solid alibi so she thinks we're not interested in her any more.'

Uncertainty flitted across Wetherspoon's face for a moment. Then he gathered the mantle of greatness about himself and said, 'Very well, a few more days. But I'll be watching events very closely as they develop, and if you haven't brought in Crondace in the next day or two we shall have to think again.' He strode away without waiting for Slider to answer, and a few steps further on, at the end of the corridor, he turned and pointed a finger. 'I'm watching you, Slider.

Remember that.'

Slider waited until he had disappeared through the swing doors to stick his tongue out. Childish, he knew, but a small satisfaction – the only one he was ever likely to get, lowly troll that he was in the hall of the Mountain King.

FIFTEEN

Sic Monday

Porson was in Slider's office when Swilley came in to say that the La Florida confirmed there had been a booking in the name of Bygod and that it had been taken up. Receipts confirmed that lunch for two had been consumed and paid for, and the till slip was timed at two twenty-two.

'So unless he had a time machine,' she concluded, 'he couldn't have got home before Mrs Kroll left. She's covered, boss.'

Porson sighed. 'That's a bugger. Oh well, can't be helped. Lucky we've got other kites to fry. Old man Kroll's still good for it, isn't he?'

'We're checking pubs and betting shops at the moment, sir,' Slider confirmed.

'We'll have to let her go, of course,' Porson said, and then brightened. 'That might make him cough – she'll be on the outside where he can't protect her.'

'But if he confesses he definitely won't be

getting out,' Slider pointed out. 'You're not suggesting we offer protection for her if he comes clean?'

Porson considered it for a golden moment, then rejected it regretfully. 'Can't do that. But he probably won't think it through. If he had any brains he wouldn't be in the pickle he's in. Just suggest that honesty's his best policy, dangle something vague – hint hint, softly softly, you get me? Nothing actionable.'

'Right, sir,' Slider said.

Porson cocked an eye at him, noting his unhappy expression, and fathomed the reason effortlessly. 'You can't worry about Mrs Kroll,' he decreed. 'We're not responsible for her problems with the Changs.'

'I know that, sir.'

'If Kroll did it, she's probably in on it.'

'I know that too, sir.'

Porson softened, not for Mrs Kroll's sake but for Slider's. 'You can have a word with Ealing,' he said. 'Let 'em know she's coming out. They must want the Changs caught as much as she does. They can use her as bait. Set a thief to catch a mackerel, eh?'

'I'll talk to them, sir,' Swilley offered. 'I know DS Barraclough quite well.'

For an electric moment both men considered what 'quite well' might mean, then Porson blinked and said, 'Good girl. Well, press on.' He headed for the door. 'And we've still got Crondace – blood in his gaff, and he's had it away on his toes,' he added. 'He's got to turn up sooner or later.'

'Trouble is,' Swilley added when he had gone, 'Crondace had plenty of time to leave the country before we ever started looking for him.'

Slider nodded, but said, 'I don't think he'll have gone far. He's not the type. What would he do abroad? Anyway, there's not much we can do about him, until Tower Hamlets gives us a lead. I'd better go and see to the Krolls.'

Mrs Kroll was extremely vocal about being let go. 'Oh, so, you believe me now, do you? Very nice! Thank you very much! After locking me up like a common criminal. I'll have you for that, you lot – don't think you're going to get away with it. You first, Mr Bleedin' Inspector Slimy, or whatever you call yourself. I'm suing you for wrongful arrest. You'll be finished once I'm done with you, I'll see to that! And what about my husband? You letting him go as well? You'd better be. I warn you, I'm not taking this lying down.'

And so on.

'I liked her better when she was under arrest,' said 'Nutty' Nicholls, the uniformed sergeant on custody. 'She was a helluvalot quieter.'

'I wish her husband was as talkative,' Slider complained.

'The strong, silent type,' said Nicholls. 'You never quite know with them. Sometimes they're hiding something and sometimes they're just stubborn.'

'That's the trouble,' said Slider. 'Keeping quiet in this case is stupid if he's innocent...'

'...but if villains weren't stupid they'd never be

caught.' Nicholls cocked a sympathetic eye. 'Maybe letting her out will give him a jolt.'

'That's what Mr Porson said.'

'Give that man a coconut,' said Nicholls. 'You going to do him now?'

'Might as well,' said Slider. 'Strike while the iron's flat, and all that. Just pop in first, Nutty, and tell him his wife's out, will you. I'll give him five minutes to process the idea and then have a go.'

Slider had a cup of tea while he was waiting, which PC Detton brought him, along with a complimentary couple of custard creams that made him feel like visiting royalty. He was only halfway down the cup when Nicholls came back and said with a chuckle, 'It's working so far. He's tearing his hair. I got more words out of him than the rest of his stay put together, though seven eighths of them were profane. Five more minutes and he'll be chatty enough to – hullo! Here's one of your hounds.'

He broke off as McLaren came in from outside, shaking himself like a dog. It was still raining steadily, and he'd managed to get pretty wet on the dash from the car – his hair and the shoulders of his jacket were distinctly damp. He looked up, saw Slider, and news leapt to his eye. 'Guv!' he exclaimed.

'Result?' Slider suggested.

'Yeah,' said McLaren in a decrescendo of disappointment. 'We got him accounted for pretty much the whole afternoon. Between the Eagle and Child and the Red Lion, and in and out of

Paddy Power and Coral's, there's not more than ten–fifteen minutes to play with. Not enough fr'im to've got to Shepherd's Bush and back, even with his van, let alone on public transport.' He stood still, looking at Slider as if hoping he might produce some way to keep Kroll in the frame – a little-known West London wormhole, or an anomaly in the space-time continuum. Then he shrugged and pulled out his notebook. 'It's all here – the times and everything.'

Gascoyne came in behind him. 'Kroll's out of it, sir,' he said, spotting Slider. Unlike McLaren he seemed pleased – perhaps just because he had done a good job. He was not as personally involved in Kroll's suspectability as McLaren was.

'So I hear,' Slider said. 'All right. Go and write it up. You've done a good job.'

They departed, and Nicholls said, not without sympathy, 'I'll huff and I'll puff and I'll blow your house down.'

'Trouble is,' Slider said, 'in my experience, once one pile of bricks falls over, the others tumble too.' *What next?* he wondered. 'We'd better get on with releasing Kroll number two.'

He was in his office still ploughing through Kroll paperwork when Atherton strolled in and said, 'Head.'

Slider looked up. 'Not "guv"? Or "boss"?'

'As in Alistair. He's covered,' Atherton went on. 'On Tuesday he lunched at the Ivy with an arts minister, spent the afternoon in his office, got changed there and went to a fund-raising dinner where he was visible up on the platform until after eleven, at which point he went on to a club with a director of the Royal Opera House and the CEO of an engineering company. A good time was had by all – with the possible exception of a posse of young ladies who may only have had a lucrative time – until nearly three in the morning.'

'And then?'

Atherton shrugged. 'Presumably he went home. But unless Doc Cameron's very wrong about the time of death—'

'It's possible, but not probable,' Slider said. 'At least, not by that sort of margin.'

'I could try and track the rest of his movements,' Atherton said. 'Whatever taxi he got home, and whether his wife remembers him coming in, and so forth, but as it stands...'

'No, as you say, he's covered. Without some evidence against him we can't justify looking at him any further. It was just a wild hope.'

'I'm not sure which way you were hoping,' Atherton said. 'With Alistair Head being obviously unworthy of the goddess Diana – who, by the way, was at rehearsal all day and apparently dined at a friend's house with a fellow cast member and his wife. And again, unless you want the alibi checked and her traced after dinner—?'

'No,' said Slider, deep in thought. He roused himself. 'They're not going anywhere. If anything did come up to implicate them ... But at the moment, we've got nothing.'

'So it seems,' said Atherton. 'No Head/Chambers, and no Krolls.'

'Which leaves Crondace,' said Slider. Two piles of bricks down.

'Or person or persons unknown,' said Atherton.

Slider closed his eyes. 'By which you mean starting again from scratch. No, let's hope Crondace comes up and sets Mr Wetherspoon's heart a-fluttering.'

'He's not always wrong, you know,' Atherton comforted him. 'Let the gods smile on their own for once.'

It was that sort of Monday, when the gods had a hangover and were out to make everyone suffer for it. Slider had gone up to the canteen and was mechanically disposing of shepherd's pie and peas and reading his own notes of the case so far when Gascoyne came in and stood by the door scanning for him. Slider felt like crouching down and hiding, but it could conceivably be good news, couldn't it? He caught Gascoyne's eye and the lad hurried over.

'It's a message from Tower Hamlets, sir.' Not long out of uniform, he hadn't got sufficiently used to 'guv' for it to come out naturally. 'DI Athill wants you to call him back. Said to say they've found Crondace.'

'Where?'

'He didn't say, sir. I thought I'd better come up and tell you straight away, though.'

'I'll come,' Slider said, abandoning the shepherd's pie without regret. Anyone but Gascoyne would have found out a lot more, even if Athill had been unwilling, but he couldn't blame the lad. He was so honest and straightforward, at least Slider would never fear he'd leak.

Athill had a faint, flat northern accent and sounded middle-aged, and Slider, who could never talk to anyone on the phone without trying to picture them, mentally gave him a beard and a round, comforting face. Tony Haygarth could have played him.

'Oh, yes – thanks for ringing back,' Athill said. 'Well, we've found your Derek Crondace. I'm afraid it's not good news.'

'How's that?' Slider asked.

'He's dead.'

Mr Wetherspoon had done a bit of glad-handing with Tower Hamlets' Borough Commander, who had put pressure on Trevor Oxley's firm to get some bodies out in the field and trace this bastard before he became a real headache. Diligent enquiry established that no-one who might have expected to had seen him since the Saturday night in the Navigation; and further probing at the Navi had established that he had been extremely drunk when he left, and that it was his custom to squeeze his bulk through the adjacent gap in the fence and make his wambling way home along the canal towpath.

Trying to retrace his last known movements had led them to a vagrant who slept under the bridge where the road crossed the canal, who said he had not seen Crondace that evening.

'Of course, he's an alky, so we didn't think his word was worth much,' said Athill, 'but on the other hand he did know who Crondace was –

seen him on many occasions, even talked to him – and as he said he hadn't seen him since, we started to wonder. There's nowhere before the bridge anyone could leave the towpath, and a witness at the pub had definitely seen Crondace get through the fence and set off. There's no boat traffic along that cut, so short of some kind of alien abduction...' He paused sympathetically.

'Yes,' said Slider, seeing it all.

'Also,' Athill continued, 'Mrs Crondace made a complaint that nobody was taking her husband's disappearance seriously and threatened to go to the press. So we dragged the canal.'

'Right,' said Slider.

'It seems he'd fallen in and got himself tangled up with a loose piece of steel piling that was half off and bent over on the bottom. Got his trouser leg caught on a bolt, apparently, couldn't get himself free and drowned. Probably in the state he was it didn't take much. They haven't done the post-mortem yet – I thought I'd better let you know right away – but from what the forensic surgeon said the condition of the body's consistent with it being that Saturday night that he fell in. He was pretty bloated. In fact, the pressure of gases would probably have brought him up in a day or two anyway, without dragging for him. The divers said—' He paused. 'Well, he wasn't a pretty sight. He'd got no ID on him, but the key in his pocket fitted the front door to his flat, and his clothes match what he was wearing in the Navi, and given we were looking for him, and his size and everything – it all fits.'

'Yes,' said Slider. 'I'm sure you're right.'

'I'll let you have the full report when I get it, but it looks as though you can write him off.'

'Yes,' said Slider again. 'Thanks.' He remembered something. 'There was some bloodstained clothing in his flat?'

'That's right, a shirt and a towel. We're still waiting for the analysis on that,' said Athill, 'but he had a cut on his forehead, so it could have come from that. Apparently in the pub Saturday night he had a plaster over it, said he'd tripped over a paving stone Friday night on his way home. Said he was going to sue the council – boasting about it. More likely he was just drunk and fell over,' Athill added with a shrug in his voice, 'blood ran down on to his shirt and he staunched it with the towel. My betting is the analysis'll show it's his own blood, but I'll let you know when it comes back if it's anything else.'

'Thanks,' said Slider. 'But if he died on Saturday it doesn't matter to us. Well, good luck with informing the wife. From what I know she'll enjoy the drama to the best of her bent.'

'Won't be me,' Athill said philosophically. 'That's what delegation's for.'

And then there were none, Slider thought as he replaced the receiver. So now it was going to have to be the hard yards, leaflets and door-knocking and TV interviews, appealing to the public for witnesses who had seen anyone going into or coming out of the house; and sifting through the inevitable flood of misinformation, self-promotion and delusion for some nugget of truth that might be useful.

And if it wasn't Kroll or Crondace – or Head – who was it who hated him enough to kill him? Well, perhaps there were others of the Crondace mindset; or perhaps he had been involved in something they hadn't discovered yet. But only Kroll had made sense of the cheque-writing. If only Bygod had managed a few letters of the payee's name before getting whacked ... But life was never that easy.

At least he would have the pleasure of telling Mr Porson it wasn't Crondace, and imagining Mr Wetherspoon's reaction when he told him. Disappointing bosses was not good for the career, but it was *such* fun.

Atherton was unusually quiet in the car on the way to Soho. Slider, who was driving, glanced sideways at him, was about to ask what was up, and then hesitated. Cursed as he was with McLaren's information, he already knew more than he wanted about Atherton's private life. If he *hadn't* known about Jane Kellock, he wouldn't have asked, would he? He'd have just assumed Atherton was having a moody and left it at that.

Or would he? Wouldn't it be natural just to say, 'What's up?' to a colleague who was also a friend? He cursed McLaren anew – now he didn't even know what was natural any more. The traffic down Kensington Road congealed ahead at the lights, and when it halted him, he said casually, 'Everything all right?'

'Everything?' Atherton enquired unhelpfully.

Slider bit the bullet. 'With you and Emily.'

'Didn't it look all right?'

Slider took that as a warning off. 'Delicious meal, by the way,' he said. 'Thanks.'

Atherton sighed. 'I just—'

Slider's scalp prickled. He held his breath, but nothing else came. *Fine by me*, he thought. But then it wasn't. It was like waiting for the other shoe to drop. Anyway, it was no use saying to yourself that men didn't do this sort of thing when a friend seemed to be hurting. At last he said, 'You just what?'

Atherton took his time, selecting his words. 'I'm beginning to feel that I'm not right for this sort of thing. Living with someone. Permanency. Being with just the one woman for ever.' Slider made an encouraging noise. Atherton went on, 'It's never worked for me before, why should it work this time?'

'Because you love Emily?' Slider hazarded.

'Yes, but – is that enough?'

'Don't ask me,' Slider said, because he seemed to be doing just that. 'I've always been married. I've always wanted to be married. I never wanted to live alone.'

Atherton sighed again. 'You see, I think it's a matter of whether you're cut out for it or not. I *like* living alone. I like having the place to myself and doing what I want without having to worry if it's going to annoy someone else.'

Slider thought of Joanna's comment about a life of lonely promiscuity. Was this angst really because he just wanted to be able to have sex with lots of women? 'But what happens,' he tried tentatively, 'when you get old and company's hard to come by?'

Atherton snorted. 'Oh yes, that's a really good reason to get married – so you'll have a captive handmaid to wait on you when you get old and ugly.'

'I didn't mean that—'

'Yes, you did. Anyway –' he became serious again – 'I *do* like having Emily around, I *do* like being with her, I'm just not sure I want to be with her all the time, without the option.' He shrugged. 'You've only got to look at how the average marriage pans out. I don't want that to happen to us. There's nothing like constant exposure to someone to dim the magic.'

Slider thought of Joanna. Sometimes it just got better and better. And he loved the intimacy most of all. The thought of having to start again from scratch with someone else appalled him. He wouldn't last five minutes in Atherton's trousers. He had never understood the thrill of the chase – not where women were concerned, anyway. The thrill of tracking down a criminal, yes, but when he went home at the end of the weary day, what he really wanted was exactly that – home.

But he had always felt that way, even when he was a young Turk. How sad was that? 'I must be light on machismo,' he muttered.

'You?' Atherton said. 'No chance. You're the original alpha male, my ol' guv'nor. You're the testosterone king, the silverback who rules the tribe with the fist of iron in the velvet glove. You're—'

'Enough!' Slider protested. 'I get the point: I

shall remove my nose from your business forthwith.'

They drove in silence for a bit, but then Atherton said, 'Trouble is I don't want to lose her.'

Slider hesitated a block or two, but then said lightly, 'Seems to me Emily's perfect for you, given how much of the time she's going to be away. Long absences and blissful reunions. Like a lighthouse keeper.'

Atherton grunted in amused response, and Slider left it at that. It was what happened in the long absences, of course – how the keeper dealt with the mermaids thronging the sea around the lighthouse.

La Florida in Wardour Street was one of those strange, dim restaurants that survives by having been in the same place for so long that no-one notices any more how dingy it is. Slider had telephoned his old friend Det Sup John Lillicrap, who had worked drugs in Soho for years and knew the place inside out, to ask him about it.

'Respectable,' Lillicrap had said. 'Never had any trouble with them. Bit of an institution with the locals.'

It was always a surprise to outsiders that Soho *had* locals. It seemed to the superficial glance such an obvious tourist place that it was hard to imagine people actually living there, but they did – and not only prostitutes, either. A vast army of ordinary working people inhabited the council blocks and housing-association buildings hidden in the courts and down the side streets behind the brash façade, and the multitude of flats and bedsits above the street level shops, clubs and restaurants.

'Does a lot of lunchtime trade with office workers,' Lillicrap went on, 'and evenings the locals mix with the tourists looking for a cheap meal.'

'Is the food not good?' Slider asked, because this did not seem to fit in with Bygod's reputation.

'Oh, it's good all right, but not fancy. Bit of a mixture – mostly Italian and Spanish but with a couple of Greek dishes thrown in, and there's generally a curry or two – all home-made. It's owned and run by a Turkish family.'

Of course, Slider thought. Who would run an Italian-Spanish-Greek-Indian restaurant in London but a Turkish family?

'Chap called Ali Berrak,' Lillicrap went on, 'with his wife Ferahna, two daughters, a son-in-law, and I don't know how many cousins and nephews and nieces. They come and go. Ali's getting on a bit now, so I don't know how much cooking he still does, but he likes to sit in there and chew the fat with the customers.'

Chew the fat? Slider cancelled tentative plans to eat there.

'What's the joke, anyway?' Lillicrap asked. 'What's your interest?'

'Trying to trace the movements of a murder victim. He lunched there on his last day with someone. So this Berrak's reliable, is he?'

'He's honest,' Lillicrap said. 'I don't know how reliable he is. Depends what you ask him, I suspect.'

'Right, thanks. I'll take my chances,' Slider said.

So he left the rest of the team to their toils – trying to trace taxi-drivers who had transported Bygod, solicitors who had known him professionally, members of the public who had witnessed his murderer arriving or leaving – called Atherton and set off for his old stamping-ground. He had started as a young constable in Central, and always returned there with that mixture of familiarity and surprise that so much was the same and so much had changed.

The La Florida was shabby, with a hand-painted fascia with the name in loopy pink writing and a stylized sun and moon to either side; there were red gingham half curtains across the bottom of the windows, menus and printed sheets about specials obscuring much of the top half; and a neon palm tree, in pink, green and yellow, flashing on and off in the glass door above the word OPEN. Inside, the low ceiling and half-covered windows made it dark, though by the time Slider and Atherton arrived it was open for business and at least half the tables were occupied. They had red gingham cloths over them, and candles stuck in Chianti bottles for evening illumination – which could have been a tongue-in-cheek glance at retro, but Slider suspected they were simply still there from the first time round. The candles were not lit now, and instead the inadequate lighting came from wall sconces with candle-shaped bulbs.

There was an appetizing smell of food in the air, and the lunchers looked like office workers, the young noisily chatting in pairs and groups, older businessmen in suits talking seriously, singletons with tablets or mobile phones to occupy them. An old, squat, nut-faced man with long but thinning hair dyed aggressively black was sitting at the bar, in a worn grey suit with no tie, and nursing what looked like a glass of pastis. He clocked Slider and Atherton at once with professional eyes, black and noticing between half-closed lids, and before anyone else had had a chance to approach them he had caught a passing waiter by the arm and despatched him to bring them to him.

'My friend! My friends!' the old man exclaimed with expansive insincerity, shaking their hands like a G-man doing a lightning pat-down. Slider wanted to count his fingers. 'Come, sit down, sit down, have a drink with me! What will it be? A glass of raki – just right for this time of day. Stimulates the appetite, readies the stomach. Two glasses of raki for my friends,' he commanded the watchful youth behind the bar. 'Sit, sit, you making the place look untidy!'

He smiled, showing several gold teeth in what was otherwise a menacing display. The boy slapped two tumblers of clear liquid and a small flask of chilled water down, followed by a bowl of olives, and removed himself to the other end of the bar.

'Mr Berrak?' Slider asked, though he knew the answer.

'Of course! And welcome to my humble restaurant. You will honour me by eating lunch here – at my expense of course.'

'Thank you – you're very kind – but we aren't here to eat.'

Berrak shrugged, sipped his raki, and gave them a stripping-down sort of look, without even the semblance of bonhomie. 'What is this about?' he asked in a low voice. 'This morning enquiries about a customer. Now you here with more enquiries in your eyes. I begin to feel persecuted. I run an honest business here – and you are not my local police friends.'

Slider tried to look disarming. 'I promise you we're not here to make trouble. And Mr Lillicrap has already told me I can trust you absolutely.'

The smile was back. 'Ah, my friend Mr Lillicrap! How is he? A long time since he has eaten here. He likes my duck curry. He likes it very much.'

'Yes, he told me it was excellent,' Slider lied. 'I wanted to ask you some more questions about the man who lunched here last Tuesday, Mr Bygod.'

'Already I told the young lady all I know. He booked the table. He came. He ate. He went. What more do you want?'

'I'd like to know something about the person he met here.'

Berrak shrugged. 'I don't remember. I don't remember him, okay? I get the name from the book, the time from the receipt. I don't know him, never seen him before, so I don't remember him.' He waved a hand. 'So many customers, can I remember everyone who comes in?'

I bet you do, though, Slider thought. He smiled. 'Of course, I'm sure you can't. But perhaps the waiter who served him can help me? I wouldn't trouble you, but it is very important.'

'How should I know who served him?' Berrak objected.

'It will be on the till slip, won't it?' Slider said pleasantly. The till, he could see, was a modern electronic one, the sort on which the bills were made up with a table number and the waiter's name in case of disputes. 'Or I could ask around your staff, if you prefer,' he added, knowing that Berrak would hate that. It would be too obvious to the punters that something was wrong. He gave Slider a scorching look, then addressed a rapid flood of Turkish to the boy behind the bar, who replied, received some instruction, and went away.

'His name is Mesud. I bring him to you,' Berrak said. 'Please sit here, drink your drink, try to look like customers, be discreet when you talk to him. He is a good boy. He is my sister's grandson so I know this. Do not upset him.'

'I've no wish to upset anyone,' Slider said.

Berrak sighed and heaved himself off the stool to make way for a slender youth who had come out from the back and who, at a barked command from the boss, perched himself resignedly, facing Slider. He was olive skinned and dark-haired with full lips, luscious black eyes and long eyelashes like a gazelle's. Close to, he was not as young as his slenderness had at first implied – he looked closer to thirty than twenty. Berrak gave him one further instruction in Turkish and went away to schmooze the tables, perhaps to turn attention from what was happening at the bar. Slider took one quick glance around and was sure that no-one was interested – had not, indeed, even realized that the police were present. Professionals like Berrak often forgot the numbing indifference of the average punter to anything but his own concerns.

'Now then, Mesud – that is your name?' Slider said, hoping that he spoke English and wasn't part of a devilish plot to make him look foolish.

But he said, 'That's right,' in an ordinary London accent. 'It's about the old bloke who had lunch here last Tuesday, is it? Uncle Ali said you lot was asking about him. I dunno if there's anything I can tell you. I didn't know him. I only knew the name from the reservations book.'

'Lionel Bygod was his name,' Slider confirmed. 'Had you seen him in here before?'

'No, not that I remember. I mean, we get hundreds through here. He wasn't a regular, anyway.'

'All right, tell me what you do remember.'

'Well,' said Mesud, frowning, 'he got here early, I remember that. He'd booked for half twelve, and it was only about quarter past, and he said was it all right to sit down and wait. Ever so polite. Lovely voice, he had, too – kind of rich, you know? Posh accent. Well, I showed him to his table – it was still quiet. The big rush starts half twelve. Well, he sat down and I offered him a drink and he said he'd wait for his guest to arrive, so I gave him a menu and left him alone.'

'How did he seem?'

'Seem?'

'Happy, sad, worried?'

Mesud shrugged. 'I dunno. He was just old. And polite, like I said.'

'All right. So he waited, and his guest eventually arrived?'

'Yeah,' he said, and some emotion flickered across his face. He lowered his voice. 'It was a lady.'

'Can you describe her?'

He glanced around conspiratorially, and lowered his voice still further, leaning in towards Slider. 'Well, I say it was a lady. She was – *big boned*, if you get my drift.' He sat back, and gave them a significant nod.

Ah, thought Slider, catching Atherton's quick glance with a strange mixture of satisfaction and disappointment. *So the lady was in fact a man.*

SIXTEEN

Trannyshock

'How do you know?' said Slider.

Mesud gave him an almost hurt look. 'Oh, come on!' he muttered. Another furtive glance. 'Look, you can't let Uncle Ali know.'

'Know what?'

'Anything I tell you,' Mesud said with a hunted air. 'He's well old-fashioned – you know what I'm saying?'

'Fine,' said Slider, 'but you haven't told us anything yet. Mr Bygod was with a lady who wasn't a lady. Can you describe her?'

'Tall. Skinny. Maybe my age – maybe more. It's hard to tell under the make-up, you know? Not old, though – not old like him. Very good wig – looked like real hair. Quite good style – nothing overdone. She could have passed most places, long as the light wasn't too good. Maybe that's why they chose this place – it's dark in the daytime, like you see. But I was in a quake in case Uncle Ali clocked her. He's not into that stuff – calls it ungodly. I mean, dinosaur or what? And he can be rude to people. That's why I made sure to serve 'em.'

'How friendly do you think they were? How

did they behave towards each other?'

He frowned again. 'Well, it's hard to say. It was a bit like a first date, to my mind. They were a bit nervous and stiff with each other. Not like they knew each other well. But it was...' He paused, thinking. 'I dunno. *Not* like a date. Different.' Another pause. 'But she was professional. I don't get it.'

'How do you mean, professional?'

'The make-up, the wig, the clothes – it was all put on right. Like I said, she could have passed, a lot of places.'

'Did you hear Mr Bygod use a name?'

He shook his head.

'Did you hear anything of what they were talking about?'

'No. They stopped when I came to the table. It wasn't a lot of laughs, though.' His face cleared. 'That was it. I said it wasn't like a date: she wasn't flirting with him, or trying to get off with him. It was more like – serious stuff. Like business.'

Slider pondered this. It didn't seem to get them much further forward, except to cast suspicions once again on Bygod's proclivities. 'Have you seen the lady before?' he asked. 'Or since?'

'She's not been in here before,' he said. 'But I think I know where she works. There's this club, down towards the corner of Brewer Street, the Gaiety. Tranny club, drag acts and so on. I go past it on my way to work from the station, and there's this poster of one of the acts, looks a bit like her.' He shrugged. 'I can't get too close and look properly in case anyone sees me. Everyone round here knows my uncle, they'd tell him like a shot if I was seen looking at a place like that. I got to be careful. Half the people in Soho are my cousins.' He gave a furtive sideways look under his eyelashes. 'He's looking at me now,' he said without moving his lips. 'Wondering what I'm telling you. Don't let on,' he pleaded. 'Make out I've not told you nothing.'

Slider gave a tiny nod, and seeing Berrak surging towards them, said aloud, 'Well, thank you for your time, anyway. If you *do* think of anything that might help us, give us a ring.'

Mesud gave a sulky sort of nod and made his escape, though not without a look from his uncle searing enough to have stripped wallpaper.

'Did you get what you want? Did he help you?' Berrak asked with his gold-studded shark's smile.

'I'm afraid it looks like another dead end,' Slider said, 'but thank you for letting us ask. If anything occurs to you about Mr Bygod's visit here, anything at all, please let us know. The smallest thing might help.'

Berrak answered with a bow. He swivelled on his small feet, hidden away down there under the swell of his overhang like the point of a spinning top, and ushered them towards the door. 'Glad to help, glad to help. Come back any time. Come back and eat. Bring your friends. Always glad to see you.' The words had as much meaning as birdsong – it was just the sound he made.

The rain had stopped at last. The clouds were still wet-looking and dark grey, but they were becoming ragged, and even as they stepped out a shaft of sunlight poked its way through a gap and bounced blindingly off the wet pavement. Water was dripping fast off every edge and vertical surface and the cars were still making that swishing noise as they passed, but everything looked instantly more hopeful in the brighter light.

'So,' said Atherton, 'what was old Lionel doing with a drag queen? He was hanging out with the alternative culture after all – and I thought he'd done with all that.'

'Maybe his lunch companion was asking his legal advice,' Slider suggested. 'Mesud said it looked like business.'

'Then why was he/she in full fig?' Atherton asked.

'Well, I don't know,' Slider retorted. 'Let's go and find out.'

The Gaiety – 'Cute name,' said Atherton – looked like any other seedy club in the area: a ground-floor open foyer with an island box office, like an old-fashioned cinema, and beyond it the entrance to the stairs down to the cellar level guarded by a steel let-down gate. The neon sign on the street over the foyer was lit, the words Gaiety and Nitely separated by a cancan girl whose kicking leg went up and down – an illusion rather spoiled by daylight since you could see all three of her legs quite clearly.

On the foyer walls were glass-fronted cases containing posters for the various acts, and below the window of the box office was a bill which shouted in bold black capitals:

KITSCH CABARET!
BURLESQUE!
TOP DRAG ACTS!
TRANNY HEAVEN!

'Just in case you didn't get it,' Atherton mentioned. He moved about, looking at some of the glazed posters of the stars. 'I'm not reassured. There's one here called Eva Brawn. And the emcee's name is Hugh Janus. Subtle, or what?'

'Why should they have to be subtle?' Slider said reasonably.

'Or, my God, maybe it's his real name!'

'Settle down,' said Slider. He was inspecting one that was on the street façade, to the right of the entrance, one that Mesud might have been able to see in passing. 'I wonder if this is it? "Danielle LaMartine, the Parisian Songbird". What d'you think?'

'I think I want to go home.'

'Stop whining. We're going in.' He had noted a security camera high up inside the foyer which had turned to look at them, so he stepped up to it and held up his warrant card. A few minutes later a concealed door in the side wall opened and a man came out. He was in formal black trousers but his white shirt was open at the neck and had its sleeves rolled up, indicating he was still off duty – the first show, Slider had noted from the box office was not until three.

'Can I help you?' the man asked, with the complete lack of servility you can afford when you're eleven feet tall and so wide they could show movies on your back. His head was shaved, his arms were lavishly tattooed with dripping fangs of one sort or another, and his face was as bumpy as a sack full of knuckles – which was probably what it had been pounded with over the years.

Slider pulled himself up to his full, unimpressive height and projected all the silverback alpha-ness at his command. 'It's not trouble,' he promised. 'We're looking for social contacts of this man.' He offered their printout of a photograph of Bygod, and held it insistently until the man took it and looked at it. 'We think he may have come here, or visited someone from your show.'

'Maybe,' the man grunted, shoving the photo back. Slider's scalp thrilled. This was as good as, 'Yes, he did,' from the likes of Knuckles, here. It was a positive lead at last. He felt Atherton stir with interest beside him.

'Was he a regular?' Slider asked.

Knuckles shrugged. 'Coupla times, last week. Never seen him before that. What's he done?'

'Nothing,' Slider said reassuringly. 'Just trying to find people who knew him. It's a matter of an inheritance. Did he come to see anyone in particular?' The eyes, grey and flat as smoothing-irons, regarded Slider with faint amusement at this suggestion that he would answer questions to which Slider did not already know the answer. So Slider added, 'We think perhaps he was interested in Danielle LaMartine.'

'What our acts do in their spare time is their

own business,' he said, which again was his equivalent of a 'yes'.

'We'd like to talk to her,' Slider said firmly, to let him know this was not a request but an order. 'Can you give us her address?'

Knuckles shrugged. 'She'll be back here later for her act. You can wait till then.' Routine stalling.

'I'd sooner talk to her somewhere quiet.' Which meant: 'Do it – now!'

Knuckles looked away indifferently down the street and seemed to speak without moving his lips. 'Flat in Old Compton Street, over the coffee store. Red door.'

'Thanks,' said Slider, with a feeling of relief that it was somewhere close by. Travelling out to a suburb only to find their quarry had been travelling in at the same time was an all too frequent annoyance. He started away, to be halted by a slight clearing of the throat from behind him. He looked back, to see Knuckles sporting a faint air of unease, which must have been pretty damn' surprised to find itself there. Slider raised his eyebrows in enquiry.

'He's all right, Danny,' Knuckles said, profoundly embarrassed to be professing such a soft emotion.

'I don't mean him any harm,' Slider said kindly. When they were out of sight down the street, he said to Atherton, 'Interesting that he reverted to "he" instead of "she". I wonder what that means.'

'That he likes him, perhaps,' said Atherton.

'I think saying, "He's all right," suggested that.

But likes him how? Why?'

'I thought you were giving up rhetorical questions. The important thing is that he obviously expects Mademoiselle LaMartine to be at home. Which means less wasted time for us.'

Old Compton Street was literally round the corner, and they were there in front of the coffee merchant's in no time. The terrace here had three storeys above the shops. The proportions and the original sash windows were eighteenth century, but the beautiful grey-brown brick had been painted white, alas, to make it uniform with the concrete new-build further down. While Slider mourned, Atherton was examining the red door and its buttons. The top one was labelled simply 'Danny'.

'Here goes,' he said.

After a long wait, the intercom crackled. Atherton leaned in and enunciated clearly. 'Danny LaMartine? It's the police. We'd like to talk to you about something. It's not trouble for you. Just a routine enquiry.'

There was another crackle, which might or might not have been a human voice answering. They waited, and Atherton was just preparing to ring again when the door opened cautiously, and a face peered out. They both held up their warrant cards.

'Sorry,' said the face. 'The buzzer's not working and it's a long way down. What's it about?'

'We'd like a chat with you,' Slider said. 'Nothing to be alarmed about.'

Eyes scanned his face and were apparently

reassured. 'D'you want to come up? It's a bit of a climb.'

'Yes, please,' Slider said firmly.

The door opened fully and revealed a tall, skinny man in his thirties, wearing black sweat pants and a baggy blue T-shirt decorated with the Pasche 'Tongue and Lip' icon in scarlet, framed by the words 'Stones' and 'Fifty Years'. His feet were bare and his toenails were painted with cherry gloss. He had the slight stoop of the shy, tall man, and looked at them with victim's blue eyes, around which there were traces of last night's make-up. His hair was toffee-fair, short, thick and tousled; his thin face had high cheekbones and a distinguished nose, with rather full, soft lips. There was nothing particularly effeminate about it, but Slider could see how he could transform quite successfully into a woman.

He let them in to a narrow hall with stairs going steeply up. Slider laid his hand on the banister and felt the glorious patina of the old Georgian wood, thinking it was probably all that was left of the original building except for some of the walls. Alas again.

'Sorry, it's quite a climb,' the young man said again. 'You might need oxygen at the top.' It sounded like a routine pleasantry: he moved easily, lithe as a dancer, but Slider felt the pull of gravity and his unexercised lungs.

They passed two landings with closed, panelled doors to other dwellings, but at the top there was barely any landing and only one door, propped open with a wooden doorstop in the shape of a cat. 'Here we are. The eagle's nest. Please come in.'

His voice was educated, soft and musical, but with just the faintest camp intonation that was probably part of the profession. They followed him into a cramped passage with, to the right, a door open on to a tiny bathroom, in front a door-less tiny kitchen, and to the left, at the end of the passage, daylight. He led them towards it, and they found themselves in a tiny bedroom/sitting room, with two sash windows on to the street, and a fireplace with an electric two-bar heater in it. It contained an iron bedstead, a cheap two-seater sofa, a coffee table and a television on a stand. There wasn't room for anything else. Slider wondered where he kept his clothes. There were books along the mantelpiece, and on the walls were vintage movie posters – *Casablanca*, *Phaedra*, *The Maltese Falcon*.

'Please, do sit down,' the man said, gesturing to the sofa. He sat down on the edge of the bed, there being nowhere else. He hunched his shoulders and clasped his hands between his knees – a boyish pose, though it probably spoke more of unease.

'I want to assure you first we're not here to make trouble for you,' Slider said.

The man nodded, the blue eyes remaining wary.

'Your name – is it really Danny LaMartine?'

'Danielle LaMartine's my stage name,' he said, 'but I was Christened Daniel. You can call me Danny.'

'And do you know this man?' Slider handed

over the picture. Danny looked at it for a long time, his head lowered to hide his face. 'Did you have lunch with him last Tuesday,' Slider went on gently, 'at the La Florida?'

'Yes,' said Danny. He looked up, keeping hold of the picture rather than giving it back, which was unusual. He looked from Slider to Atherton and back again, his expression puzzled and a bit anxious. 'But why are you here? What's this about? Has something happened?'

'I'm very sorry to have to tell you that he's dead,' said Slider.

The blue eyes filled with tears, the lips quivered, but he remained looking at them steadily, even straightened his shoulders a little, as if facing justice. He nodded. 'I see,' he said.

Atherton stirred. 'You don't seem surprised.'

'He told me—' Swallow. 'He said it wouldn't be long. I thought I'd see him again, though. I thought—' Now he squeezed his eyes shut, and two tears, forced out, tracked slowly down his cheeks. 'We wasted so much time,' he said in a gaspy voice, trying not to cry. 'If only – we'd met – sooner.'

'How long have you known Lionel Bygod?' Slider asked, through a suspicion that was working its way to the surface.

The eyes opened, swimming with tears, and a quavery smile quirked his lips. 'All my life, I suppose,' he said. 'He's my dad.'

Slider made the judgement, conveyed to Atherton by a look, not to tell him right then that the death was not due to natural causes. He seemed ready to talk, and here was the chance, he felt, to clear up a lot of puzzles, a chance which might be lost in the bewilderment and shock that would follow the revelation of murder. There was no guile in the face to suggest he knew anything about the death. In fact, it was a face of great sweetness. Slider remembered Diana Chambers using that epithet about Lionel – not a word generally applied to a man, and having the more force for that.

'I didn't know he had a son,' Slider said.

'For a long time, if you'd asked him, he probably would have said he didn't.' A look of bitterness. 'I shouldn't have left it so long. I wish I'd come back sooner. If I'd known then what I know now ... It was my mum, really, more than Dad in the beginning, but he went along with it. I suppose – well, it was shock as much as anything. I can see that now, but at the time...' He gave a quavery smile. 'There were faults on both sides. I was as pig-headed as Mum in my own way. Everything had to be the way I wanted it.'

'Tell me,' Slider invited.

There had been tensions in the small family for a long time. June's ambitions and desires were different from Lionel's, as were her tastes, and as their divisions grew they each, perhaps unconsciously, tried to recruit Danny as an ally.

'Mum wanted me to go into the law and make lots of money,' Danny said, 'and I suppose Dad did too at first, but I wasn't brainy enough. After a bit he realized that and stopped pushing me, but Mum never did. And then when I said I wanted to be an actor, he was all right with it, because he loved the theatre, but Mum hated the whole idea, and blamed Dad for "infecting me" with the acting bug.'

Unhappily, he told of the other strains between his parents that he had hardly understood at the time. June had wanted more children, but none had been forthcoming, for which she had blamed Lionel. Gradually, the idea had sunk into her brain that he was lacking in sufficient manly force to quicken her; and perhaps some vague notion, garnered subliminally, that effeminacy was endemic in theatreland, made her equate his kindliness and his interest in theatre with latent homosexuality.

'She had an old-fashioned hatred of "queers", anyway,' Danny said, his hands clasped between his knees again. Slider saw it was a defensive pose. 'I mean, there are a lot of people like that, even now. The difference is, they won't say it openly now, but they still think that way. Mum didn't mind admitting it. And she used it as a stick to beat Dad with.'

'Do you think she really believed he was that way inclined?' Slider asked out of interest.

He frowned. 'I'm not sure. I don't think she did at first. It was just something to shout at him. Later – well, I don't know. I wasn't around to see, but from what he told me, I think she probably believed the whole ball of wax.'

The crisis came when he was eighteen. 'They were planning a big party for me, for my majority. Mum was in raptures about it – it was going to be huge. She loved that sort of thing. She was even willing to get Dad to ask some showbiz celebrities for the sake of the splash it would make. Well, anyway, as the date approached I thought—' He paused. 'I mean, at this distance it looks cruel, like the worst possible timing, but you see, I couldn't bear to let them go on with the party without knowing. I *had* to tell them before they spent all that money. I mean, it would have been worse afterwards, wouldn't it? They'd have felt – cheated.' He looked an appeal, but got no answer from either man. He looked down. 'So I told them. Two days before the party I came out to them.'

Slider was contemplating the impact that would have made, and the courage needed to face the music. Atherton asked, 'How long had you known?'

'I don't know – a long time. Certainly since I was thirteen or fourteen. I'd had a lot of girl *friends* – I always got on with girls – but I was never interested in them in that way. And I suppose gradually I realized it was boys I wanted. I had one or two experiences – very minor, just fumblings, really – and when I got to eighteen I thought, I'm never going to find other people like me, never going to find love and a life on my own terms if I don't tell them, come out into the open. And then this horrible party was looming and it was the spur I needed to get it done.'

'And they didn't take it well?' Atherton asked.

He shuddered. 'Understatement. Mum went raving mad.'

'And your father?'

He frowned in thought. 'Well, he didn't rave –

that wasn't his way – but I could tell he was shocked. I suppose any father would be. He didn't say anything, really. He went very quiet, but he couldn't meet my eyes. I hated that. He tried to calm Mum down, but – well, he'd never quarrelled with her in front of me. He was very loyal. So he wouldn't say much. What I mean is, he tried to keep the peace, but he didn't defend me. And I felt he should have.' He shrugged. 'To be fair, I didn't give him much of a chance to come round. I didn't want to stay in a place where they were ashamed of me. So two days later, on my birthday, I left. I just took off, cut myself off from them, and never went back.'

'Where did you go?'

'Liverpool first. As far as I knew they didn't know anyone from there, and I thought it would be the last place they'd look for me – if they *did* look for me. And there was a young scene there. I had my savings, I got myself a job as a barman, and I hung around the Playhouse and the Everyman. Then I got a job waiting tables in the Everyman Bistro and got to know everybody and – well – finally I got a part. I took the stage name Danny Martin. Martin's my second name. It was a great time for me. I was out, I was acting – I'd got everything I ever wanted.'

He had also got a lover, an older actor who took him under his wing, taught him, introduced him, set his feet on a career path. However, he was a lot older than Danny, and it didn't last: the usual spats and jealousies soon led to a break-up. Danny by then felt confident enough to stand on his own, and a move seemed a good idea, so he went to Manchester, got some rep work there, and found a new lover.

'It was hard to make a living, though, and eventually Steve and I decided to try Australia. I had nothing to stay in England for. I did think about contacting my parents before I left, but I thought they wouldn't really care, so I just went.'

In Sydney the burlesque scene was really taking off. Drag acts, following the success of *Priscilla, Queen of the Desert*, were all the rage, and Danny discovered he had a talent for that sort of thing that would be likely to earn him a better living than straight theatre.

'And it has,' he said. 'I've not made a fortune but I've got by all right.'

He moved on from Steve, but made other friends, and had quite a following in the burlesque world. He was happy. Then about a year ago the death of his partner of five years had left him feeling restless and a bit lost. He'd decided to come back to London. He'd got a cabaret job easily enough, and this little flat; and, lonely, had started to wonder about his parents, particularly his father, whom he had always felt had more sympathy for him than his mother.

'By then I felt sure that he'd have come round eventually if I'd given him the chance. I wasn't so sure about Mum, but I'd always felt closer to Dad. In any case, it was a long time ago, and attitudes have changed a lot. So I decided to get in touch and see what happened.'

'How did you find him?' Slider asked.

'Well, it wasn't easy. I didn't know at the time,

but he'd given up his practice and sort of gone into hiding, and Mum had remarried and moved. I couldn't find either of them, and after a bit I was sort of in despair about it. And just as I was thinking of giving it up, I saw him.'

It wasn't as much of a coincidence as it might have seemed. Living as he was in the heart of theatreland, he had taken to going to see plays again, rekindling his love of the legitimate stage. He had been queuing for the box office at the Gielgud to get a ticket for Diana Chambers in *Hay Fever* when he had seen Miss Chambers herself heading down to the stage door accompanied by a tall, distinguished figure who was unmistakably his father. He had abandoned the queue and followed. They had gone in by the time he got there, but he asked the stage doorkeeper if that had indeed been Lionel Bygod with Miss Chambers.

'Well, of course, I know how to get talking to backstage people,' Danny said. 'He didn't mind telling me it *was* Dad, said he knew everybody and was often there, so I asked if he would give him a note next time he saw him. I didn't have paper and envelope, but I did have a handbill in my pocket from the Gaiety, with my picture on the front, and I thought I might as well take the bull by the horns, if there was ever going to be a chance of honesty between us. So I wrote on the back something like, "This is me. I'm sorry I ran away. I really want to see you again." And hoped for the best.'

Nothing happened for a bit. 'I thought they hadn't passed on my note. Then I thought he still didn't want to see me. Then I thought it was a bit feeble to give up after just one try, so I was going to write another note, a proper one, and take it down there. And that night when I was doing my set, I looked out and there he was. My father. Sitting at a table, watching me. It was the weirdest thing I've ever done, go through my Danielle LaMartine act with my dad watching. I don't know how I got through it. But at the end he applauded, and when I looked at him, he smiled and nodded. So I knew it was all right.'

SEVENTEEN

Reigning Men

He got up abruptly and walked to the window, his bony shoulders hunched, his fists stuffed in his pockets. The wet sky was like dirty dishrags. The traffic was slowing in afternoon density and there was no more swishing, but you could hear the engine sounds quite clearly. The window was large and single glazed, and Slider noticed there were no curtains. Living here you would not be separated from the world outside, any more than a pigeon on the window ledge.

'I shared a dressing room, I couldn't take him there,' Danny said. 'In the corridor between the loos and the fire exit – that's where I first talked to my dad. He cried. It was awful. I'd never seen him cry. He kept saying he was sorry – he was so, so sorry.'

He stopped. Slider said, 'Do you want to take a moment?'

Danny took out a handkerchief and blew his nose briskly, and turned back to them, his eyes a little pink now, his eyelashes endearingly wet. 'No, I'm all right.' He folded his arms across his chest, tucking his hands under armpits for comfort. 'I want to talk about it. There's no-one I can tell except you.'

'Go on, then,' Slider said encouragingly.

Danny took a breath and resumed. 'He said it was all his fault. He said he'd searched for me, gone all over London, the theatres and bars and the gay scene. That was brave of him,' he commented in parenthesis. 'But of course, he didn't know where I'd gone. He just assumed I'd have gone to ground in London.'

'People mostly do,' Slider agreed.

That night, after Danny's last set, they had gone to a gastropub nearby that stayed open late, and in the privacy conferred by the press and noise of a crowd of young people having an expensive good time, they had talked. 'We had so much to catch up on. I told him about my life, he told me about his.'

'Did he tell you about the Roxwell case?' Atherton asked.

Danny nodded solemnly. 'God, yes. That must have been awful for him. And it was because of me, in a way, that he took it in the first place. After I ran away, he started doing a lot more *pro bono* work, and especially defending people that everyone was against. He said it was a way of trying to make it up to me, because he should have stood up for me and he didn't. I understood, sort of. But I said to him, my life's been fine, you don't need to feel sorry for me. It's you that's suffered, really. I told him that I felt bad because all those years he must have been wondering if I was all right, and not knowing if I was alive or dead. He sort of nodded, and he took out his wallet and showed me a photo of me he had in there.'

Danny reached down and picked up something from the bedside cabinet and offered it to Slider. It was of a skinny, fair-haired boy of about ten in swimming trunks, grinning and sun-squinted, clutching a bucket and spade, with a blowy English beach for background.

'He gave it to you?' Slider said. It must have been the one Diana Chambers mentioned. So that was why they hadn't found it in his wallet.

Danny nodded. 'He said he didn't need it any more. It makes me want to cry to think he'd been carrying it around all these years.'

They'd talked until late, tentatively finding each other again. Bygod had told him of the worsening relations with June, how they'd split up, how she was now with a new man.

'Did you contact your mother?' Slider asked.

He shook his head. 'I thought about it, but Dad said she still feels the same about – you know, people like me. She hasn't softened at all. And he said the bloke she's with is a bit of a rough diamond, not the sort to welcome a gay tranny drag queen as a stepson. So I didn't. He says she's all right, she's happy in her way, so I reckon it's better to leave sleeping dogs lie, really.' He brooded a moment. 'We were never close. It was Dad I thought about all those years, him I missed. And reading between the lines, she's been pretty shitty to him, one way and another. I mean, leaving him in the middle of all that Roxwell business, just when he needed support the most...'

'Did he tell you about Diana Chambers?' Atherton asked.

Danny sat again on the edge of the bed, his hands under his thighs, and shook his hair back from his face. He looked like Princess Di, Atherton thought.

'Yes,' he said. 'But that was after he and Mum spilt up.'

'I didn't mean it as a criticism,' Atherton said. 'What did you think about it?'

'I thought, "Good old Dad!" He told me it had to be a big secret, because she's married to Al Head, the director. She never wanted a divorce, so there was no question of them getting married, but from the way he talked she's his big love. I'm glad for him. And of course she's a fantastic actress.'

This last obviously conferred extra kudos on his father. He had obviously forgotten, absorbed in his narrative, that his father was dead. His earlier words, *There's no-one I can tell except you*, revealed a loneliness that put this little room, which was really quite snug in its way, into a new light. He had come home to find his father, called from his new world by the pull of an older love, and what did he have now? A tiny room in the most indifferent city in the world, an underground job in the most transitory of professions, and all the life-building to do again, from the bottom. The effort, Slider thought, would sicken in prospect.

They had parted in the street after closing time, Danny seeing his father into a taxi before walking home. A couple of days later they had met again, this time Lionel coming in the late morning to his flat, where they had sat and talked until Danny was due at the club. The third meeting was again for a drink after work, though they hadn't spoken for long that time. Danny was tired, and Lionel had seemed a bit low, out of sorts.

'But when he was leaving, he said next time we met, he was taking me out to lunch. And he asked me to dress up – he said he wanted to walk into a restaurant with a beautiful woman on his arm.'

'How did you feel about that?' Slider asked.

Danny shrugged, with a faint smile. 'Oh, I didn't mind, really, though it was a bit weird, I mean, him being my dad and all. I think he was trying to show me he completely accepted me. You know, my life and my job and everything. He didn't need to – I knew he was all right with it. But he was so keen on it, said he wanted me to be the way I really was when I was with him, so I said okay rather than argue any more. So we made the date for Tuesday, at the La Florida. It had to be somewhere round here, because my first set was at half past three that day.'

Atherton sat up. 'So you're saying, when you met last Tuesday, that was only the fourth time you'd seen him?'

Danny nodded. He chewed his lip and his eyes filled with tears again. 'It's only been two weeks. All those years apart – and now he's gone! I thought we'd have – we'd have more time.' He fumbled out his handkerchief again.

Atherton gave Slider look that said, *Now do we tell him?* which Slider ignored.

'Tell me about that lunch,' he said.

Bygod had started out cheerful, almost light-hearted in manner, and had tried to charm Danny into a similar mood. But Danny, already feeling slightly awkward at being with his father in his women's clothes, sensed something in the wind, and the lunch had got off to a sticky start. A glass or two of wine, and the kind attentions of a very sloe-eyed waiter who had obviously clocked him, had relaxed him a little, upon which Bygod had said he had something to tell him.

'It's serious, but I don't want you to be sad about it, because I'm not,' he'd said.

Then he told Danny that he had cancer, and that there was nothing to be done about it. Danny had been stricken dumb at the news, but Bygod had gone on talking, talking, easing him through the first shock.

He said, 'Everyone has to die some time, and I'm not afraid. I've done everything I wanted to do with my life, and I'm just marking time now. I'm ready to go.'

Danny, trying not to cry, had said, 'But I'm not ready to let you go.'

And Bygod said, 'The only sad thing about it is that we've only just met again, and I'd have liked to have had more time with you. But we've a few months yet, and we'll make the most of them. We mustn't waste any of our time together regretting the past or being afraid of the future.'

The speech, Slider guessed, had been carefully chosen in advance, by a man who knew, personally and professionally, about the power of words. That Danny could now remember them and repeat them proved their worth.

Then he'd said that he had changed his will and was leaving the bulk of his estate to Danny.

'I said, "I don't want to hear about that," but he said, "You must. You may not care about money now, but you will some day." And then he asked me if I didn't have some pet ambition that money would help with.'

'And do you?' Slider asked.

He gave the faint, troubled smile again. 'As a matter of fact, I do. And telling him about it helped me to get through the next half hour without breaking down, which I suppose is why he asked.'

'What is it – your ambition?' Atherton asked.

'I'd like to open a place of my own, a club – but not round here, not in Soho, and not in a cellar. Maybe Earl's Court or Notting Hill, somewhere like that. A smart place where nice gay couples can come and eat and watch the cabaret, maybe dance.' He shrugged. 'I've been thinking about it for a long time, but of course there was no way in the world I'd ever get that sort of money together. But I used to have fun planning the acts and thinking how I'd decorate the place and so on. I know someone back in Sydney who'd come and be my chef...' There was almost a glow in his face as he thought about it. 'Dad got me talking about it, and when I finally ran down he said, "There you are, then. Money *is* worth having after all. You'll be able to make your dream come true." He said, "Maybe you'll call it Bygod's," and he smiled. And I said–' the tears welled again – 'I said it was a good name for a club.'

There was a pause while he mopped up. Then Slider said, 'So your father said he had actually made out the will? Or was he just talking about doing it?'

'No, he said he'd done it. He said he'd left something to Diana, and some bequests to charity, but most of it to me. He said when it was all done and dusted and the tax paid, I ought to end up with enough to set up my club – maybe one and a half million.' He shook his head. 'Of course, I've always known the old man had money, but I never realized it was that much.' He lapsed into a brooding silence.

Atherton broke it. 'Did he give you a copy of the will? Or did he tell you where he'd put it?'

Danny looked up. 'No. I never asked. I suppose he thought there was plenty of time – that's what I thought, anyway.' He frowned. 'Why are you asking me that?' The long-delayed suspicion caught up with him. 'I mean, not to be rude, but why are you here anyway? I wouldn't have thought it was the police's job to break this sort of news. Is something wrong?'

So the moment arrived, in which he had to be told. Since Atherton had been so eager for it, Slider let him be the one to tell. And he used the period of exclamation, explanation and tears to think through what he had learned.

They arranged for him to come to the station the next day to do next-of-kin things, but told him he did not have to identify the body, since Mrs Kroll had been able to do it. 'I'd like to see him, anyway,' Danny had said. 'I think I owe him that.'

'That can be arranged,' Slider said. 'And there should be no difficulty about releasing the body, so you can go ahead with the funeral.'

A grave look had settled on his face as he realized he was now responsible for such grown-up things. His long boyhood was finally over.

Outside, the slanting autumn sunshine was gilding the ragged edges of the clouds and the air was distinctly cooler. The golden part of autumn seemed to have passed.

'You shouldn't have told old Berrak it was a dead end,' Atherton said as they stepped into the street. 'Now it's gone and turned into one just to spite you.' They had asked Danny the usual questions, but he had not known of any enemies or fears Bygod might have had.

Slider found himself savagely hungry – they had not had any lunch in the end. 'Fancy a quick bite?' he asked. The good thing about Soho was that there were plenty of old-fashioned sandwich bars where you could get a freshly-made one and a cup of coffee, and sit on a high stool at the window and watch the world hurrying by.

When they were settled, Atherton sipped his coffee, took a bite of his ham and mustard, and said, 'Well, where does all that get us?'

'It clears up a few small questions,' Slider said, savaging his corned beef and tomato.

'And leaves the main one unanswered. It's a good thing he has an alibi, given he's the main beneficiary from the death.'

Slider said, 'I suppose we'll have to check with the club that he did actually go on that afternoon, but I have no doubts about him. What possible motive could he have?'

'Suppressed rage all these years towards the father who effectively turned him out,' Atherton said.

'What I was thinking,' Slider said, ignoring that, 'is that according to Diana Chambers, Lionel told her he *was going* to change his will, but he told Danny he *had changed* it. He saw Diana on the Thursday, and Danny the following Tuesday, which suggests he actually made the new will some time over that weekend.'

'Unless he was just being careless with his tenses,' said Atherton.

'He was a lawyer. I'd say he knew the importance of using words accurately. Anyway, assuming the will *was* actually drawn up between Friday and Tuesday—'

'I suppose he'd do it himself?'

'Can't see any reason why not. But he'd still have to find two people to witness his signature.'

'That could be anyone,' Atherton said.

'Indeed. But none of his friends said anything

about witnessing a will when they were asked about next-of-kin.'

'He could have got two people off the street.'

Slider made an equivocal face. 'Yes, and I know novels talk about people doing that, but I imagine it would be harder than it sounds. In real life, most people approached by a stranger on the street and asked to come into their house and witness a document would pin their ears back and scarper like hares. Anyway, I don't think Lionel would consider doing that. I think he'd want people he'd know would be around, at least for the next few months. People he knew.'

'So – what? You think he *didn't* make the will?'

'No, as I said, I don't think he'd have said he had if he hadn't. It's just a little puzzle.'

'The bigger puzzle is, where is it? The natural place for him to have put it was in that document safe, with a copy going to Danny, or whoever the executor was.'

'Yes, I wonder why he didn't give Danny a copy that Tuesday,' Slider said. 'Forgot, maybe. He had a lot on his mind. As to where it is now, the obvious conclusion is—'

'That the murderer took it. Which means (a) that he knew about it and (b) that getting rid of it was to his advantage,' Atherton said. 'But we don't know who the money was left to before. The ex-wife springs to mind.'

'But any will made while he was married to her would have been made invalid by the divorce,' said Slider.

'Maybe he made another will later leaving

everything to her.'

'But then where is it? No point in stealing the new will if the old one isn't there to be found.' He shook his head. He thought about what Joanna said: *Who wouldn't wait for the cheque? Someone who would get the money anyway*. But there'd be no getting the money without the will. 'It's a puzzle.'

'Well,' said Atherton, 'all we have to do is wait for someone to turn up brandishing the old will, and nab them.'

Slider gave a crooked smile. 'Mr Wetherspoon will be ecstatic about such a passive approach. Gives him so much to talk to the press about.'

Joanna had got home just before him from an afternoon recording session in Barnes. He found her in the kitchen reading a book at the kitchen table with George, who was in his jammies ready for bed, his hair brushed into gold silk feathers.

'Everything okay?' he asked, kissing the top of her head. 'You looked tired.' He looked critically at his son, who seemed as stout and rosy as a barrel of apples. 'Has the boy been a good boy? Dad gave him a good report, I hope?'

'Your dad,' Joanna said portentously, 'wants to speak to us.'

'What about?'

'He didn't say. He dropped George off when he heard me come in and said he'd come back when you were home. That's the "us" in "speak to us".'

'You're unusually snarky, my love,' Slider observed, sitting down beside her and taking

George from her. The child weighed a ton. 'What does Grandad feed you on?' he murmured. George regarded him drowsily and gave nothing away.

'I'm not snarky, I'm worried,' Joanna retorted. 'When someone wants a formal talk like that, you obviously start thinking of bad news. Like the withdrawal of babysitting privileges, perhaps.'

Slider shrugged. 'If that's what it is, we'll weather it. I've told you. We'll work something out.'

Joanna snorted. 'I was talking to some of the others at the break this afternoon about teaching, sounding out whether there's enough around and what it pays these days. Just in case.'

'That's a bit premature,' he said.

'They all rolled their eyes. From the orchestra to private teaching is a big step down.'

'Haven't you *ever* taught?'

'Oh yes, years ago, when I was first out of college and needed the dough. I had this kid, once, Damien – his mother thought he was a genius. He produced the worst noise you can make with catgut without the rest of the cat being present.'

Slider laughed, glad she had retained her sense of humour.

'I'm not kidding,' she went on, seeing he was enjoying it. 'They had this Jack Russell, used to sit outside the door and howl all the time he was playing. Damien's mother stuck her head in one day and said, "Couldn't you play something the dog doesn't know?"'

He patted her hand. 'That's better. Shall I put him to bed while you make us both a gin and tonic? I had a hard day too.'

'Oh dear, the middle-class resort to alcohol,' she said solemnly. 'It's a slippery slope, you know.'

Slider stood, hefting George up against his shoulder. He smelled of apples and sweetness. Slider thought of Lionel Bygod perhaps putting Danny to bed the same way, and ached for the love of fathers and sons, and the sorrow that is love's ultimate ransom.

'He's all bathed and everything,' Joanna's matter-of-fact voice called him back. 'Here, take the book.' When they reached the door she said, 'I've got four more recording sessions for next week. And Tony Whittam says the orchestra's in line for the new James Bond film. He's pretty sure we'll get it.'

'Jolly good,' Slider said. Wasn't it? Was she trying to remind him how much they would lose without a babysitter? Or was she just imparting glad tidings? He smiled back at her, and went out, stumped upstairs with his hundredweight of son, thinking about the new baby to come and how much more they'd need the money when it arrived. Joanna worried that she would not get the work after she had taken time off to have the baby, that her name would drop out of the fixers' minds for newer, fresher players. He hated the idea of their child coming into the world as a burden rather than a blessing; he worried that she was already doing too much, but knew that she would not slack off – the self-employed could never afford to say no; and he didn't want her to know that he was worried, in case that upset her.

'It's good to have problems like this at home to take your mind off your problems at work,' he informed George, who took the information silently but with a sage nod, his mind on Pooh and Piglet and events in Hundred Acre Wood.

Slider heard the distant sounds of his father arriving as he was tucking George in after the story. There seemed to be natural-sounding conversation going on; but of course, neither of them would ever be uncivilized. He kissed George, turned off the light, and went down to find everyone in the sitting room with gin-and-tonics. Everyone included Lydia, and his father was smiling so much it was a wonder his face didn't fall in half. It didn't take all Slider's detective skills to work out that it probably should have been champagne rather than G&Ts.

'I'm guessing congratulations are in order,' he said as he stepped in, receiving his glass from Joanna.

'That's right, son,' said Mr Slider. 'Lydia's done me the honour of saying she'll marry me. I don't know why, but I'm not asking, case she changes her mind.'

'That's wonderful,' Slider said. 'I'm so pleased for you.' He kissed Lydia, who kissed him back with new enthusiasm. She was small and solidly put together, like well-made furniture, with wiry, curly dark hair threaded artistically with grey, and careful make-up. He didn't know how old she was – younger than his father, certainly. It was odd to think of Dad kissing a new woman, sleeping with her – in the future if not already; and of course, why not, except that it was one's *father*, and parents always existed outside the bounds of sex. He turned his mind away from that contemplation. 'So, what are your plans?' He saw Joanna turn her face minutely towards him at the question. But might as well get it over with.

'A quiet wedding,' Lydia said. 'We're too old for a big fuss. Just something *nice* – family and a few friends.'

'We thought, some time next month,' Mr Slider said. 'So we can have a honeymoon and be back before Christmas.'

'Honeymoon where?' Slider asked.

'Oh, somewhere warm,' said Lydia. 'Not sure where *is* warm in November. Florida, maybe? I've never been to America.'

'And then,' Mr Slider said, looking from Slider to Joanna and back, 'if it's all right with you, we'd like to settle down here – in the flat, I mean. Lydia's got a house, but we've discussed it and we'd like to live in the flat, so as to be near you.'

'My son's in Devon and my daughter's in Canada,' Lydia added, 'so it would be nice to be near George's family if I can't be near mine.' She smiled at Mr Slider fondly. It was a shock to Slider to hear him called George again, for the first time since his mother died. Slider's name was George too – George William, but he'd always been called Bill to distinguish. So little George was the third generation.

'And that way,' Mr Slider went on, 'we'd be able to look after the children for you whenever you like.'

'My only grandchildren are in Canada,' Lydia said wistfully. 'I miss seeing them.'

'So that's what we thought,' Mr Slider concluded. 'If it's all right with you two.'

'If it's all right!' Slider exclaimed. He looked at Joanna and saw to his disconcertion that she was trying not to cry, so he spoke for them both. 'Of course it's all right! It's perfect! We'd like nothing better than to have you here. If you're sure the flat is big enough for two?'

Lydia laughed. 'You haven't seen my house – a little modern box. I had to get rid of all my nice furniture when I moved in – it just wouldn't fit. The rooms in the flat are so big in comparison. And there's the garden, too.'

'Anyway,' Mr Slider said with the ghost of a wink, 'we're only little people. We don't take up a lot o' room.'

Later, in bed, Slider said, 'So there's all your problems solved in one fell swoop. Now, if someone could only show me who killed Lionel Bygod and how to prove it, between us we'd be totally worry-free.'

'Wouldn't that be bland and boring?' Joanna said, nesting against his chest. 'A worry-free life?'

'I'll take it,' Slider said. 'Are you happy?'

'About your dad and Lydia? Very. She seems good for him.'

'But she's no pushover,' Slider said. 'I sense a

hint of steel inside that should keep his life interesting.'

'I hope it will sustain her when she's doing her share of babysitting,' Joanna murmured sleepily. 'I can't get over it – sitters on tap.'

'I told you we'd work something out.'

'"We"? I see the hand of Father Christmas in this. It's a miracle not of our making.'

'But we're such nice people, you see,' said Slider. 'If we weren't, they wouldn't want to live on top of us.'

'Underneath,' Joanna corrected, but she was asleep, really.

EIGHTEEN

A Mall and the Night Visitors

It was distinctly colder on Tuesday, with a high pale sky, strangely translucent, like onions cooked in chicken fat; and a brisk wind that found out every gap around door and window. Joanna hunched herself into a chunky sweater to get the breakfast. 'We'll have to think about putting the heating on,' she grumbled. George in his chair, crust in hand, waiting for his egg, looked impervious. He seemed to have his own inbuilt central heating and never felt the cold. He sang to himself and supplied his own rhythm section with the spoon.

Some days it was agony to drag yourself away from the knobbly normality of home and face a world in which the sane rules did not apply, in which people did unspeakable things, and so often for pitifully meagre reasons. Everything Slider had learned so far suggested Bygod was a nice, even an admirable man. He drove with his mind slipping loosely over words, images, impressions, half out of gear – often the best way to allow cells to bind together. The day let him through indifferently, as if watching events in some other part of town. He parked in the yard, scurried through the sharp wind into the building, and mounted to the familiar 1970s' ugliness of his office, his desk, and his pile of paperwork, where he sank gratefully below the surface as into a tepid but welcome bath.

Connolly was the first to disturb him, lounging in looking smart in a black cloth trouser suit over a lime green roll-neck. She had dangly earrings that looked like tiny bunches of green grapes. Slider stared at them blankly as his mind drifted back up.

'I've found the taxi that picked up your man on Tuesday after lunch, boss,' she said. 'Cruising black cab picked him up in Shaftesbury Avenue just before three o'clock. He musta walked straight down to Shafters after leaving the restaurant. Cabbie left him home to Shepherd's Bush, got there about quarter to four. So far no-one else has come forward to say they picked him up again that day, so...'

'It looks as though he was home between three forty-five and seven,' Slider said, picking it up.

'Gettin' whacked,' Connolly concluded. 'Narrows it down a bit, so.'

'It does. Better have another look at any CCTV footage we've got, refine it to those hours. I'll talk to Mr Porson later today about leaflets, now that we've got the time fixed a bit better.'

'Right, boss. Oh, and I got on to Melbury Cars in Ken High Street, and the last time he hired a car was the Sunday right before he died. He picked it up ten o'clock and brought it back seven in the evening with two hundred and thirty miles on the clock.'

Slider didn't know if he felt pleased or sorry. Now there was a whole lot more stuff to check, and who knew if it would yield anything as useful as a lead? Two hundred and thirty gave you a radius of about a hundred miles from the centre of London, which was a large world, and so full of a number of things. 'Run and get me the road atlas, will you?' he said. 'And pass the car's reg number to McLaren and Fathom, get them to start looking for it on the ANPR for Sunday.'

'Right, boss,' said Connolly.

'Oh, and ask Swilley to come in.'

'OK.'

'And see if you can rustle me up a cup of tea.'

Atherton came into his room just as he was trying to mark out a hundred mile radius on the atlas with a drawing-pin and a piece of string. Annoyingly, of course, he couldn't get it all on one page, except on the overview page, which didn't give any useful detail.

'Bit of a pointless exercise,' Atherton commented. 'Why not wait until you get a ping from the ANPR?'

'I just wanted an idea of where he *might* have gone,' Slider defended himself.

'He *might* have gone anywhere,' Atherton said, leaning to look over his shoulder.

'At least we can be sure he went *somewhere*,' Slider countered. Like anyone else who lived north of the river, he was looking to the north of London first – south always seemed a direction of bleakness and desperation. And – lookie here – what was around ninety miles directly north of London, straight up the A1? 'Stamford,' he said aloud. 'With Colleyweston, where he was born, just three or four miles to the west of it.'

Atherton looked. 'What are you suggesting?'

'He knew he was dying. He'd just seen his son and made his will.'

'We assume.'

'And it was a lovely day that Sunday – a lovely autumn day. Maybe he went for a nostalgic look around at the scenes of his youth – why not? Stamford's a fine old town. And it's pretty country. Green hills. The woods changing colour. A nice day out to say goodbye.'

'You're such a romantic,' Atherton said. 'Do not forget he met and married the lovely June, loyal spouse and the joy of his heart, in Stamford.'

'Yes, but given that Colleyweston is not a metropolitan hub, he probably had most of his youthful Saturday nights out in Stamford, too.

He probably had a lot of memories.'

'Might have had some friends in the area,' Atherton admitted. 'You could be right.'

'It's just an idea. Ask McLaren to look for the car in that area first. And try ringing round the pubs and restaurants. If he went that far, he probably ate somewhere up there.'

Atherton shrugged and turned to go, saying over his shoulder, 'If he paid cash, as was his usual method, they won't have any record of his name.'

'But he was a good tipper,' Slider pointed out, 'and they tend to be remembered.'

If Sinar Serhati was disconcerted by another appearance of the police at the Piazza, he didn't show it. He greeted Swilley with a white smile and a wide gesture of welcome, gestured her to a seat at the nearest table, and offered her coffee again.

'No, thanks,' she said. 'I've just got a few more questions to ask you. Won't take long.'

'For you, *bella signorina*—' he began gushingly, and then, catching her eye, broke off short, shrugged, and said, 'Sorry. Force of habit. But please, sit down, and tell me how I can help. I suppose you haven't found out yet who killed poor Mr Bygod?'

'We're getting there,' Swilley lied. 'Just need to clear a few things up. Now, you said the last time Mr Bygod was in here was on the Saturday before he died. He had lunch.'

'That's right.'

'Was he alone?'

'Yes, he often lunched alone on a Saturday. I think he liked having the time to himself. He'd have half a bottle of wine and some spaghetti and some olives. He said once it reminded him of Sorrento when he was young.' Serhati glanced round at his restaurant, and the greyness of Shepherd's Bush outside, and shrugged. 'He was a nice man,' he concluded.

'Okay.' Swilley nodded. 'Now, on that day, did he have any papers with him?'

'Papers?' Serhati prepared a negative, then clapped a hand to his mouth in almost comical dismay, his eyes wide above it. '*Dio mio*, I forgot! Not at lunch, but earlier. Should I have told you? Will I get into trouble?'

Swilley, interested that he exclaimed in Italian rather than Kurdish, concluded that the restaurant had got deeper under his skin than he knew, and said, 'Just tell me now. It might be important, it might not.'

'He came in in the morning, early, must have been about half past eleven – I was just opening up – to book his favourite table for one o'clock. We are busy Saturday lunchtime – it is best to book. Then he said he had a favour to ask me. I said, "Sure, anything," and he asked if Tiago and I would witness his signature on a document. Tiago is one of my waiters, he was helping me lay the tables. Anyway, Mr Bygod signed and we signed and that was that. He said he was going to do a few errands and he'd be back at one o'clock, and went away.' He gave a rueful shrug. 'I'd forgotten all about it. It didn't seem important at the time so it went out of my head.'

'Did you see what was written on the document?'

'No,' said Serhati. 'I don't know what it was. It was folded kind of long and thin, and all there was on the part he showed us was a line for his signature and two lines for ours. He explained we were just signing to say we had seen *him* sign it. Tiago said afterwards it was probably some financial thing, a deed, maybe property or something.' He looked at her hopefully. 'Is it all right? I just forgot, is all.'

'No, that's fine,' she said. 'Don't worry about it. So, when he came back to lunch, did he mention this document? Did he say anything about it?'

'No, no, he never mentioned it again.'

Telling Slider about it on her return, she said, 'It looks as though that could have been the will, boss. Your hunch was right. What made you think of it?'

The fact was that what looked like a hunch was usually the result of long experience and subconscious filtering of ideas, the pay-off for basic hard work. There was no such thing as a free hunch.

'The timing just seemed right, that's all, given that we knew he went in there on the Saturday,' said Slider. 'And he knew them, and knew they'd be around for a while. Pity Serhati didn't see anything else, though – the executor's name or anything.'

'Or even that it *was* definitely the will,' Swilley added.

'Two witnesses, in the presence of the signatory and of each other,' said Slider. 'I don't know what else it would be.' He pondered for a moment. 'Well, thanks,' he concluded. 'I don't know that it helps much, except to help confirm that he *had* made a new will before he went to see Danny on Tuesday.'

Swilley stirred discontentedly. 'But if Danny was his only kin, he'd have got the money anyway. Diana Chambers is the only one who needed him to make the new will. And she'd have wanted it to be found.'

'I know,' Slider said unhappily.

Porson was unexpectedly consoling. 'Can't be helped. Sometimes you have to do it the hard way. Needs must what can't be endured.'

'I'm afraid they were hoping for a quick turn around at Hammersmith,' Slider ventured.

Porson scowled, his eyebrows leaping together like two rams in combat. 'You let me worry about that. Everyone always wants a result yesterday. But you can't break eggs without straw. Better to do it right than do it quick. Have you got anything left?'

'We seem to have eliminated the obvious. But we know he had lots of people coming to him for help,' Slider said.

'The more the merrier. Gives you more to work with,' Porson said, undismayed. 'Better start charting 'em all, get working on their movements, alibis, etcetrea. Progress of elimination.'

'Yes, sir.'

'And we'll go ahead with the leaflets. Get

something sketched out, will you? We'll put a couple of people out in the street handing 'em to passers-by, do the bus routes, get 'em through all the letterboxes on the block. Give the carpet a shake, see what falls out.' He seemed to take heart from Slider's air of gloom. 'Buck up, laddie. You know how it goes – eventually someone'll come forward. Someone must've seen chummy go in or come out, even if he doesn't remember it now. Slow and steady wins fair lady.'

Slider murmured agreement and took his faint heart back to his own office. He had hardly sat down when the phone rang. He recognized the tortured RP vowels of June Bygod/Buckland before she had got any further than asking if he was him.

'How can I help you?' he asked, with a little wisp of hope curling upwards that she might have some information, might have remembered someone who wanted Lionel dead – preferably a sinister man, seven feet tall with red hair, a scar on his face and an unusual tattoo on the back of his hand.

'Oh, I was just wondering,' she said, with a deprecatory laugh. She sounded nervous. 'Have you made any progress?'

The spark was doused. 'We are following up a number of leads,' he said as quellingly as politeness allowed.

'Yes, I'm sure you're working very hard,' she said. 'But I wondered if you had any idea when all this will be over. I mean, it's upsetting to think of poor Lionel's killer walking about loose out there. It would be nice if it was all sorted out and we could put it behind us, get on with our lives.'

I didn't know you cared, Slider said, but not aloud. 'I'm afraid I can't tell you at this stage how long it will be.'

'No, of course not,' she said, as if disappointed. 'I expect these things take time. I suppose if you don't find out who did it, eventually you'll have to write it off – close the file or whatever the right expression is?'

'No murder case is ever closed, madam, until it's solved,' he said firmly.

'Oh, quite, but – you'd sort of put it to one side, wouldn't you?'

'We're a long way from that stage yet,' he said. 'Don't worry, we'll track the culprit down all right. And now, if you'll excuse me, my other phone's ringing.'

He disconnected himself, and sat staring at the wall for a long moment, pondering. What had she meant by the call? Did she think they needed geeing up? Or was it—?

Atherton came in. 'Bullseye!' he said. 'You win your choice of a cut glass vase or a fluorescent pink teddy.'

'How's that?' Slider frowned, still far off in thought.

'Your hunch,' Atherton said. 'Which seems to be getting more pronounced, by the way. It's the lack of ergonomic chairs. Stamford,' he elucidated, seeing Slider was still only halfway back. 'You guessed right. He had lunch at the George in Stamford. Waiter remembers him from his large tip, description matches, and he said Bygod mentioned in a chatty way that he'd lived in the area as a lad and had many fond memories of the place.'

'Oh,' said Slider.

'You don't sound pleased at being proved right,' said Atherton.

'I can't see that it helps,' Slider complained. 'Unless he met someone there – and that's a whole lot more things to check.'

'Well, he lunched alone,' Atherton said. 'And from the timing of the meal he must have gone straight there, but of course he may have gone visiting afterwards.'

'Or was just driving about, looking.'

'There is that. But if he visited someone, it might have stirred up an old enmity. Someone he knew an old secret about, who later decided old Li was better off out of it.'

'I suppose we'll have to get the local police to make enquiries about his movements,' Slider said with a sigh. He didn't like it when a case went out of his area. Foreign police couldn't be chivvied like your own firm. 'But it does open up a whole new area of possibilities.' He looked across as McLaren sidled up to the door and tapped tentatively on the frame for attention. 'Yes?'

'Guv,' McLaren said, 'I think I might've got something.'

'I'm buying,' Slider said.

McLaren came all the way in, printout in hand. 'Well, I was looking for the hire car up the A1, like Jim asked, and there's cameras on the big roundabout where the A1 crosses the A411. I got him going up and then again coming back.'

'As you would,' Atherton said impatiently.

'Yeah, but no – fact is, he gets pinged there three times.' He looked at Slider hopefully. 'He goes north in the morning, straight up the A1. But coming back in the afternoon he turns off, down the A411 towards Chipping Barnet. Then about an hour later he comes back along the A411 and turns south on the A1 towards London.'

'Chipping Barnet,' Slider said triumphantly to Atherton, 'is where June lives, in a delightfully bungaloid residence right on the main road.'

'The main road being the A411,' McLaren said, eager there should be no mistake.

'Yes, I get it,' said Atherton. 'So he has his jaunt – perhaps meeting some old friends or perhaps not – and on the way home—'

'It's only a mile out of his way, if that,' McLaren interpolated.

'—he drops in to see the lovely former Mrs Bygod—'

'Something she omits to mention to us when asked,' Slider said happily.

'—to tell her – what?' Atherton reached for the end of his sentence.

'There is one obvious topic,' said Slider. He paused, thinking.

Eventually, McLaren broke the silence, saying, 'Shall I go on tracing the hire car, guv?'

'What? Oh, no. Not for the moment. I've got something else for you to do. Get on to the DVLA and get the numbers of June's van,

Buckland's van, and the Range Rover that's parked on their front, which I imagine is registered to Buckland. Then look for any one of the three on the Tuesday in the vicinity of Shepherd's Bush Road.'

'Right, guv,' McLaren said, a light going on behind his eyes.

And to Atherton, Slider said, 'I want you to have a look at Buckland's business, Barnet Multibelt Limited. Get Gascoyne to help you.'

Atherton frowned. 'You're thinking the ex-wife? Isn't that revenge served unreasonably cold?'

'Just do it.' He waved them away. He stared at the wall a bit longer – it was being unusually helpful today, that wall – then got up and went to his door. Out in the CID room, Swilley, at her desk, looked up and caught his eye. He beckoned and she got up and came towards him.

'There's something I want you to check,' he said.

It was late before the various strands came together. Connolly and Fathom went for a tray of teas and everyone assembled in the CID room for the reports to be shared.

First McLaren. 'It turned out to be the Range Rover – lucky, cos it's easier for the camera to see in. They're both there – you can see 'em nice and clear on two of the cameras. He's driving. They've done the M1 and North Circular, he comes off at Dudden Hill Lane, then he must've done some back route he knew through Willesden. But we catch him again on Scrubs Lane, then West Cross roundabout, and Jerry gets him on the bus camera in Shepherd's Bush Road.'

Fathom looked modestly pleased. 'Five to four that was.'

'So Lionel had only just got back,' Connolly remarked.

'Then we got 'em going the other way starting twenty-five past four. Only, going back, *she's* driving,' McLaren concluded.

'Thirty minutes. Longer than they needed for a straightforward bash 'n' dash,' Atherton observed.

'Maybe they had a chat that turned into a barney,' Connolly suggested.

'What have you found out about Buckland's business?' Slider asked Atherton.

'Buckland owns it. He had a partner way back, but bought him out ten years ago. Did pretty well for a while. But there's been a sharp downturn since the financial crash, and the business is struggling now. He closed his office two years ago – he does some of the paperwork, and he's got one secretary working out of her own home, part time.'

'She's the one I talked to,' Gascoyne said. 'I got the impression she's more than just a secretary, if you get me.'

'Might be useful to look into that,' Swilley said.

Gascoyne nodded. 'Anyway, she says he's doing it all himself now. Had to let his men go, does the skilled stuff himself, has a boy to help him when there's heavy lifting to do, but she says he's useless – the boy. One of a series of useless boys. She was quite defensive about him working too hard, but proud that he never minds getting his hands dirty. Got the impression he's a bit of a hero to her.'

'He took out a second mortgage on the house two years ago,' Atherton went on. 'It's in his name, by the way. And there's a court case in process against him – a dispute with a big logistics company about some work he did for them.'

'She mentioned that,' Gascoyne put in. 'She says they're just trying to get out of paying because money's short since the crash. She says there was nothing wrong with the installation. But it's costing him in lawyer's fees, and she says he's "worried to death" about it – her words.'

'Anything against him?' Slider asked.

'He's got no criminal record,' Atherton said, 'and there's nothing about him on Crimint. Just this dispute – and he's two months behind with the mortgage payments.'

'But he *is* married,' Swilley said. They all looked at her. 'And I don't mean to June.' She read from her crib sheet. 'Philip Arthur Buckland, age sixty-two, married in 1969 to a Wendy Harper in Willesden Town Hall. They were divorced in 1979. He married again in 1984 to a Patricia Boyes, divorced 1992, married a third time – he was a glutton for punishment, this bloke—'

'Dick-happy, more like,' McLaren muttered.

'—in 1993 to a Gillian Cunliffe, from whom there has been no divorce to date. So he could still be paying for her,' she added, looking up.

'So him and your woman June aren't married?' Connolly said. 'Well, well. Livin' in sin, the little splapeens!'

'Not married,' Swilley confirmed, looking at Slider. 'And the other thing you asked me to check, boss – her and Lionel were never divorced, either.'

'Ah,' said Slider, with satisfaction.

'"Ah" is the mow juice,' said Porson, making them all jump. He had slipped in quiet as a cat with the inevitable cup of tea in his hand. 'I've been wondering along those lines myself.'

'It was the missing will that was puzzling me,' Slider explained. 'The only person who would automatically get his money was his wife. Then when Mrs Bygod telephoned me this morning to ask how long it would be before the murder was cleared up, I started to wonder. Everyone talked about his "ex-wife", but we were just assuming there had been a divorce.'

'But why wouldn't he divorce her,' Connolly said, 'after the way she treated him?'

'Diana Chambers said he never held grudges. And he had no-one else. Diana was his great love and she wouldn't marry him, his son was gone. Why go through the palaver of a divorce when there was no need from his point of view? And from hers – I imagine Buckland had had his fill of marriage by now and preferred just to live together. And as long as she stayed married to Lionel, anything he had would come to her in the end.'

'Until the point,' Atherton gloated, 'when he came to tell her their son had resurfaced and he was changing his will to leave everything to him.'

'Blimey, that's a bit rough,' McLaren said. 'I mean, even if she was a cow, he'd let her expect to get it all them years...'

'He left something to Diana Chambers,' Atherton said. 'Maybe he left something to June, as well – we don't know. But not enough, when she was expecting to get the lot.'

Slider took it up. 'Buckland's business is in trouble, they've got their old age to provide for, she's been relying in a quiet way on Lionel coming good in the end, and suddenly he turns up and tells her it's not going to be. Probably he told her he didn't have long to live, as well, so she knows she has to move quickly.'

'So she plans to kill him?' Swilley said. 'My God, that's cold.'

'Well,' said Slider, 'I'm not sure if it was that. They were at the flat a long time – I suspect they went to plead with Lionel, or argue with him, at any rate. But he was determined to give the bulk of the money to the son June hated and disowned. Maybe the contemplation of what they were losing was just too much, Buckland lost his temper and whacked Lionel on the head. Disaster. Then all they could do was snatch the new will and leg it.'

'Hmm,' said Porson. 'Well, there's plenty of questions for them to answer, anyway – enough to bring 'em in.'

'I've an idea,' said Slider, 'that if we put pressure on them separately one of them might turn on the other. I didn't get any great sense of harmony in that house.'

'Good point.' Porson looked at his watch. 'Getting late. What do you want to do?'

'I find it always unsettles people more if they're picked up at night rather than in daylight,' Slider said.

'Buckland's out on a job this evening,' Gascoyne said. 'The secretary mentioned it. Putting new belts into the checkouts at a supermarket. She was letting me know how hard he works, out day and night while June sits at home doing nothing. She doesn't like June.'

'It's a big club,' Connolly muttered.

'Even better,' Slider said, growing cheerful. 'We can pick 'em up separately and keep 'em apart until the right moment.'

The Harmony Shopping Centre in Willesden was showing its age. Built small and cheap at the beginning of the fashion and overtaken in the nineties and noughties by larger, more luxurious malls, it now sported cracked tiles and chipped floors, planters where nothing grew but rubbish, and enough streaked concrete to turn even Le Corbusier blind. The big names had abandoned it, a lot of shops were boarded up, and the smaller traders left behind gave it a ramshackle air. Even the supermarket was only a PaySave, a small, local chain. It alone had lights on inside. Barnet Multibelt's van was parked in the loading bay outside it at the back, and the security guards let them – Mackay and two uniformed officers – in the same way, raising the metal shutters for them with the look of alert glee that usually comes over people when they realize someone else is in trouble and they are going to witness them copping it.

Back at the station, Slider was warned that both teams were on their way back with their quarries. 'Good. Process Buckland, put him in the pokey, get his fingerprints checked against the lift from the door in the flat. When June comes in, put her in the interview room and I'll come and talk to her first.'

He let her wait a bit before going in, with Swilley to intimidate her with her tallness and beauty. June Bygod was looking small, dishevelled and cross anyway, and gave Swilley a look of extreme disfavour. She transferred her angry gaze to Slider and evidently thought he would be the softer option, because she tried to smile, though it was plainly an effort.

'What's all this about?' she demanded. 'Why are you dragging me out of my house at this time of night?'

'Sorry about that,' Slider said, sitting down. 'I wanted to ask you a few questions.' He allowed himself to look her over, guessing it would annoy her to be discovered in a shapeless pair of slacks and an elderly jumper covered in dog hair, make-up rather worn after a day's use, and no jewellery.

She bridled. 'Well, there was no need to come rushing over practically in the middle of the night. Why couldn't you call tomorrow and be civilized? I'm perfectly willing to help you, but I don't see why my leisure time should be interrupted. I was just brushing my Lhasa Apso.'

Slider heard Swilley turn her snort of laughter into a cough, but couldn't help glancing at her hair, which was sticking up at one side, perhaps where someone had guided her head into the back of the car. She put a hand up to it automatically and snapped, 'And that's another thing! Sending uniformed policemen like that! What will the neighbours think?'

'I think you're losing sight of an essential point,' he said. 'We are investigating a murder. That's rather more important than your poodles and pekes, wouldn't you say?'

'I don't have a peke.'

'The murder of your husband, what's more.'

'Ex-husband,' she snapped.

'Really? But you're not married to Mr Buckland, are you?'

'What's that to do with you? It's not a crime. A lot of people live together these days. If Phil and I choose not to get married, that's none of your business.'

'Of course, you couldn't marry him even if he wanted to marry you,' Slider went on smoothly, 'because you and Lionel were never divorced. Why was that?'

She was silent, calculation flickering behind her eyes. No use claiming they were divorced if the police could prove otherwise. And besides, she needed to be married to Lionel to get the money. Her eyes shifted off a point to the left of Slider's head. 'We just never got around to it. We're as good *as* divorced, anyway. We've lived apart for seventeen years. What more do you want?' The eyes came back, more confident now. 'If that's all you wanted to ask, you could have done it on the telephone.'

'Actually, I didn't really want to ask you questions. I brought you here to tell you a few things. You wanted to know about the progress of the case, didn't you?'

'Yes,' she said, but it seemed she sensed something was not as it appeared, because she didn't relax. 'Have you – have you caught someone?'

'We confidently expect to be charging someone very soon,' Slider said. 'Some new evidence has come to light.'

He waited, to make her ask, 'Oh? What's that, then?'

'A car. A black Range Rover with two people in it. We think we'll be able to identify them when we've enhanced the photograph. And most importantly, a fingerprint inside the flat.'

'Oh?' said June, but it took her two attempts to articulate the sound. Her mouth must have suddenly got very dry. Her eyes disconnected as she seemed to think furiously.

Slider smiled sinuously, and told her. 'It was on the door to Lionel's study. Whoever wiped the door knobs held the door steady with an ungloved hand. Funny how often it's the little mistakes that trip the criminal up.'

She didn't say anything, but her eyes grew hot and her lips tight at the word criminal. It was also funny, Slider thought, how little criminals ever thought of themselves that way.

Hollis met him outside the interview room, eyes

bright. 'It's a match, guv,' he said eagerly. 'Buckland's prints.'

'Thank God for that,' Slider said. 'Did he give any trouble?'

'He blustered a bit at first, but then he went quiet. Got a bit thoughtful. I'd say he's worried.'

'Has he said anything?'

'No, guv. He's not a happy bunny, though. They've given him a cup of tea and left him to stew.'

'All right. Give me two minutes to get to the screen room, then bring June in to him and leave them alone.'

It was quite cosy in the screen room, with Atherton and Swilley at the monitors and the others packed in behind. Mr Porson was there as well, with a cup of tea at which Slider looked with envy. His own mouth was dry – he'd had nothing since the meeting, and he'd done a lot of talking since then.

'All set?' Porson asked, and took a luxurious gulp.

'She'll be brought in in a moment,' Slider said.

In the lit room, Buckland was sitting at the table, wearing the regulation paper suit, and looking as low and scared as a beaten dog. Interesting, Slider thought, that he wasn't holding up better: it suggested he had not had any close dealings with the police before. He took a sip at the tea in front of him, and replaced the mug abruptly as the door opened and then closed behind June.

He started up, his expression veering between

hope and bewilderment. 'Juney? What are you doing here? What's going on? Have they—?'

He got no further before she was across the room and fetched him a clout, across the side of his head.

'You idiot!' she hissed. 'You bloody stupid useless moron! You left a fingerprint!'

'You what?' he protested. He had sat down again, perforce, and had his hand to the side of his face.

'A fingerprint! All your bloody fingers and thumbs, you stupid bastard.'

'I never!' he said. 'What are you talking about? I wiped the thing and the doorknobs, and I never touched anything else. I had my hands in my pockets.'

'You wiped the doorknob, but you held on to the door while you did it!' she cried in exasperation raised to such a power it seemed as if her head might explode. 'They just told me. They've got a full set of prints off it. It's only a matter of time before they match it with yours—'

'They took 'em when they brought me in,' he admitted, looking frightened.

'Well, you're stuffed, then,' she said, folding her arms over her chest and giving him a tight nod.

He reddened. 'What're you talking about, *I'm* stuffed? It was *you* did it.'

'Only because you're such a lousy coward you'd never've had the balls.'

'*I* was never going to! You were the one that lost your temper and bashed his head in!'

'It doesn't matter now,' she cried. 'The point is

they've got something on you. There's no point in both of us getting done for it.'

He was on his feet, his face suffusing with anger. 'Oh no you don't, my girl! You're not landing this on me! D'you think I'm an idiot?'

'You *are* an idiot! This is your fault, and if you were any sort of a man you'd take it and let me out of it.'

'You killed him, not me!'

'I only did it for you, didn't I? It's your business that's down the toilet.'

'Like hell you did. I'm not taking the blame for you—'

She flew at him, battering him ineffectually with her small plump fists and making a mewing noise, while he tried to restrain her.

'I think we've got enough, don't you?' Slider said.

'Better get in there before they murder each other,' Porson growled as the eager couple grappled in apoplectic rage. 'Love and marriage, eh? Go together like a horse and wassname.'

'Carnage,' Atherton offered.

Night ran into morning and morning became all day with the interviews, the processing, the conferences and the paperwork. Slider didn't get home, but at times like those policemen were capable of running just about for ever on a tank empty of everything but adrenalin.

However, at a late lunch hour he emerged from Porson's office and returned to his own to find Joanna there. She kissed him and said, 'Congratulations. Now I'm going to come the wifey and make you go upstairs for lunch. Emily's here too, she's just gone to winkle Jim out.' She cocked her head a little. 'Don't look like that. You can spare half an hour, can't you? You've got the villains under lock and key.'

He allowed the tense frown to slither off his face. 'Of course I can. Actually, I'm more thirsty than hungry. I keep getting brought cups of tea and not getting round to drinking them.'

'You'll be hungry when you've stopped being thirsty. Come on, I'm dying to hear all about it.'

'What day is it?' he asked as they headed for the door.

'Wednesday. Why?'

'Oh good. It's hotpot Wednesday.' He answered her questioning look. 'Wet food – easier to suck off the spoon.'

'So at what point,' Emily asked, toying with green jelly that she had picked up at the counter without thinking, 'did she decide to kill him?'

'Hard to say,' said Atherton. 'She may have had it in the back of her mind all along, that it would come to that. She claims it was a spur of the moment thing, that she lost her temper because he was being so unreasonable.'

'So she didn't mind talking about it?'

'Couldn't shut her up once she'd started. You often find that. Once they've broken that first barrier and admitted it, they just want to tell you everything. Boasting about how clever they've been – despite the fact that they're sitting there in custody, which is not the cleverest position to be in.'

Monday morning's post at the Buckland house had brought several nasty bills, plus a *billet aigre* from the mortgage company. Heated discussion over the next thirty hours had resulted in the expedition to visit Lionel, plead with him for money and, if he wouldn't see reason, for one of them to steal the will while the other distracted him. Slider thought that even the apparently good-tempered Lionel might have become annoyed at the second such appeal to his purse in one day, and found it easy to refuse the wife who had always made it clear she despised him.

'But it was a cockeyed thing to do anyway,' Emily complained.

'You want criminals to be logical?' Atherton countered.

'Seriously. She knew the son had reappeared, you say? So even if she took the will, he'd only got to come forward and claim, and he'd get the dosh.'

'She didn't think he would come forward,' Slider said, replete with hotpot and feeling a bit sleepy now. 'He'd been in hiding for so long, I think she just expected him to disappear again – and he might have, you know. He might never have heard of Lionel's death, and if he did hear about it in a roundabout way, he's quite diffident enough to think Lionel had changed his mind again. He didn't seem like the sort to relish making a fuss.'

'For that sort of money?' Emily objected.

Slider shrugged. 'Anyway, he might have found it difficult to prove he was Lionel's legitimate son. Possession of a birth certificate – even if he had one – might not cut it, if his mother denied him.'

'She still really hates him, then?' Joanna asked.

'She has the rigidness of mind of the not-very-bright,' said Slider. 'To her he became a non-person, and she holds to that. He simply doesn't exist.'

'But then,' Emily put in, '*why* did Lionel tell her? If he knew how she felt about the son, why did he go and tell her, not only that Danny had reappeared, but that he was going to leave him all his money? I mean, she was never going to take that well.'

'He was curiously naive for a solicitor,' Slider agreed. 'Diana Chambers said he was utterly truthful, without regard for the consequences. I suppose he thought June had the right to know about Danny. And if he knew she had been expecting to inherit his money all those years, he'd think she had the right to know he was changing his will, too.'

'It strikes me as a bit mean, disinheriting her completely,' Joanna said. 'Not that I'm condoning her – I mean, she's obviously bonkers as well as unpleasant – but still.'

'He thought she was all right with Buckland. And he wasn't cutting her out completely. He told her he was leaving her twenty thousand.'

'Oh, well, that's all right then,' Joanna said, with a wry look.

'He even offered to give her an advance to tide her over – that was the cheque he was writing.' Slider pushed his plate away and pulled his tea towards him. He'd left it too long again, and it was cold. 'Destroying the will wasn't a completely pointless idea, you know, even if Danny had come forward and been able to prove his identity. Because the intestacy rules would still have given her more than under the new will. She'd have got all his personal possessions, plus two hundred and fifty thousand, plus a lifetime interest in half the rest of the estate. A not insubstantial amount. But of course she wanted it all. Funny how often murder comes down to greed,' he concluded, pushing the cup away again.

'You're not to get depressed about it,' Joanna said, laying a hand over his. 'You're just tired. You've done a good job.'

But Lionel Bygod is still dead, Slider thought, though he didn't say it aloud for fear someone would mention that he hadn't had much longer to live anyway. Those months had been his, and no-one had the right to take them away. And he would have spent them getting to know his son again.

'So what will the result be?' Emily asked, abandoning the jelly without regret. 'Will they go down?'

'Oh yes, no doubt about it,' Atherton said. 'I suppose the defence might try to parlay Buckland down to manslaughter, because he gave her up so readily, and he didn't actually strike the blow. But he'll still go away for a long time, and she'll get life.'

'So, that's good then,' Emily said, looking at Slider.

Atherton looked too. 'He gets like this,' he told her. 'Adrenalin withdrawal. Plus the Universal Guilt syndrome – but he always has that.'

'I *can* hear you,' Slider pointed out.

It wasn't just adrenalin withdrawal. He had spoken several times both to June and Buckland since they were charged. Buckland was miserable and frightened, June furious and defiant, but neither had the slightest remorse, or pity for their victim. Buckland simply had no room to think about Lionel in the clamour of his own woes; June still hated and despised her former husband, and utterly repudiated her son. Her attitudes had not softened a whit, and he wondered tiredly if people could ever fundamentally change. It made so much of what he did seem pointless. You could revenge the dead, but what good did that do them?

He tried to console himself with the thought that father and son had at least been reconciled for that brief time. He hoped very much that Danny would open his club, and that he would call it Bygod's. A gay tranny cabaret club would be a curious, ironic but somehow satisfying memorial to the mild solicitor who championed the underdog.

Atherton was still studying his guv'nor's bent brow. 'Mr Porson's throwing buckets. I don't know what more you want,' he complained.

Slider pulled himself together. 'A hot cup of tea would be nice for a start.'

CPSIA information can be obtained at www.ICGtesting.com
Printed in the USA
LVOW10*0926200315

431250LV00011BA/415/P